PLOTS

We gratefully acknowledge the support of the Canada Council for the Arts and the Ontario Arts Council for our publishing program. We also acknowledge the financial support of the Government of Canada.

Cover design: Val Fullard

Plots: A Robin MacFarland Mystery is a work of fiction. All the characters portrayed in this book are fictitious and any resemblance to persons living or dead, is purely coincidental.

Library and Archives Canada Cataloguing in Publication

Curtis, Sky, author
Plots / Sky Curtis.

(Inanna poetry & fiction series)
(A Robin McFarland mystery)
Issued in print and electronic formats.
ISBN 978-1-77133-537-9 (softcover).-- ISBN 978-1-77133-538-6 (epub).--
ISBN 978-1-77133-539-3 (Kindle).-- ISBN 978-1-77133-540-9 (pdf)

I. Title. II. Series: Curtis, Sky. Robin McFarland mystery.
III. Series: Inanna poetry and fiction series

PS8605.U787P87 2018 C813'.6 C2018-904349-0
C2018-904350-4

Printed and bound in Canada

Inanna Publications and Education Inc.
210 Founders College, York University
4700 Keele Street, Toronto, Ontario, Canada M3J 1P3
Telephone: (416) 736-5356 Fax: (416) 736-5765
Email: inanna.publications@inanna.ca Website: www.inanna.ca

MIX
Paper from
responsible sources
FSC® C004071

PLOTS

A ROBIN MACFARLAND MYSTERY

a novel by

Sky Curtis

INANNA PUBLICATIONS AND EDUCATION INC.
TORONTO, CANADA

To my funny and feisty Aunt Patty,
with love.

1.

AS I STRETCHED MY LEGS under the covers, I recalled a line from a novel I had just read. *The silky sheets slid over her soft skin as she stretched her lithe body.* Okay, let's be real; the sentence didn't apply to me. First of all, my sheets weren't *silky*. They were a tough grey from being washed with blue towels. A mistake, I know. And *slid* over my skin? No, *slid* wasn't quite the right word, either, my being fifty-six and all, sprouting various doo-dads all over my body. Skin tags. Bumps. Scaly bits. All of which snagged on sheets. No sliding here. And *lithe body*? *Hahahaha*. But still. I stretched and felt good.

A day off from work. Sunday. No desk. No computer. No boss. No following hot leads about—oh my heavens, be still my beating heart—home furnishings for the newspaper. Today, the Home and Garden section of *The Toronto Express* could do without my ever-insightful epistles. Right now, the top story was doorknobs. Wowzer. Doorknobs. The new building code mandated levers, not knobs. *Poof!* Doorknobs were gone. Last week, it was the demise of ashtrays. So, now the world was free of doorknobs and ashtrays and I, lucky me, was free from my job. Today I would not be the harbinger of such absolutely riveting news. Today I was free, free, free.

I lay in bed and watched a shaft of springtime sunbeams float slowly through the opening in the blinds covering my window. I pondered the suggestive word *shaft* for a second. Or two.

Okay, a bit longer than that and where was Ralph anyway? Right. He had a double shift yesterday and then went straight home to his bed an hour after our dinner.

My bed was so peaceful. As I stretched my legs, my mind danced with the dust motes and I connected the blood in my veins to the pulse of the slow inner music of the universe, to a oneness with all things in the world. It felt harmonious.

Naturally, this feeling of peace didn't last. It never did with me. I began to think, and thinking was my downfall.

I was thinking about the sunbeams, and as lovely as they were, they had escaped through a small gap in my, quote unquote, "Room Darkening" curtains. Tiny sparks of anger burst in my chest. The light had woken me up. The lovely start of morning was infected with the more familiar angst that stayed with me all day. This anger, this worry, this tightening of my upper torso, this hornet's nest of chaotic emotions, always seemed to begin with being ticked off at my curtains. Morning after morning, I opened my eyes and said to myself, "Fucking curtains." Why would the package say "Room Darkening" if they weren't? I should write an article for the *Express* about the stupid curtains. Expose the false advertising.

But I knew it wasn't the drapes that were churning me up. It was something within me that had lain dormant all night long, snoozing under the rock of sleep like a poisonous snake. A few minutes after the sun came over the horizon the viper lifted its head, tasted the air with its forked tongue, and then slithered towards me, its rattle going a mile a minute, jangling every nerve in my body.

The drinking helped. Every night I got sloshed. My own little party. And it saved me. From what I wasn't sure. Maybe my thoughts. Maybe the snake.I was getting help for the drinking. I wasn't worried about my health. No, my liver seemed to be made of Teflon, deflecting the alcohol. But I didn't like the image of an eighty-year-old grandmother hoofing seven bottles of wine from the store to her car every week, probably in her slippers because her bunions were so bad. In a tatty coat over a polyester nightgown. Hair in pink sponge curlers. So dignified. No time like the present to stop. Last fall I had started seeing Sally Josper, a naturopath, for my pesky problem.

But then my path of righteousness had gone by the wayside because of a wild situation at work, one that involved not one but two murders. And almost mine. The initial theory about the motivation for the murders was the theft of Canada's fresh water from Lake Ontario, but that lofty hot button concept collapsed under a wave of reality. The murders were caused by the usual dirt: jealousy and shame. The story sold papers like hotcakes. Death and sex on the front page. All by me. My brief foray into being a crime reporter had been a dizzying success. Did I like it? Yes! I liked the notoriety. Sure, who wouldn't? But no! I didn't like the notoriety, who would? I liked and needed a peaceful life, and the flamboyance of the case was anything but. I was happy to be back in the quiet folds of the dull Homes and Garden section. Bring on the doorknobs, yessiree. Shafts of light and doorknobs.

Hmmm. When was I seeing Ralph next? I'd love to polish *his* knob. Robin, shut up. You are sex crazy.

I didn't hate my job, don't get me wrong, but there were frustrations. For example, now that it was spring and the snow was melting away, people were looking around their properties and noticing what needed improvement. Decks were high on everyone's list. Last week I wrote about the new polymers for outdoor decking. The fake wood never needed staining, lasted for decades, well, actually forever, so of course it ended up in a landfill, tossed by a bored homeowner who wanted the new style of decking. Glass barriers instead of banisters. Black metal railings instead of wood. My editor, Shirley Payne, the boozy-floozy who didn't miss a trick, cut out the political environmental bit in the, I must say, well-written article. We had advertising from the company that sold the decking, she said. *Snip, snip*, out went my comments. So, yes, there were trials. At least I didn't drink during the day like some newspaper people. Beers and burgers at lunch. Not me, I was purely an evening drinker. How puritan.

The drinking situation was not so bad that it interfered with my day-to-day functioning, but I think Ralph was beginning to notice that my wine with dinner, a demurely sipped glass, somehow expanded into a whole bottle guzzled down by the end of the night. I didn't want to lose him because of Merlot. And he, I noticed, was knocking it back as well. Was he doing this to keep up with me? Or had he come to the relationship with his fondness for alcohol? I didn't know. Couldn't remember. Anyway, after all the interruptions to my resolve to stop drinking, I went back to see Sally a few weeks ago and started over.

I wasn't sure she was helping me, but I was sticking to it. She told me to write three things I was grateful for every morning. Apparently I was a crabby bitch. So I did it. I actually enjoyed it. I had bought a little notebook from Dollarama with a robin on it, symbolic, being my name and all. I religiously wrote down three things I was grateful for every day. I could feel my brain changing, but it was as slow as altering the direction of an ocean liner.

At my last appointment, I told Sally how I used to feel a snake stalking me, but that it no longer sank its fangs into my jugular. How I used to spend my days feeling its venom coursing through my veins and wrapping tightly around my throat, cutting off my air supply, but that now there was only a rattling in my blood. She had tilted her head and looked at me as if I were a little nuts, which I had been trying to disguise. And then she said I was talking about anxiety and to remember to breathe. I was sort of ticked off that I had something so mundane. I liked my snake in the veins context better. She also told me that in addition to the gratitude exercises, I also needed a new totem, whatever that meant. Something to do with animals. I loved animals, so maybe she was right.

As I lay in bed this pretty Sunday morning, I made the effort to clear my mind and do the gratitude job Sally had given me. She had told me that the first step to sobriety was to literally change my mind. Neuroplasticity. The buzzword of the century. But maybe it worked, so today, yet again, I was grateful for my little dog, Lucky. My hand searched over the duvet for my cute pup and played over his head, stroking his silky ears and scratching under his collar. I was also thankful for meeting Ralph Creston. Several nights a week he stayed over, but I didn't know if he was *The One*. We seemed to get along okay. His saving my life last fall might have something to do with it. That awful day I had had an allergic reaction to almonds. I couldn't reach my inhaler because my hands were bound behind my back and I was lying on my kitchen floor, face down. I had tried flopping over so I could stand up, but only made embarrassing slurping noises on the polished wood. Ralph showed up in the nick of time and administered the drug. I sucked on the canister as if my life depended on it. It did.

Ralph had a lot of baggage from his previous marriage, and I was still unpacking my personal suitcase from mine. God knew I had steamer trunks of it. But if you threw out all that crap, I wondered if he was a good match for me. Sure, he was kind, gentle, smart, brave, funny, generous, the works. Plus, he didn't smoke or indulge in recreational hunting and fishing. Those were deal breakers for me. I didn't know his religious beliefs yet, but as long as he believed in the interconnectedness of life, I was sure we'd get along. I had recently become a Nichiren Buddhist slash Unitarian with a side dish of Christian traditions. Being a cop, he probably understood that what affects one person affects us all. We'd have that conversation eventually, I was sure, because I had to check it out. So far, he didn't seem like a narcissistic guy who thought the rules didn't apply to him, but the relationship was still young. We'd only been going out for eight months.

Don't kid yourself, Robin, you should know by now. Well, I didn't.

Which brought me to today's third thing I was grateful for. I was beginning to know what I liked. This in itself was a bit of a miracle. My life had been spent surviving, first in my family of origin that was outwardly perfect until anyone sat at our dining-room table and witnessed how my father treated my mother and us kids. And then in my marriage, also outwardly perfect until anyone sat at our dining-room table and witnessed how Trevor treated me and the kids. You marry your father. That's what they say. And, in my case, it was true. Trevor was constantly criticizing me for everything I did. Just like dear old Dad. In this lifelong atmosphere of disdain, I had lost who I was.

But somehow, over the past five years, without Trevor and being on my own as a single parent, I had gained some self-confidence and dignity. I knew what I liked, most of the time, except about Ralph, and I was going to speak up about it. I would no longer nod compliantly if someone said something I didn't agree with. I wouldn't be with someone who demeaned me. No more trying and trying, begging really, to get a man to accept me and love me. I liked who I was and I was grateful for it. I was no longer going plead to be loved. Either love me for who I am or find somebody else. I read that on Facebook.

Those were my three things. Secretly, I was also grateful for that butter tart I ate yesterday. So delicious. It should be *numero uno* on my gratitude list, but of course, I couldn't write it down. Shame, you know. Another buzzword of the century. I was way overweight, but that butter tart was worth it. I justified eating it even though I could feel flab being pressed up against my rib cage by my extra firm mattress. I told myself that the enzymes in butter were good for my digestion. And that bacteria from colds attached to the fat in butter and then were eliminated. That we needed plenty of oils in our diet. Then I wondered, briefly, why I hadn't eaten two tarts of the magnificent health food.

I reached for the robin notebook, which was beside my crusty wine glass on the bedside table, and wrote down my list. I made sure I actually felt gratitude for each thing. They say the mind doesn't change unless one spends at least twenty seconds actually feeling the gratitude. Sally told me that. And it was true. I could feel my brain opening up and relaxing. The snake slithered away into the murk of my subconscious, its rattle barely audible.

Making my gratitude list had gotten easier because I ensured I enjoyed things during the day. I planned ahead, channelling Pollyanna. And what was on my agenda today? I flipped through the pages of my mental calendar. Right. My family had been invited for Sunday dinner, kids and parents. I suppose I should ask my narcissistic brother Andrew and his fashionista wife Jocelyn to come. I hadn't asked him for dinner since he'd been home from Europe. Germany consortium or some shit.

That would make nine people for dinner. My four kids, my parents, my brother and his wife, plus me. I'd make a big vegetarian lasagna, a huge salad, and a dozen rolls. Watermelon, if I could find one, for dessert.

With resolve and a cheery outlook, or the best I could muster, I got out of bed and flung open the fucking curtains. Yup, it was a beautiful day in May. The pastel tulips that lined my garden path were swaying in the lovely breeze. I ate some granola and called Andrew, and yes, lucky me, he could come. Fuckhead. At least my parents would be happy to see him.

My brother was a colossal jerk. Arrogant. Self-righteous. Argumentative. Carried a grudge. A typical white fat cat, Rosedale kind of guy, with his studied and deliberate philanthropy. He wore his donations to good causes like a badge of honour. The type of guy who pranced by homeless people in his Harry Rosen suit, muttering "Get a job you lazy good-for-nothing," while funding a new shelter. I personally thought he was unstable, bordering on OCD with a dash of psycho thrown in. But he was my brother and my parents adored him. Of course they did. My father thought he was the best thing since sliced bread and my mother went along with my father. Always.

It was a typical Sunday. I did laundry, gardened, ate lunch, walked the dog, went to the store to buy some ingredients for dinner. Yes to watermelon and no to butter tarts. I was ready for the whole gang by the time the doorbell rang. It was my parents. Great. Here we go.

"Hi Mom, Dad, how was the trip here?"

"What, you think we can't manage? Your mother's a great driver."

Really? They no longer had a car. My father had lost many marbles and along with them his driver's licence. My mother's vision was deteriorating because of macular degeneration, and she too had no licence. But I was non-aggressive. I dug deep within myself and tried to find my father's subterranean Buddhahood. "I know she is, Dad."

See, I could do this Buddhist thing.

I gave my mother a hug, hoping to erase the puzzlement from her face. I could feel her rib cage. She was so thin. Is this what happened to people in their early eighties? A disappearing act? Probably not me, I loved food too much. I was going to be a substantial old lady. "Come on in, out of the cold air," I said. It was only mid-May and some evenings were still chilly.

"Crisp," my father barked. "Not cold, crisp. In the autumn we say 'crisp.'"

Robin. Don't react. Pick your battles. Don't correct him about the season. He strode into my living room as if he owned it and then suddenly braked in mid-step, looking lost. My mother hurried over to him and put her arm through his, leading him to the chair in the corner, where he always sat. He shook her off, leaving her with a tightly shut downturned mouth. "Janice, I always sit over here, by the kitchen door."

"Of course you do, Duncan, my mistake," she whimpered, hurt. He was such an ornery asshole. Always had been.

The door burst open and in flooded a tidal wave of kinetic energy. My kids. All four of them at once, plus Maggie's partner. They were laughing and pushing and flopping down on the furniture, as if they lived there, which of course they had done. Maggie, my oldest, and her newish beau, Winchester, stuffed themselves into the La-Z-Boy in the corner opposite my father. They were clearly in love, arms and legs intertwined, like ribbons of milk in coffee. Calvin, my second oldest, sprawled on the couch, arms hanging over the back, a ready grin on his open face. Bertie, the baby, sat at the other end of the couch, legs tightly crossed a nd arms across his chest. Oh dear, we'd have to deal with that later. Evelyn, the second youngest, was repeatedly tapping her eyebrow and grinning.

I twigged immediately; she'd been to a cosmetic surgeon and had the tattoo over her eyebrow lasered out. "Oh look, everyone. Evelyn had her skull removed."

My mother peered at Evelyn through watery lenses. "Her skull? Removed?"

"No, Mom. A tattoo of a skull."

"Oh." My mother wrung her hands.

My father wasn't about to miss this opportunity. "Don't be so stupid, Janice. Of course it wasn't her skull. She's sitting right there, head attached, beside that black man."

He was referring to Maggie, not Evelyn. This was rapidly turning into a comedy of errors.

Calvin suffocated a laugh with his hand.

My mother's head jerked over to Maggie, leaving in the air behind her the conundrum about the skull. "Hi dear. Who are you with?"

Maggie, bless her soul, didn't tell her grandmother she'd met Winchester several times before at other Sunday dinners. "This is my new boyfriend, Winchester."

"Nice to meet you, Winchester. I see you are a Negro."

It would appear that one's eyesight, body fat, and social filters all disappeared over eighty.

A wide smile spread across Winchester's handsome face, exposing strong white teeth. I was sure he did that for effect. "Yes, Ma'am. Ah's black."

Everyone laughed, except, of course, my mother who didn't get the joke. Maggie jabbed him in the ribs with her elbow. Winchester had no more of a Jamaican accent than I did. He smiled fondly at her. He knew the score with people like my parents. I found my heart warming to him as I worried about them making a life together and the obstacles they would face.

I left the room to get some hummus and pita with Calvin's laughter following me into the kitchen. He was so gregarious. I could hear him telling everyone about the second week in his new job. He worked for a software design company in a converted loft in Liberty Village at the foot of Dufferin Street and had, if he craned his neck, a view of the lake. The old warehouse floor had been divvied up with partitions and the overhead ducts and the floor vents had been painted flat black. *Presto*: cool office spaces. Apparently one of his colleagues had shouted, "Mouse." All the dogs then started barking—this was one of those pet friendly work environments—because racing down an aisle was a dachshund with a computer mouse in its mouth. I entered the living room at this punchline while carrying the appetizers.

My father said with the patronizing authority of one who knows, "Those dachshunds are good mousers. Bred for it, you know."

A look flickered across my mother's face and her lips compressed as she clamped them shut. No, she wasn't going to correct my father. Not now, not ever.

I put the plate of goodies down on the pine blanket box that served as a coffee table. The kids dug through the mound of pita like a bunch of bulldozers and I went back into the kitchen to get the lasagna out of the oven. Maggie followed me.

"We'll be okay Mom, Winchester and me. Really we will, don't worry."

I turned my head to her. "You saw how your grandparents are."

"I know Mom, but that generation is dying out. It's different now. Multiracial is the norm, especially here in Toronto."

"I sure hope so, honey. Here, get the rolls out of the oven for me and put them in that basket on top of the fridge. I wonder where your uncle is."

"Uncle Andrew? Aunt Jocelyn? They're coming?" She plastered on a fake smile. No one in my family liked them.

"He said they were, but you know how busy he is with his international consortiums." I said "international consortiums" in a low and important voice.

We laughed together. Andrew was so conceited.

There was a sudden commotion in the living room and I felt a gust of cold air swirling around my feet. Andrew. Speak of the devil. Right on time. As usual.

I tugged my lips over my teeth in what I hoped passed as a smile and sauntered into the living room carrying the lasagna, followed by Maggie. "Come sit, everyone. Dinner is ready. Hi Andrew. No Jocelyn?"

Thank God. I couldn't stand her either.

Andrew untangled himself from my mother's arms—he was always the favourite—and slid across the floor over to me. "Naw, she's in Korea, some electrical thing. Thanks for asking me, sis. This looks wonderful." He sniffed the lasagna as it passed by him on the way to the table and busked my cheek.

Frankly, my brother made me sick and I wanted to scrape off the saliva he'd left on my face. He was one of those rich conservatives who plundered the world for everything he could get, right down to the granite countertops in his fancy-shmancy kitchen. I didn't know how his wife could stand him. But then, she was much the same, wasn't she, wanting all the newest gadgets and gizmos. I think their barbecue cost more than my car. I know it did, given I drove a grubby, paint-challenged Sentra from a previous decade.

"Thanks for coming, Andrew." See, I could be civil. Finding the Buddhahood in a disgusting human being. That was me. Being a good Nichiren Buddhist. Yuppers.

Everyone slowly wended their way to the table and took their seats. Chairs scraped on the floor and napkins were put on laps. I sat at one end and watched as Andrew headed for the other. Maggie slipped in front of him and took the spot. It was her turn, after all. The kids rotated their positions, a practice I had begun almost immediately after Trevor had been killed. I wanted them all to understand the importance of sitting at the head of a table. It was where the tone of the conversation was set. Andrew appeared to be gracious as he sidestepped and took a chair in the middle of the table, next to our mother, although I caught a fleeting flare of fury flash across his face. My, my. See what I mean? Unstable.

After everyone had passed around the dishes and served themselves, the conversation resumed. They all had a story to tell about their week, with Evelyn's visit to the cosmetic surgeon's taking top billing. Bertie's problem was a girl. Calvin loved his job. Maggie hated hers. After the dinner, plates were cleared away and the watermelon was brought in. Andrew dabbed his lips with his napkin and cleared his throat. Oh no, he's going to pontificate about something or another.

"We need to talk about the cottage," he said.

"Oh?" I was surprised. This was a new one.

"Yes. When I came home from Europe a couple of weeks ago, I went straight up north for a few days. I had a small cocktail party there one evening with a few local professionals, one or two clients, and some of my Toronto real estate and entertainment friends. Anyway, I discovered that the land next to us has been sold. A theatre friend of mine told me. I think the new owner is planning to develop it."

"What?" yelled my father. His hearing was deteriorating along with his volume control knob. "They can't sell Crown land. It's CROWN land."

"Well," said my brother, "we always thought it was Crown land, but it wasn't. I researched it in town as soon as I heard. It has been owned by a family from Rosedale for years, neighbours of mine in fact, and now they have sold it. To a developer." Andrew said the word "developer" as if he were saying, "criminal." For all his conservative bluster, I believed he did value nature. That was his one redeeming quality. "This is going to create a bad feeling in my neighbourhood. So much for my annual Victoria Day barbecue."

It was all about him.

I chugged my wine.

2.

ON MONDAY MORNING, Shirley Payne, my highly sexed editor, was perched on the corner of my desk, legs tightly crossed, her khaki pencil skirt hitched up and exposing more thigh than I personally would like to see, although the males in the room were trying to look as if they were not looking. Vexing sexual harassment charges, don't you know. Her satiny, electric blue blouse stretched tight across her huge hooters. She was tapping her capped teeth with the end of a pen, her tongue darting out each time she tapped.

This mating display was for the benefit of Doug Ascot, the editor of the crime pages, who was glancing at her from his corner office, kitty corner to my desk. He was pretending to read something riveting on his computer, but even I could see his eyes dart this way and that so he could watch her in his peripheral vision. Under his desk his legs were crossed and one hand was nonchalantly resting in his lap. Did I detect movement? Pulleeze. Their hot affair had been the fuel for office gossip for years, which every now and then burst into flames if they fought.

Doug was the boss of my best friend, Cynthia, or "Cindy" Dale, a crime reporter. Cindy's desk was next to mine, although right now she wasn't in the office. She was no doubt chasing down some drug lord or getting shot.

Shirley tugged down her skirt while wiggling her right foot in its bright red four-inch ice-pick high heel. "I was thinking of that story you wrote some time ago. The one about the corrupt condominium developer."

I remembered it well, mainly because the guy had hit on me to ensure favourable press. Did he think I was born yesterday? "Yeah, I remember it. He was a sneaky asshole."

Shirley lifted her eyebrow. "Yes, he was that. The story went over well and now it's early spring." She admired the thin silver chain around her ankle. Was she wearing nylons or was that a spray-on tan?

And where was she going with this?

"It's at this time of year that developers are hunkering down, getting their ducks in a row for the summer build."

Ah-h-h. A clue. "That makes sense."

"Nothing much is going on in Toronto, other than the world-leading condo building boom, *haha,* but I've kept my ear to the ground. There's nothing too newsworthy. No one dicking around with building materials or permits, no greasing of palms at city hall, nothing, really. But a lot of *Toronto Express* readers have cottages. They'll be opening them up soon. Next weekend in fact. And mostly everyone loves the wilderness. So..."

She was waiting for me to put it all together, to make the idea mine. She'd been on a managerial motivation course recently. So transparent, but I obliged, "Maybe there's something dirty happening in cottage country." I knew there was, but I didn't want to give voice to it yet, not until I checked it out. And not with my brother. I'd go to the town planner in Huntsville myself. But how to get the paper to agree to this and give me time away from the office? I could manipulate too.

Shirley smiled at me like a benevolent yet patronizing teacher who's underachieving pupil finally gave the right answer. "One never knows. So many issues in the north. There's a lot of conflict about real estate development. Write this down. Land grants, native rights, water pollution, light pollution, traffic congestion, boat traffic, taxes, electricity costs." She took a breath. "Golf courses. Fertilizer. Algae blooms." She patted her stiff, porcupine-needle hair down as she recited this list, watching me take notes. "Yes, real estate development is an issue that pops into my mind. But take your pick on the angle, Robin. I'm sure you'll find something up there to write about."

Two could play this game. With luck, I could finagle some money out of the paper. "It would involve travelling, and perhaps overnight accommodation. Would there be an expense account?"

"Don't you have a cottage near Huntsville? And isn't Huntsville in the centre of the Muskokas? That would be a perfect location to hunt down a story. Real estate probably."

The Muskokas? The only people who said "the Muskokas" were rich white people who wanted to belong to the rich white club. For the rest of us, there was just one Muskoka. Anyway, I'd tried. Clearly, she wanted me to front the expenses. But at least I'd get out of the office and up north, legitimately, and not have to fake being sick before taking off for the upcoming long weekend. Not that I ever did that, oh no, not me. "So, you think Huntsville is a good place to start?" I was nailing it down.

"Sure," Shirley said, batting her fake eyelashes. They looked like spider legs in death throes. "Huntsville would be perfect. You could work from home away from home." She honked out a laugh.

I had to hammer this baby down and went for the jugular. "So, the paper doesn't have to pay for my accommodation, right?" I wanted to make sure she knew she was getting a good deal.

Shirley laughed, delighted. "It's so wonderful. You know how we're strapped for cash and getting squeezed out by the internet."

Bullshit. The paper had accommodated the internet explosion of news just fine. There were dozens of new young digital reporters. Tons of irritating advertisers. "I'll need an expense account for gas and food on the road."

Shirley's eyes flinted over. "Gas, yes, food no. You would have to eat anyway, and you can take a sandwich if you need to go on a side jaunt. I'll get you a gas card with a hundred bucks on it."

Better than I expected, considering I'd be driving up there anyway. Free gas, *whoop-de-do*. It's not like my scab-encrusted Nissan Sentra drank it thirstily.

"Deal."

Shirley tilted her head to the side, her straw-coloured hair scraping her shoulder, acknowledging the agreement.

"Why don't you head up tomorrow? There's nothing much happening here. Finish up that article on fire-retardant sprays for fabric today. And don't forget to mention our advertiser's products."

I mentally deleted the paragraph I had written about the cancer-causing components of the sprays. "Sure thing. I'll get that done today and head out. How long do I have to prowl around and come up with something?"

Shirley lazily swung her arched foot back and forth and looked up to her right, head slightly tilted, putting on her thinking look. She was probably reflecting on how alluring she was. And maybe she was, to Doug, who was watching our little interchange with a small smile on his lips, hand still in his lap. Maybe he was thinking that with me away he and Lady Hay Hair could play unobserved.

"How about the rest of this week? Four days. Check in with me on Friday around three. That should give you time to find something good, research it, and then write the story. If it's not enough time, there's always the long weekend."

The rest of the week away from the office? At the cottage? With pay? Holy smokes. I nodded and stuck out my lower lip in a considering sort of way. "Should work."

"Great." Shirley slid off my desk, her thighs making a farting noise as they rubbed along the Formica surface. I did my best to suppress the tsunami of giggles flooding my mouth. I was so immature. She yanked down her skirt as she stood up, her head held high, pretending nothing had happened. "See you next Tuesday, then." She cavorted over to Doug's office and shut the door behind her. Time for a romp in the hay.

I focused on my computer and tried to unravel myself from the notion of fire-retardant sprays coming in aerosol cans, which were highly flammable. How did they test the product? Spray the couch, throw a match at it, and then run like hell with the can in hand? I was seeing an exploding inferno of flames around a chesterfield when a sudden tap on my shoulder sent me into my next life. I jerked back in my chair and clasped at my heart.

Cindy threw back her frenzy of red hair and laughed at me. "Gotcha!"

A flicker of irritation fired through my veins before her infectious laughter hosed it down. "Yup. That was a good one. Where've you been?"

"I was checking some facts with a source before I submitted my article on the Red Tarantulas, which I've finally done."

Cindy was well-known as a crime reporter, and she had been writing a series on Toronto's gangs. She had to tell someone her good news because her boss was probably right now in a lip-lock behind his office door with my boss, Shirley Payne.

"How many more gangs are you going to research?" I hated this topic she was covering. So dangerous.

"I think I'm finished. I've done five. The Blazing Snakes. The Machetes. The Fly Boys. The Beach Boys. And the Red Tarantulas. That's one for the four corners of the city, plus one for Innisfil in Lake Simcoe. Sure, there's about ten more I could do, but these are the main guns and I don't want to completely terrify the good citizens of Toronto. They are already frightened by the huge uptick in gun violence."

I was so relieved she was done with gangs. "Oh, thank God. I can't wait until you get back to covering simple drive-by shootings, crack house busts, and domestic disputes involving paring knives." We both laughed.

"Actually, I'm going to take some time off now. I've been at it for months, and I didn't get much of a winter holiday. Actually, no vacation at all. Time for a break."

"Going to hang out with your kids, see some friends, go on some dates? Maybe find a partner? Have a fun staycation?"

Cindy was unashamedly gay and sadly single. "Yeah, right. No, I thought I'd hike in the Arctic. Isn't that what lesbians do on their holidays?"

I smiled. "Only if they're wearing Birkenstocks with socks. But really, any plans?"

Cindy pulled out her desk chair and brought her sleeping computer back to life with a sweep of her hand. She wasn't going to look at me. "No, nothing at all. Maybe I'll head south to Puerto Backyarta."

I laughed. But a plan was unfolding in my head. "I'm not going to be around next week either," I said tentatively.

Now she turned her green eyes to me. "What? You're taking a holiday too? You, Lady Workaholic?"

"Nope. Working. Trying to find a good story in cottage country. Real estate development."

"No guff. Muskoka? Sanctioned by Shirley?"

"Cindy. Listen to me. First of all, no one says 'no guff' anymore. And yes, sanctioned by Shirley. She even suggested it. Well, she manipulated the conversation so I would suggest it."

"Doug was on the same management course. So obvious." She rolled her eyes.

I took the plunge. "Would you like to come with me? Up to Pair o' Dice? There's tons of bedrooms at the cottage. I mean, if Doug lets you take the time off that is."

"Paradise? Is that the name of your cottage?"

"Yeah, only it's like a *pair of dice*." I said it slowly so she would get it.

"Is someone a gambler?"

I shook my head. "No, nothing like that, someone way

back when thought it was cute." That someone was me, but I wasn't going to admit it. "Do you think Doug will let you off for the week?"

"Oh, he will. I've already hinted around it for the past pay period. It's a bit much, you know, working for weeks and weeks without a day off."

"You deserve it! There are lots of bedrooms and I would love the company."

"You've said 'lots of bedrooms' twice now. I get it. I don't get to sleep with you."

Cindy and I had a running joke about how she was desperate to get in my pants. I didn't bother to reply. She lifted a corner of her mouth. "Okay, okay. I'll go ask him now."

"No, wait. Lady Hay Hair is in there with him."

Suddenly, his door whooshed open and Shirley swished out, her hair looking like a startled hedge hog, her cheeks on fire. She was straightening her hot, shiny, blazing blue blouse. She smoked by my desk. "Don't forget. Fire-retardant sprays on my desk before you go."

I wondered if she knew what she'd said given how hot she was. Probably not. But then, you never knew. She looked like a bimbo, but she was a pretty smart boss. Looks were so deceiving. Did I hear her laughing as she shut her office door? Yes, she got it. Then I heard her lighter click as she fired up a cigarette.

Cindy shook her head. "Smoking. She's too much. How do you work with her?"

"Oh, she's okay. Tough, sure. But really supportive. When it counts."

Cindy nodded grudgingly. Last summer, Shirley had a good reason to fire Cindy for plagiarism, a journalist's guillotine, but had kept her mouth shut. "I'll go see Doug."

"Fingers crossed." I watched her knock on Doug's door and hoped he wasn't too compromised. Cindy waltzed in and I could see he was pushed right up against his desk, his legs tightly tucked under. Good camouflage. Made me think about Ralph. Guess I wouldn't be seeing him for a week or so. I'd have to talk to him about that. Later.

I wrote a few sentences on autopilot about fire-retardant sprays while my mind worked out the logistics of Cindy coming with me. Had I been too impulsive? I did that. I made offers before I thought about the impact on me. Going out for a drink with a friend was one thing. Being with them in the same cottage for four or five days was quite another. But Cindy and I had known each other for decades. We were best friends. We'd get along. As long as she kept her hands off my wine.

But what about Ralph? Maybe I should ask him up for a few days. How would that work if Cindy were there? He worked shifts. Four days on, four days off. Maybe he had a stretch of time coming to him. And that smacker on Saturday night, boy-oh-boy, what a humdinger of a kiss. So much promise! Hot hot hot. Speaking of which, I had to get this fire article done or I wasn't going anywhere. I pushed my mind towards the benefits of fire-retardants on beds so they wouldn't burst into flames. If only I were so lucky! Some days it was hard to keep the mind from wandering.

Cindy grabbed my shoulder from behind while I was deep in thought. Again, I jumped. "Stop that," I yelled. Maybe I wouldn't be able to handle her for a week straight. "Don't frighten people." I used my mommy voice.

Cindy looked suitably chastised. "Sorry, I thought it was funny. I see it wasn't. Sorry."

"That's okay. What did he say?"

"I can go. I can take the rest of the week off. I have to do a small edit on this last article and get it in on his desk."

"I have the same instructions. I have to get this article done, and then I'm free."

"What's it on?"

"Fire-retardant sprays."

"Oh yeah, that stuff is great. I think there's a company that makes a good one out in BC. Nanaimo. Non-toxic. People spray it on uniforms and bedding and wood doors and stuff like that. I think it's used on what they call 'Class A materials.' It's purchased a lot by schools and institutions."

"Maybe you should write the article. Where did you pick up all this information?"

"At one point, when I was growing up, I wanted to be a firefighter and I researched all kinds of stuff then."

"You wanted to be a firefighter?"

"Why not? I'm strong. Tall. Brave. I liked the idea of rescuing people and saving historical buildings from burning down."

I rolled back my chair and looked at her through new eyes. "You surprise me."

Cindy shuffled her chair under her desk, head down. Maybe she was a little embarrassed to be caught outside of her glam persona. "What? You assumed I wanted to be a ballerina when I grew up?"

We both laughed. At almost six feet tall, she would never be a candidate.

"Or a..." she paused for effect and rocked her head back and forth, setting off boomeranging curls, "...hairdresser?"

We laughed even harder. Cindy's red hair looked like a fireball that had met with a wood chipper.

"Okay, let's get these babies done and head on out." I started singing softly, "I'm gonna leave this city, gotta get away."

Cindy started to sing over me, "*Over* hill, *over* dale, as we hit the dusty trail."

I stopped my singing. Her last name was Dale and she was hinting hard. "Stop dreaming. Ain't going to happen. I might be over the hill, but I'm not over the dale. I have a *boy*friend."

She said, "Shit."

It was going to be a long week.

3.

I PACKED UP THE CAR with everything I thought I'd need for the week, my computer and Lucky's dog food being at the top of my list. His sensitive stomach literally backfired if he deviated from his diet. It wasn't pretty. I tossed a few frozen containers of homemade soup into the food bag. And some bread and mayonnaise. Potato chips. Wine. And more wine. It was my fruit. I needed to cover all the food groups.

But it didn't matter if I'd forgotten anything, Huntsville was a bustling centre of commerce now with almost twenty thousand people. In the last few years, the town had acquired Walmart, The Home Depot, and Shoppers Drug Mart. Even the old Beer Store in a potholed parking lot had been abandoned for a spanking new one, out by the hardware store. And there was a new liquor store, all shiny chrome and glass, a few years old, by a Staples. I wondered what all this development meant in terms of the town's priorities and goals for future demographics. No more redneck underbelly?

As I got into my shitbox car, I began to worry about the bugs up north. I knew there'd be lots this time of year, but I hated insect repellent. I hoped there'd be a wind off the lake to blow the blackflies into the woods. On the other hand, then the wildlife would come into the open to get away from the bugs. Just what I needed. A bear joining me for my morning coffee on the dock. I wished I had a gun. No, I didn't. I'd never seen a gun in my life and wasn't about to want one now.

I pulled in front of Cindy's house in midtown, slightly north of Yonge and Lawrence. It was only ten years old, a solid four-level stone pile that had replaced a charming two-storey frame house. Her whole neighbourhood had undergone a metamorphosis in the last twenty years with Tudor-fronted bungalows for small families torn down and replaced with McMansions for small families. Every time I saw one of those huge homes looming over a stalwart next-door bungalow, my first thought was of vacuuming. Who wants to clean such monstrosities? But I guessed if you lived in North Toronto you could afford a cleaning service. Or at least have central vac. I personally had never even seen central vac in my life and felt blessed when my thirty-year-old Hoover worked on the rare occasions I hoofed it out of the closet. Having asthma, I had wooden floors and washable rugs.

Cindy had been married to a dentist until he had probed the mouth of his hygienist with a fleshy instrument. But Cindy won the mini-castle in the divorce settlement, along with a chunk of change every month. It was my guess that he'd felt guilty because he'd cheated on her. So, although she earned a reporter's salary, she still had the North Toronto fixings, years later.

Me? I loved my Cabbagetown neighbourhood with its mixture of welfare recipients, transients, toothless homeless people, smattering of immigrants, and financially stable young professionals. A little extra moolah would have been nice, but I was pretty proud of myself for making a go of it, not that I was jealous of her windfall. I tried to convince myself of this as I looked at her detached stone edifice and did a short Buddhist chant to clear my unkind thoughts.

It was a beautiful Tuesday morning with sunshine streaming through the translucent leafy arch over her street. Toronto had rules about tree removal for construction of new-builds, and believe me, I knew all about them, having done a story on the specific kind of fencing required to be put around a tree on city property to protect it when a home was being torn down. I knew some useless stuff.

It was a perfect day for going to the cottage. I couldn't wait to get to the lake even if I couldn't swim yet. The ice had gone out late this year, the third week in April, so the water would be frigid. Anyway, I was supposed to be working. I talked myself out of feeling ashamed for wanting to have a little enjoyment while I worked. A hundred-dollar gas card hardly qualified as an expense account that could be misused.

I texted Cindy that I was in front of her house and waited for her while Lucky slept quietly in the back seat beside my so-called luggage. One of my kids had borrowed the one family suitcase, so my clothes were stuffed into a green garbage bag. Lucky was resting his wet brown nose on the corner of one, leaving little droplets of condensed sweat. The next car I owned was going to be a SUV with a huge cargo area where he could stretch out on a nice soft duvet. Beside my Louis Vuitton matching luggage. Oh, the stuff of dreams.

While I waited for Cindy to emerge, I checked my weather app for the Huntsville forecast. A long row of suns! Temperatures in the high teens! Almost summer! It was going to be a beautiful week, sunny and warm at least until the long weekend. The nights looked warm too, which meant they would be buggy as well, but hey, I could handle it.

Cindy's oak door swung open and she staggered out, pulling a huge suitcase on wobbly wheels. She was wearing blue jeans and a bright pink tank top that clashed with her red hair. Three bags were slung across her shoulders. An insulated food bag and a flowered makeup bag hung over her right shoulder, and a large leather satchel, which she referred to as her purse, over the left.

I jumped out of the car. "Here, let me help you."

"No, no," she panted as she rolled the suitcase down her flagstone path, its wheels bumping over bits of moss. "I'm balanced. If you remove anything, I'll topple over."

I sidestepped around her and behind the car to open the trunk. With a grand gesture I swept aside an old tarp, some empty plastic bottles, and a pile of newspapers to make room for her stuff.

She grimaced. "I see you've cleaned out your car especially for the trip."

The bags slipped down her arms onto the sidewalk. Then, with a grunt, she leveraged the suitcase on her knee over the bumper where it tumbled on to the embarrassingly crusty floor of the trunk. She pitched the food bag on top of the suitcase and lugged the 'purse' and her makeup to the passenger side of the car. I slammed the lid down leaving paw prints in the grime and dusted my hands off on my jeans. I'd get around to washing the winter salt off the car, one day. We hopped in simultaneously, like synchronized swimmers, our doors banging shut in unison.

I couldn't wait to get out of the city. I charged up Avenue Road to the 401, zoomed off the westbound exit, wove in and out between the eighteen-wheelers and then peeled onto the 400 heading north. I played dodge'em with the traffic for a bit while Cindy rummaged in her flowered makeup bag for her mascara. She pulled down the visor to look for a mirror, saw there wasn't one, shrugged, and proceeded to mascara her lashes. She never once looked in the rear-view mirror. She never once poked herself in the eye. Her hand was completely steady as I swerved and sped up, braked and slowed down. Years of practice, I guessed, getting ready for work while driving to the office.

"Stop trying to wreck my beautiful makeup job," she finally yelped as I zoomed around a huge Dodge Ram.

"I don't think I could if I tried. You clearly have tons of experience with car salons."

"Well, I do get up late some mornings. It's harder eating and putting on blusher at the same time while driving, so this is a snap."

"You're never late, that's for sure." I was being kind. She snorted.

The traffic eased off just past Barrie, and I set my cruise control for one hundred and nine kilometres an hour, nineteen over the limit of ninety. Who drives at ninety kilometres an hour? The cops were few and far between this Tuesday morning and I knew they only stopped people going twenty over the limit. By the time we passed Orillia, the stress of the city was behind us and our shoulders dropped from around our ears. I hummed a few bars about country roads taking me home. I was so happy about heading north. A paid vacation, no less.

"So," Cindy interrupted my revelry, "any story ideas?"

"That's for me to know and you never to find out. You're on holiday. I'm the one working."

Cindy thought about that for a bit. The miles ticked by. We passed some roadkill. The poor raccoon's feet were straight up in the air, frozen in rigor. We both saw it and we both said nothing. The silence expanded as the pavement hummed below us. A few miles later, Cindy cleared her throat. "Good to get your feet up."

I choked back a laugh.

Then she said, "I'm always after a story."

We drove in silence for another twenty minutes with this defining pronouncement echoing in the car. When we got to Gravenhurst I said, "You're right."

"Right about what?"

"You're always after a story."

"Oh that. Yes, I always am. So..."

"I'm not sure it's a story, but it might be."

"If you're not sure, then it is. Believe me, I can make a story out of a blade of grass."

"Well, the property next to my family's cottage was purchased by a developer."

"Ah, conflict between the natives and the urbanites. Environmental meltdown. Displacement of wildlife. Light pollution.

Animal protection. There's a story there, for sure."

"It could be a three-way conflict between the natives, the locals, and the urbanites. You gotta be careful, Cindy. People are touchy. Especially about development."

"Sorry."

She sung the word. And then corrected herself, "Indigenous. Indigenous people. Not natives." She never wanted to offend. "What's he going to build?"

"It might be a she. That's what I'm going to find out. Maybe a golf course and condos."

"Golf course? Watch out. Tree huggers hate those things. The land is shaved clean of all growth, depleting a natural resource so people can hit a tiny white ball around. We need trees for oxygen. Golf courses harm the ozone layer. Plus, the fertilizers run off into the lake, creating algae blooms. Plus, the lake is used to water the greens, draining the aquifer. Plus, wherever there are more people, there is destruction. Air. Land. Water. All in all, really bad for the environment."

"Geez, Cindy, I didn't know you knew so much about development. Where'd you pick all this up?"

"At one point in my life, I wanted to be a forester."

"I thought you wanted to be a fireman, I mean, fighter."

"That, too."

"What, a man or a fighter?"

She ignored me. "How many acres is it?"

"I'm not sure. It's so large my family always thought it was Crown land."

"How do you know it isn't?"

I put on an uppity voice. "Andrew said so."

Cindy laughed. "Well, check that out too. He's not always right. Surprisingly." She couldn't stand Andrew. Or most men for that matter. "Sometimes Crown land is sort of taken over by a family, you know, over time, like a hundred years and the title has been obfuscated and then they go and sell it in a private deal. So, maybe it is Crown land. And you can't develop Crown land unless you meet certain criteria, like providing employment for disenfranchised groups or something."

"'Obfuscated.' Pretty big word this early in the morning."

"Or maybe the person who bought it isn't a developer at all. Maybe they're an investor. It is Muskoka, after all. *National Geographic's* best summer trip. Maybe someone bought it to sit on and cash in sometime during the next decade. Maybe it isn't a story and you'll be stuck doing a review of all the new ice cream parlours in Huntsville."

I set my mouth in a tight line. "I doubt it. Andrew might be an asshole, but he probably researched it."

"We can go to the Town Hall and check it out."

"What do you mean, 'we'?"

Cindy merely smiled and looked out the window. The miles rolled by, past hundreds of trees. Finally, she asked, "How much longer?"

"God, you're whining. You sound just like my kids. About twenty minutes."

"I'm starving. What do you want to do about lunch?"

Cindy was always starving.

"I brought some stuff like soup, bread, and mayo. There's usually a can of tuna or something lurking around in the cupboard. We can make it when we get there."

"How old's the tuna?"

"Don't worry, the health inspector has been by." Although Cindy had terrible table manners, she was a bit paranoid about her food quality. But maybe she had a point about the tuna. If there was a can, it had probably been sitting there all winter. Can one eat a can of food that's been frozen? I had no idea. I tried to remember what I had read about Arctic explorations where a stash of cans was found. Did it say that the cans were perfectly edible? I didn't ask her to google it.

We drove along in silence. I was daydreaming about sitting on the dock. Who knows what Cindy was thinking about.

Probably lunch. Or guns. As we got closer to town, Lucky suddenly leapt up and barked. Cindy jumped a mile. Guns, then.

"What the...?" She pressed her hand to her chest.

"It's Lucky. I guess you didn't know he was in the car."

"Geez, Robin, Why didn't you tell me?"

"You'd think you'd notice. Anyway, it serves you right for yesterday." I said, smiling. I took the next exit off the highway and soon we were cruising down Huntsville's main drag. "He always barks when we get close to town. He loves it at the cottage."

Cindy turned around and scratched Lucky's ears. "You going to the cottage?" she crooned. Lucky wagged his tail and barked again. "You going swimming?"

Lucky didn't bark.

"He hates the water. Besides, it's too cold still. He likes barking at deer."

Lucky barked.

Cindy's head was swivelling from one side of the street to the other. "Wow, look at all the stores that are out of business."

Brown paper was taped to windows with masking tape in about thirty percent of the stores. But I brushed it all off with a wave of my hand, "Oh, the merchants always shut down once the snow flies. No one can survive here during the winter."

"What, candlesticks in the shape of moose and mosaic house numbers don't sell well to the local population?"

"You're right. It is sort of their own fault, not researching the year-round market."

"Maybe that's the story. There's no post-secondary education available here, so how on earth can people know how to properly plan a sustainable business? Or maybe the story is about the prohibitive cost of tuition, which contributes to the cycle of poverty in the north."

"I guess there's all kind of newsworthy articles lurking about in Huntsville, but I want the big one. I know you're the crime reporter and I am the lowly House and Garden hack, but I got a taste of the big time and I want it again." Sort of.

"I thought all the attention last fall on the Everwave case was a bit overwhelming for you."

"That was in Toronto. This is small-town Huntsville, two and half hours away. It would be different here." I was defensive.

"Probably worse, if you ask me. Small towns are hotbeds of rumours and backstabbings. Plus, silly billy, the story is going into a Toronto paper. Believe you me, it will have the same hoo-ha as the murders you solved. Whatever the story is."

"I didn't solve those murders last fall on my own. You helped, remember? Look, there's the Town Hall, that building with the clock tower." I turned off the main street at the most easterly set of lights and headed out of town on Highway 60. I showed terrific self-discipline as I drove right by the ice cream takeout joint.

Cindy was sulking. I knew why.

"Okay, okay. You can come with me."

She pulled out her lipstick. "We getting close now?" Cindy tugged down the window visor and flipped it back up. No mirror. Again. She puckered in the rear-view mirror while dabbing her lips with a tube of Hot Fuchsia Garden. It matched her tank top perfectly. The mosquitoes would love her for sure.

"Looking good for the coyotes?"

"You never know who you're going to meet. Be prepared, that's my motto."

"Not many gays in Huntsville."

She turned at me with her green eyes wide open. "Are you kidding? I researched Huntsville before coming. There's a baseball team called 'The Lizzies.' That's at least ten people, if you count the pinch-hitter. A lot of ho-mo-sex-u-als," she said, stringing the word out over five slow syllables, "retreat to small towns. People are more accepting, believe it or not. In fact, the smaller the population, the more open the society seems to be, to all types of alternative lifestyles, including gays. People are simply people where people are scarce."

I knew she was wrong. "You might be right. But those who hate, hate harder. And this is much truer in the United States," I said.

Cindy snorted. "Canada isn't the United States."

She could believe what she wanted. I turned off the highway onto a sideroad and came across a neighbour, trudging along, carrying a heavy shopping bag. I turned to Cindy, "My neighbor, Dick Worthington. From England. Moved here as a child about fifty years ago. Permanent resident. About sixty."

"A match for you?"

I crowed. "No, he hunts. I don't do hunters."

"White trash then?"

"In a nutshell. You'll see." I slowed the car down and came to a stop beside him. "Mr. Worthington. Nice to see you. How was your winter?"

His voice was deep and gravelly from years of smoking and drinking. His hands were leathered mitts sticking out from the frayed cuffs of his red-and-black plaid bush jacket. Buttons strained over his beer gut. A greasy strand of grey hair had escaped from his ponytail and was limply hanging at the side of his face, caught in his bushy eyebrow. "Had a pretty easy time of it." He laughed, exposing yellowed teeth. "Five cords of wood only. I've really been to town." He laughed at his joke and held up the bag in his hand. "Big sale on in the sporting goods store. Bought me some stuff for next season. A new orange cap. Camouflage gloves. Bear bait. Gutting knife. And this." He pulled out a long strip of leather. "A belt for my new knife."

"Didn't you do well." I pretended to admire his purchase. Some people. "We're here for about a week, opening the place up." I was trying to make normal conversation. Dick Worthington gave me the creeps. He was a little off. Not the sharpest tool in the shed. And maybe there was no shed.

His black beady eyes shifted under his pink eyelids. "Your brother was here a couple of weeks ago. Had a big shindig with the locals and some famous people. Actors and investment types. Fun. Lots of food and drink. I guess you heard about the property next to youse." Angry spittle was forming in the corner of his mouth.

"Yeah, I heard about it." I kept my voice neutral.

"Well, I'm mighty pissed off. That's my hunting ground. I've lived here for fifty years, hunting there, and I'm going to continue to hunt there." His rasping voice rose a whole octave. "No one is going to stop me. Anyone who tries..." He let the sentence drift off and nodded a few times, looking me straight in the eye with his pinprick pupils, seeing if I caught his meaning. In case I didn't get it, he shook his bag of hunting goodies.

Geezus. Rural justice. What a nutbar. He'd kill so he could kill?

"Well, must be going. See you around." I tooted the horn twice as I pulled away from the dirt shoulder.

"You didn't offer him a lift?" Cindy was being sarcastic.

"He'd say no. He likes to walk."

Soon the road got thinner and thinner. Bits of grass tufted in the middle hump of the pavement and the asphalt edges crumbled into the foot-wide gravel shoulders. Pieces of black tar were scattered throughout the pebbles, probably pushed there by last winter's snowplowing. I buzzed down my window.

We drove past a small pond and listened to the red-winged black birds trilling. A blackfly flew in through one window and was blown out the other. A crow cawed in the distance. The fragrance of growing grass filled the car as we passed an open field, slowly turning green. At the top of a hill, we could see blue water sparkling prettily against the fresh new purplish-pink buds in acres and acres of forest.

I flung my arm out the window, "And what you see over there is about seven hundred acres of soon to be developed land. My family's cottage is over the brow of the next hill."

"How many acres do you guys have?"

"I'm not sure, really. A few hundred. Andrew would know. Exactly."

My scruffy Sentra ground up the next hill and once past the top we turned right onto the small private road leading to the family cottage. I never did like the entrance to the place. It reminded me of the scary scene with the flying monkeys in *The Wizard of Oz*. Dark forest blocked out the sun and tree branches seemed to reach out to us. Shadows jumped in and out of patterns of sunlight on the forest floor and an animal darted across the road in front of the car. Probably a fox or a coyote. No, only a squirrel. I could see its bushy tail disappearing behind a tree. The tires crunched over the gravel, throwing up loose stones that periodically pinged against the muffler. A tingle crept up my spine into my scalp, and I could feel my ears pinning back. Something seemed ominous to me, something a little off-kilter. Maybe it was running into Dick Worthington. I was glad to get into the sunny clearing around our old frame building.

"We're here," I announced with more gaiety than I felt. I doubt I fooled Cindy for a second.

"That's a pretty long driveway in from the main road." She was admiring the view. "What lake is this?"

"Peninsula Lake. Thanks for coming Cindy. I mean that. I'd forgotten how isolated it was here."

"I'm so glad you asked me. I don't often get to go to a cottage in *la-di-dah* Muskoka. Let's unload and get settled. Maybe some lunch before our hike in the woods."

"*Our* hike in the woods?"

Cindy was opening her car door. It lurched on it hinges and then stuck.

"Bang it with your shoulder."

She heaved her body against the grimy metal. "Yes, our hike. We have to check out the land that's going to be developed, especially the waterfront. That way when we go into the Town

Hall we will be orientated to any maps and plans."

"We cut a few paths over the years in what we thought was the neighbouring Crown land. But I don't know Cindy. At this time of year? All the animals are waking up from their hibernation. They'll be hungry. There'll be bears."

"Naw, they're not interested in us." She sounded tentative. "Bears hardly ever attack people. Maybe once a decade, a crazy bear will attack. You know, one that's been eating flashlight batteries. But don't worry, we're safe from them. I read up on that when I was thinking of being a forester." She was trying to convince herself.

I opened the car door for Lucky and he bounded out before I could grab him. He loped away and then raced in tight circles around the lawn in front of the cottage, his leash flapping behind him, a silly grin on his face. We both watched him and laughed. He came when called, amazingly, but probably to get away from the swarm of blackflies flying around his head. We grabbed our luggage and hurried up the bumpy path to the steps to the kitchen door. I took a deep breath of the sweet northern air.

We were here.

4.

I OPENED THE SCREEN DOOR on its creaky hinges and then inserted the old brass cottage key into the lock of the back door, sweeping my arm in front of me to usher Cindy in. She marched past me directly into the kitchen, her head whipping this way and that as she checked out her surroundings. Making herself at home, she unzipped her insulated food bag and pitched items into the fridge.

"Not too shabby," she said while slinging some lettuce into the vegetable cooler.

"Thanks." I loved the place and was grateful that she appreciated it.

My family's cottage was circa 1895, and had the wide plank floors, large rooms, a fieldstone fireplace and the casement windows of the period. I flung open a window over the kitchen sink and the red-checkered gingham curtains flapped in the light spring breeze. The view was simply beautiful, a peaceful combination of hills and rocks, water and sunshine. I took a deep breath and filled my lungs with the perfumed air of the forest. When I turned around, I could see that the kitchen gleamed. The scent of pine polish lingered on the wooden cupboards. Underlying this was the smell of disinfectant. Andrew might be an asshole, but he cleaned like a demon. He must have spent hours cleaning after his fancy shindig two or three weekends ago. The countertop was spick and span, not a single mouse turd in sight.

"This fridge is spotless," said Cindy, her head buried deep in its interior.

"That's Andrew. OCD."

"Well, I didn't think it was you."

Should I be offended?

I dragged my green garbage bag past her, through the living/dining room combo, called a "Muskoka great room" by pretentious real estate agents, and up the stairs. "We're up here," I called as my bag thumped on the steps. Lucky followed me with his long tail slowly sweeping back and forth.

"Coming." The fridge door slammed shut and Cindy clomped up the stairs after me, her rolling suitcase carried in her hand. At the top of the stairs she exclaimed, "Oh this is so lovely. No wonder you love your cottage."

The wooden floors were luminous from the light shining through a mullioned window at the end of the hallway. There were six bedrooms on this floor, three on each side of the hallway, and two bathrooms, all with wooden plank doors facing onto the long corridor.

"Here, you take this room," I said while opening up one of the doors. "And I'll take the one next door to you. These are the better rooms because they are lakeside with a pretty view. Let's use the same bathroom. That way we'll only have to clean one when we leave."

"Oh, I don't mind," said Cindy as she walked into the bathroom across the hall from her bedroom. "I can clean my own bathroom. This one is nice."

She was such a princess.

I left her testing the taps and said, "Up to you." I hoofed my green garbage bag onto my bed, ripped it open because I couldn't get the knot undone, and stuffed my clothes into the dresser.

Cindy poked her head into my room. She eyed the mangled garbage bag on the bed. "Trying out a new brand of soft-sided luggage?"

I laughed. I should have been embarrassed, but I wasn't.

"Where are the sheets?" she queried. "I always feel settled after I make up my bed."

Uh-oh. The sheets at this time of year were guaranteed to have mouse poo in them. "Ah, hang on." I dashed to the linen closet and flung open the door before Cindy had a chance to get there, grabbed the top sheet and shook it out. Nothing. I grabbed the next sheet and shook it out as well. Nothing. Phew. Two pillowcases were next. I shook them too. Nothing. We were safe. It looked like the mice hadn't got into the cupboard. Or maybe meticulous Andrew had already washed the winter out of everything. I dumped an armful of clean linen on Cindy's bed.

"Here, I'll give you a hand."

The two of us made up her bed and then, while she finished unpacking, I rummaged in the linen closet for some other sheets and made mine. When I was done, I looked out my window and admired the view. Every hill, every tree, and every rock had been permanently etched into my retina from a lifetime of looking at this landscape. I turned my head until all the silhouettes lined up with my memory. The grass leading down to the little sandy beach where I played as a child was still somewhat flattened by the weight of the winter snow, but here and there fresh green sprouts made their way through the undergrowth. Three large crows, or at least I thought they were crows but maybe they were turkey vultures, circled on the breeze, high above the lake, lazily riding on the soft wind. The copse of weeping willows to the right of the beach was still leaning precariously as a unified group over the water's edge. I marvelled at the tenacity of their roots. These four trees had been threatening to fall into the lake for as long as I could remember.

Cindy tapped on my door and I reluctantly turned away from the window to face her. "Oh hello, Mrs. John Wayne." She was wearing hiking boots, blue jeans rolled up at the cuff, and a navy-blue hoodie. The hoodie was so old, the zipper curled in a wave down her front and there were little white pills of fluff on the sleeves. In her hand she held two bug hats, probably from Dollarama. She was ready for her walk.

I looked down at my thin-strapped summer sandals and lightweight linen skirt. "I'll be a minute."

"Put on anything blue. Bugs don't like blue." She held out her arms to illustrate her point.

"Did you wash your hoodie with the towels? Wash your towels separately. That way you won't get pills. I work for the Home and Garden section and I'm an expert on laundry. Unfortunately. But don't worry, mosquitoes and blackflies don't really like me. I take vitamin B."

Cindy laughed. "It was my son's, and God knows he doesn't separate his laundry. If he does it at all. The jury's out on vitamin B repelling bugs, so good luck with that. I brought you a bug hat." She tossed it on the bed, turned on her heel, and thundered downstairs, where I could hear her banging away in the kitchen. She was opening and shutting cupboard doors, probably checking out the cooking utensils. Cindy liked to cook, which suited me just fine. I loved to eat. A perfect symbiotic relationship.

I dug out some jeans and a sweatshirt, threw them on, and slid my feet into my Timberlands. Frankly, I was starving. Maybe Cindy had manufactured something delicious from the slim pickings. As I went downstairs I saw a tattered filament of a spider's web lazily wafting from the corner of the stairwell. It was with a flash of malicious glee that I registered that Andrew wasn't perfect after all. My daily practice of finding the Buddhahood in everyone was a tad rusty today.

Cindy was hovering over a pot on the stove, stirring one of my frozen soups slowly while it melted. It smelled heavenly. She had chosen the eastern one with coconut and cumin. Perfect! There was a bowl of tuna salad and washed lettuce leaves draining on a plate. Some slices of bread from a fresh loaf were on the bread board, waiting for assembly.

"I left the sandwiches for you to do," Cindy said.

"I think I can manage that." I grabbed a knife and spread the tuna on bread, shook out the remaining water from the lettuce, placed it haphazardly on the tuna, and slapped the bread together. "I didn't know you ate fish." Cindy was a vegetarian.

"Sure I do. I'm not, like, a pure vegetarian vegetarian. I eat milk products and eggs as well. But no meat. I can't stand the idea of eating an animal that has legs."

"Some fish have legs. Evolution, you know. Eons ago a fish walked out of the water and onto land. That might be where we began."

"That's where my husband began," she laughed.

"Mine too." I carried the sandwiches to the harvest table while Cindy brought in the soup. "Thanks for making this, Cindy. I'm starving. Driving always makes me hungry." Everything made me hungry.

"You helped."

I snorted.

Over our lunch we discussed our route. Or at least I did. "There's a trail marked with orange tape tied around trees on the land that's been sold. Remember, we always thought it was Crown land. My kids made the path years ago when we wanted a long hiking trail through the woods. It's a loop and takes about forty-five minutes to complete on foot." I looked at my watch. "It's after twelve now, so we'd be back in time to head into Huntsville and go to the Town Hall. They probably close at four. How does that sound?"

Cindy slurped her soup. Her table manners were outrageous. One day I would lose it and snap at her. "Sounds fine by me," she said. "Are you worried about bears?"

Of course I was.

"Naw. We'll be fine. I'll carry an air horn with me and, if we see a bear or a coyote, it will scare them off."

"What's an air horn?"

"It's a canister of compressed air that blasts a really loud noise. They use them on sailboat races to indicate the start. They are also used by boats in trouble on the water. They are deafeningly loud."

Cindy shoved some sandwich into her mouth and spoke while chewing, "So, better than pepper spray or bear spray?"

"Don't talk with your mouth full." Oops. My non-judgmental Buddha detachment misfired.

"Sorry."

She wasn't.

"Bear sprays can backfire on you, especially if you are downwind and they get in your eyes. So I think an air horn is a better option. The worst that will happen if you make a mistake with it is your ears will ring for a few days."

She gulped down another mouthful before she spoke, swallowing pointedly before speaking. "You're sure it will scare bears away?"

Not at all. "Positive. Animals and humans alike! Didn't you see that show on the police researching the use of loud decibels to neutralize criminals? Believe me, it will work. We always have a canister here at the cottage. We take it when we are heading into the woods."

"Where do you get one?"

"Oh, any boating store has them. Ours came from the marina section at the Canadian Tire here in town. They aren't expensive. We buy the small size that fits into a pocket."

"So, they're pretty common then."

"Oh sure. It's just that most people use them only on boats, not knowing they are really effective in scaring off animals." I thought for a bit. "In fact, I've never used one on a boat."

"Yes, but have you ever used one to scare off a bear?"

"Well, no, but I know it will work. All the research indicates it will."

Cindy gathered up her bowl and plate. "Righto, then." She didn't believe me. Neither did I. "Let's wander into bear-infested woods with a horn for boats. Yippee. I feel so safe."

I rolled my eyes. "No, really, it will work."

"I'm taking a big stick." She thought for a second. "Or a hatchet."

"Oh my, hand-to-hand combat with a bear. Good luck."

"Maybe I should take off my hiking boots and put on running shoes."

"You can't outrun a bear, Cindy. They can travel faster than a car if they put their mind to it."

"I'll climb a tree?"

"Bears climb trees."

"Okay, dart into the lake."

"Bears can swim."

"So, I give up. If you run into a bear you're basically dead."

"Well, no," I said, hoping I wasn't lying. "Face the bear, wave your arms, and look big. And make as much noise as possible." I stretched behind me for the air horn on the sideboard and waggled it to illustrate my point.

She reached for my plate and bowl. "Consider me educated."

I followed Cindy into the kitchen with the glasses. "If we get separated, look for the orange ties on the trees and eventually you will find your way home. If you can't find any ties, head downhill. You will come to the lake and see our place."

"Why would we get separated? We're walking together, right?"

I knew what she was like, Miss Independent. "Well, you never know." I decided to be the devil's advocate. "Maybe if I get attacked by a bear, you'll have to run to safety."

Cindy ran the water in the sink and squirted in some dish soap. How lucky was I that she cooked *and* cleaned!

"You just said you can't outrun a bear."

"The bear would be busy with me."

Cindy stopped washing the dishes and looked me up and down. The seconds ticked by. Then she looked at her own body. Considering. "Yup. They'd pick you over me."

"That was rude."

"So, let's go on our bucolic walk in an enchanted forest." She dried her hands on a tea towel hanging on the stove handle and then wiped them on her jeans. "I'm ready when you are."

I picked up a bottle of insect repellent from the window frame and held it up. "You want some?"

"Are you kidding? That stuff's poison. We have bug hats, plus I'm completely covered." She showed me her arms again.

"So I see. And yeah, I never use it either. I never put it on my kids either. Sunscreen as well. The amount of crap in those products, unbelievable. It's a wonder they can get away with it. There should be food guidelines applied to stuff that goes on skin. Imagine putting this shit on your body."

"Insect repellent stinks, too. Air pollution. I'm almost ready to go. I have to go to upstairs for a sec before we head out. I'll be right back."

Cindy ran up the stairs while I dried some of the dishes and put them away. I was looking forward to a walk in the forest with all its lovely smells of dusky earth and evergreen. To think that this forest was going to be razed, making way for a stupid development of some kind. Condominiums or a golf course. Geezus.

The more I thought about it, the more enraged I became. I loved the land. I could feel anger frothing in my chest, ready to erupt. This would not be good for anxiety, from which I periodically suffered, like now, before going into the woods in the spring. Bears woke up in the spring and they were hungry. Yes, I was a true Canadian, and loved the wilderness, but I was also realistic. I started to breathe slowly into my belly and count to eight as I exhaled. In four, out eight. In four, out eight. I shut my eyes and breathed in and out, feeling the anger melt away.

"What are you doing?"

I jumped out of my skin.

"Oh, a little meditation to open my heart to nature." Cindy

already thought I was a spiritual nutcase, so why not feed her impression? God forbid she should know I was scared out of my wits. I don't know why I was. I'd walked this trail hundreds of times.

She wasn't fooled. "I'm scared of bears too. Let's go."

With that, Cindy snatched the air horn and a bug hat off the sideboard and marched out the kitchen door. The porch door slammed loudly and Lucky looked up from his corner of the couch, his soft brown eyes questioning me.

"No, you're not coming this time Lucky, you rest here for a bit. We'll be right back," I said hopefully, as I snatched my bug hat and followed her.

Cindy was heading onto the path leading to the right edge of the property. She looked over her shoulder as she walked toward the woods. "Hurry up," she shouted. "I see an orange marker tied around that sapling over there. Is that where we go in?"

"Yup." I raced ahead of her. When I got to the orange tie I touched the tape as if it were a mezuzah that would keep me safe. Then I acted like an orchestra conductor, bowing from the waist down as I gestured into the woods with a stick I'd picked up off the lawn. "Follow me. This marks the doorway to the trail."

I took the first step in, holding the branches so they wouldn't snap back on Cindy. I looked ahead into the dark bush and immediately felt as if something were not quite right. Everything looked the same as it always did; shadows shimmered on the forest floor and sparrows hopped from tree to tree, squawking at our intrusion into their sanctuary. But I was convinced something was off. I don't know why I felt so jangled. My animal totem, whatever that was, was jittery.

5.

I TOOK A FEW STEPS deeper into the bush and then looked behind me. Cindy was grimly parting branches, her head thrust back on her neck, out of the way of twigs that might lash at her. I gave her what I hoped was a jaunty smile. "Isn't this fun?"

"Some trail." She spat out the word.

No, Cindy wasn't happy.

"Well, it *is* a bit thick here. I think it filled in over in the fall. But it will open up when we get out of the scrub and into the maple bush," I said merrily. "The next marker is up ahead, see it?" I pointed up the incline and to the left. "It's right over there, tied around that tree."

She hissed, "How far to the maple bush?"

I sang, "Once we get to the top of this little hill, to that marker, and then down the other side. It's not far. There's a bit of a marshy area and then another incline." I tried not to let her see I was panting. "It's at the top of that." It was tough going.

"Whatever you say, Radisson."

I guffawed at her reference to an early Canadian fur trader. "If we had come here six weeks ago, there would have been buckets on the trees. Somebody in town taps them every year for maple syrup. Really, this land has been treated as if it belonged to no one and everyone for years and years."

"Bugs aren't as bad as I thought they'd be," said Cindy, swatting at her head.

Was she being sarcastic? Or honest?

"As soon as there's a hot day or two, there'll be less. When the ground dries up, the blackflies are gone. They breed in water. So, they will be out in full force once we head down the hill a bit to the marsh," I said, by way of an explanation. I was slightly ahead of her and there were already swarms dive-bombing my head. Good thing I had put on the bug hat.

Suddenly, Cindy took off her bug hat and shook it madly. "Fucking blackflies. One must have got in somehow."

I quickly tightened the drawstring around my throat. "Get that hat back on, Cindy. A bite on an eyelid could turn you into a Cyclops." Then, I added, "Don't worry. Once we get past the marsh it will be way better."

"You wish."

When I reached the swampy ground, my feet squelched through mud with every step. But as soon as I had waded into the mud, I was out again on solid ground, stirring up dust from dried crusty leaves and heading to the top of the next incline. Ahead, I could see sunlight penetrating through the canopy above, leaving dappled shadows on the forest floor. A light breeze fanned my face and the bugs were diminishing.

"Almost there," I shouted over my shoulder. There was no sarcastic reply, so I twisted my body around to look for my friend. No Cindy. "Cindy?" I called. Where was she? "Cindy?" I shouted, this time louder. No answer. Last thing I needed was for my red-headed friend to be lost in the woods. She was very tall; how could I not see her?

I sighed and retraced my steps. Damn her anyway. Plus, she had the air horn. But worry seeped through my anger. She wasn't exactly a wilderness gal. Down into the marshy gully, up the small incline, over the brow of the next incline. No Cindy. "Cindy," I yelled, throwing my voice into the forest. It echoed eerily, bouncing off trees. I heard a rustling in the leaves and I spun around. A squirrel scampered off. Suddenly, I felt very alone. It was far too quiet. Fear crept up my spine and crawled over my skull. Where was she? I should have trusted my instincts; something hadn't seemed right when we'd entered the woods. I listened hard. The wind rustled through the branches and a deer bleated in the distance. Where was my friend? I scanned the leaf-littered ground and lower branches, looking for signs of her: a torn thread, a lost shoe, something. I sniffed the air, trying to catch a whiff of bear. Or worse, a coyote.

"Yoo-hoo. Up here. The view is fantastic." Her voice warbled through the trees.

I craned my neck and looked up, high into a huge jack pine. Cindy was sitting with legs dangling on each side of a large branch, her back leaning against the trunk. Shit. "What are you doing? You're over fifty years old. Get the fuck out of that tree. You scared the daylights out of me."

"I can see for miles. I haven't climbed this high since I was ten. This is beautiful country. So many lakes, all sparkling in the distance. Come on up." She gestured expansively at the landscape with one hand while the other was nonchalantly curled around a branch. My throat constricted.

"No," I shouted. Was she nuts? I didn't do trees. First of all, I was fifty-six. Secondly, I get a nosebleed on a footstool. "No way. I don't like heights. Come on down. I want to do the whole trail in time to get to town. I'm working, remember?" It sounded like a lame cover for my fear, which it was. I could have throttled her.

She swung a leg over the branch and with dizzying speed shimmied down the tree, swaying from branch to branch and finding footholds for her swinging feet. I could hardly watch. Finally, she was on the ground, brushing herself off and wiping her hands on the seat of her pants.

"Fantastic. So fun."

"For you, maybe, but you frightened me. You can't take off and go your own way, Cindy. You have to stick with me. Things happen in the woods. Don't do that again."

"Sorry." She apologized but it sounded as if she were saying,

"Whatever...." I was tired of her fake apologies.

"No, I mean it, Cindy. What if you had fallen out of the tree? Broken some bones?"

"Oh, come on, don't be a worrywart. You would have found me. Called for an ambulance."

I shook my phone at her. "No signal. Besides, what if something had happened to me while you're up in the sky, ogling the landscape? It's only you and me here, and we need each other for safety."

She looked suitably chastened. "You're right. Sorry."

"Okay. Now follow me and stick close." It was like talking to a child. I put my useless phone back in my pocket and headed over the incline, checking over my shoulder, making sure Cindy was following me.

"'Closely.' Not 'close.' Adverb modifying a verb."

I shook my head. "Geez, Cindy. Knock it off. You know what I mean. Besides, I think you're wrong. 'Stick closely'? Naw. Doesn't sound right. Maybe 'stick close by.' That sounds better. You need a dangling gerund in there." I thought for a minute. "Not that 'by' is a dangling gerund."

"No *dangling* gerunds for me," she panted. "I'm gay."

Oh, what a card she was.

We made our way through the marsh and up the next steep incline. When we were over the brow, we looked all around. The forest view stretched forever. I loved this vantage point. I grabbed her arm and started to point at landmarks. "See over there, that uprooted tree? There used to be a den of foxes living there. When the tree fell over, it left a gaping hole at its base, a perfect spot for a home. And up that tree? See it? That dark blotch against the sky? That's a raccoon nest. Last year she had five babies. So cute."

"Squirrels' nest," Cindy said with authority. "Those were baby squirrels."

"How would you know? I like my raccoon nest thesis better."

"I wanted to be a biologist for a while."

"Sure you did. After being a fireman and a forester."

"*Firefighter.* Watch your language. What's that down there?" Cindy asked pointing to a hump in the forest floor about halfway down the hill. "Looks like some kind of brownish-yellow rock or something. Are there such things as yellow rocks?" She squinted. "Is it a rock?"

I followed her gaze and saw what she was looking at. It sure looked like a yellow rock. Sort of the colour of breastfed baby poop. "I've never heard of yellow rocks around here. Maybe in the Middle East. Sandstone. Here we have grey ones and black ones and even some pink ones. But yellowish? Not so much. Besides, you'd think I'd remember it being there. Let's take a closer look."

Cindy took off down the hill at a slant and I followed, our feet rustling in the new green shoots springing up through the dried leaves. The musky smell of forest floor rose as I kicked up the leaves, hurrying to catch up to her. She covered the terrain like a gazelle, loping down the hill on her long legs over to the yellow rock. I covered the terrain like a dachshund, skidding down the hill on my short stubby legs. When we got closer, I could make out some material. "It looks like a bunched-up pile of fabric—the colour of a Carhartt jacket. You know, one of those denimy woodsy coats? Someone must have become hot while walking in the woods and ditched it, intending to pick it up later and then forgetting it. I've done that."

Cindy said, "I know those jackets. They're pretty durable. Sandstone. I think that's the name of the colour. Or Carhartt Brown. I always wanted one, but the bottom snaps don't do up on me. Besides, I think it would make me look like a biker chick."

I eyed Cindy up and down. In her hiking boots, baggy jeans, leather belt with its huge silver buckle, and scruffy navy-blue hoodie she already looked like a biker chick. "Wouldn't be a stretch."

She ignored me. "Do you think we should leave it or hang it up on a tree? That would make it easier for whoever lost it to see it."

"If it were mine I would want someone to hang it up, you know, so if it rains it won't get all muddy."

"I know, but some people are weird about their possessions. They don't want people touching them. I mean, what if some guy left it there on purpose, as a marker or something? Maybe it's on a rock. It is sort of humped up into a mound."

I agreed, "Yeah, it does look like it was left on a rock. I don't know why he bothered. Look how stained the back of it is."

"What is that? Mud? It'll be hard getting that out."

"You're such a mother. Did you bring your stain remover?"

"You're the one who noticed the stain. Are we going to hang it up or not?"

I thought for a minute. People could be possessive about their stuff. And people who wore Carhartts were people used to going in the bush. And those people could be hunters. With guns. "Okay, let's do this. Let's leave it where it is and finish our walk. We may bump into the guy and then we can tell him where it is, just in case he forgot. If we don't bump into anyone, then we can hang it up on our way back. The trail loops around up ahead and comes back on itself, so we'll pass by it again."

"Suits me. Let's go. Is that an orange marker up ahead? Over there?" She pointed to her right.

"Yes. We go over that way and eventually come to the shore. It's pretty rocky on the way, and lots of scrubby bush, but eventually we come out at a pretty little beach."

"Beachfront, huh? That's worth a mint." Cindy stopped and pirouetted around in a full circle, her hand shielding her eyes and looking up. "I'm pretending I know how to determine our direction by looking at the sun," she said, laughing. "Don't have a clue. Which way are we facing?"

"West. Well, more like southwest."

"Southwest facing beachfront. Sun all day long. Sunsets. Prime, prime, prime."

I grabbed her by the arm and pulled her towards the marker. "Come on."

We scrambled over some rocks and plunged into the bush. The orange marker could be barely seen up ahead, a small slice of the edge of the tape barely visible through the thick branches. Blackflies were attacking us in full force again. I wished I'd put on some bug spray after all. Maybe that skin product made by Avon that people swore by.

"Whoever dreamed up that blue theory and bugs was full of shit," said Cindy madly swatting at her head.

"I'm with you on that. But we will be out of this bush soon and at the waterfront. There will be a breeze and the bugs will be blown back into the woods."

"How do you know there will be a breeze? You a shaman or something?"

I laughed. "No, but there was a light wind through the trees back there and a light breeze in the forest usually means a gale at the shore."

Finally, we made it to the water. We sat on a large piece of driftwood that had been bleached by the sun and took off our bug hats, shaking our heads to loosen our damp hair off our scalps. The fresh gusts of wind kept the bugs at bay, and we relaxed from our constant vigil against them. I stretched my left arm out and said, "All this land to the left of us belongs to this huge plot. And if you look over there," I pointed right, "you can see my family's cottage."

"Wow, I didn't realize we'd come this far. Are we in the middle of his land?"

"Yeah, about that. There's probably three thousand feet of waterfront to the right of us, and more to the left. He has about a mile, or slightly over."

"Did you ever notice that waterfront is measured in feet, not metres?"

"I know. And fruit and vegetables are sold by the pound, not by kilos."

"A truly bilingual country."

I stretched my legs and hoisted myself up, trying not to groan. I really had to lose some weight. "Let's head back. The trail circles around a bit that way and then joins up to where we were when we found the jacket."

"I'd forgotten about that. I wonder if it will still be there."

"I haven't heard anyone scrabbling about in the bush, so probably."

We put our bug hats back on and took off into the forest again. I would have to talk to my kids about clearing the trail a bit in the summer. No, wait, this wasn't land we could use anymore. In fact, Cindy and I were trespassing right now. We followed the orange markers for five minutes when I noticed a plastic spray bottle half-buried under some sprouted maple keys. I wouldn't have noticed it if I weren't focused on placing my feet carefully between roots so I wouldn't trip.

"Hey, look at this." I picked it up. "Just what we need. Bug spray. It's the same brand of insect repellent that I found on our kitchen windowsill." I held it up to my face. "It has a word written on it with black magic marker. 'DOG.'" I took the lid off and took a whiff. "I don't care how bad the bugs are, I would never use this kind. It stinks."

I handed it to Cindy to smell. "Ugh. That's disgusting. No wonder someone used it on their dog."

She screwed the lid back on tightly and handed it to me. I debated about throwing it deep into the woods but Cindy, the litter police, probably sensed what I was about to do and shook her head just once. I put it in my back pocket.

"No point in leaving litter around," I said to appease her. "Look, there's the jacket."

Sure enough, the jacket was still humped up on the ground. Cindy marched toward it. "I'll get it and hang it up."

I followed close behind. When we got to the jacket, we could see that its edges were covered with earth, and only the corduroy collar was available for grabbing. She tugged at one corner of the collar to lift it out of the earth. She grunted. "Seems to be buried in the dirt or something. I can't seem to lift it."

"Here, I'll help pull." I wandered over to the front of the coat. "It's probably been here awhile. It sure is caked in mud. And it's kind of ripped too. Probably someone's favourite coat and they couldn't bear to part with it even though it was long past its prime." I bent over to inspect the collar. As I got closer to the jacket, I nearly gagged. The stench coming off the material was unbelievable. "It smells pretty bad." I wrapped my fingers around the opposite edge of the collar that Cindy was holding.

"Okay, let's pull on the count of three."

Cindy nodded at me, her auburn curls bouncing on her forehead, inches from mine, and said, "Sounds good." We both took a breath. "One, two, three."

The coat made a sucking noise as it lifted out of the muddy earth. The smell got worse and worse. It was so heavy. Why would a jacket weigh so much?

And then we screamed when we saw what was holding the coat down in the earth.

A bloody torso.

6.

WE MADLY SHOOK OUR HANDS and hopped up and down in tight little circles, screaming at the top of our lungs. My whole body was vibrating. I had never in my life seen a headless torso. It was awful. There was a stump were the neck had been severed. The skin around the stump was shredded and there was a bit of white bone protruding. It had teeth marks in it, much like the ones Lucky left on his marrow bones. It was like the severed neck of a store-bought chicken, but on a much larger scale. I thought I was going to throw up.

As suddenly as we had started, we both stopped screaming and dancing around. Cindy was walking around the jacket-covered torso, kicking at the ground with her feet.

"What are you doing?" I shouted. "This could be a crime scene and you're disturbing it in a pretty major way. Don't disturb the crime scene."

"I'm looking for other body parts. They must be around here somewhere."

"Cindy, we should get the police."

"Naw, the guy was killed by a bear. The police can wait."

"How do you know he was killed by a bear?"

"Claw marks on the front of the body."

That shut me up. I hadn't seen the claw marks and I certainly wasn't going to check now. I was completely repelled by the neck stump. But I wasn't convinced of her theory. Bears in

Ontario simply did not randomly attack people. If my fingers worked— if my phone worked—I would google the statistics. But I knew the statistics were really low, like one attack every forty years or something. While I was thinking about this, Cindy kept parting the plants on the forest floor with her foot. She was determined to find something.

"Bingo," she shouted a few minutes later. "Come see."

Did I want to? No, but I was propelled forward as if by some unseen force, like a moth to a flame. I knew it would turn my stomach. I knew it was against my newly found Buddhist belief that one needed to stand apart from the negative in the universe and simply observe, but on I went anyway, my feet moving of their own accord, my stomach lurching with every step.

Cindy stood proudly beside her trophy, pointing and grinning. "Stop while you're ahead," she said.

I took one look at the skull's black soulless eye sockets, felt my stomach heave, and tossed my tuna sandwich into a small bush.

Cindy tutted and shook her head, "Don't disturb the crime scene," she mimicked before continuing on her meticulous search. She stopped at the base of a large maple, struck a pose, and gestured at some roots as if she were showing off a prize on a TV game show, smiling with all teeth showing. I wiped my mouth on my sleeve and took some deep breaths. How could she handle this?

"This isn't as bad as the head, Robin. Come and look."

"No." This wasn't working for me.

"No, really, it's okay. You won't get hurt, the guy is completely armless." She threw back her head and laughed.

I guess we all handle death differently. She made jokes. I barfed. And I did so again. Only this time, I tried to throw up on my old barf, just in case this was a crime scene. Out of the corner of my eye, I could see that Cindy was proudly pointing at a bone, not long enough to be a leg, leaning against the root of the tree. There were bits of red muscle attached. I heaved again, only now nothing came up. Even so, I bent over and drooled over the wet patch of wilted lettuce and semi-chewed bread. Why hadn't I brought a tissue?

Cindy continued on her search, using her right foot to stir up the leaves in front of her as she slowly walked in a widening circle around the jacket, her eyes casing the ground and all around. A few more minutes went by and then she shouted triumphantly, "*Ta-dah*!" Her head was tilted upwards, looking up to the sky. About twenty feet up, in the crotch of two adjoining tree branches, was a long white bone. It was missing the hip joint but still had a few long white tendons attached to the other end.

I could feel my stomach rise in my throat and then fall again. This was a human being we were looking at. Cindy was finding pieces of a dismembered person. A somebody. A living creature who had a mother, maybe a wife, maybe children. This was horrible.

"Cindy, stop."

"Robin, really, it's okay. The person is dead. He doesn't care. Come see. Maybe this is your story. You'll get a leg up in your career if you take a close look at the facts." She laughed. "Leg up. Get it?"

It wasn't funny. "No. This is horrible. How can you be so flippant?"

She continued on her search, one foot gently probing the earth in front of her. The air was filled with the sound of Rice Krispies crackling as she walked over the dry leaves. After a few minutes, she stopped and dug into the earth with the toe of her hiking boot. She then turned her back on her find and started to kick backwards at the spot with her heel. "Hey Robin, I found something else."

"I'm not coming to look." I was deep breathing, trying to get the whistling out of my ears. "You are really disturbing the crime scene. If it is one." I thought it was. Bears did not attack people. Except bears that had been eating batteries.

"There. Finally, I got it." The sound of her kicking at the earth stopped and I hazarded a peek. She was on her haunches, stirring at the damp earth with a stick. "Hey, Robin. Come here. Let me give you a hand," she laughed. I wished she'd shut up. "I see a ring. Beside a finger. Maybe the poor schmuck was married." She dug in the earth with the stick and then picked up the ring. "Nope, it's a ruby ring. Weird for a guy. But, you never know. Come take a look."

No way would I go over. "This is so disgusting. How can you get so close?"

"Oh, honey, this is nothing compared to seeing the face of a drug lord shot off by some gang member." Cindy had seen a lot while writing her series on gangs. She stuffed the ring in her front pocket.

I'd had enough. "Listen, we had better go back to the cottage. I want to call the police. And get an ambulance or something."

Cindy threw back her head and laughed again. I detected a touch of hysteria. Maybe she wasn't doing that well. "This guy doesn't need an ambulance. He'd give an arm and a leg to live again. He's dead in the water. *Hahaha.*" She was pointing to a foot lying in a puddle and then looked at me to see my reaction to her pun. I wasn't appreciating the joke. "Is the EMS for you? You need a *wah, wah, wahmbulance*?"

Did she ever stop? She was almost maniacal. I shook my head. Maybe this was her way of coping with the shock of it all.

"Let's go, Cindy." I took off down the trail and hoped she'd follow. I had gone about twenty yards when I heard her foot-steps in the dry leaves behind me. I turned around to make sure it was her. You never knew. Maybe the bear was still around.

I didn't understand this situation. Not at all. If it had been a bear, what on earth had the man done to antagonize the creature? Did he have a salmon sandwich in his back pocket? I had personally never heard of a bear attacking a person. Sure, there were always stories circulating about bears tearing through campers' tents to get to their food packs. Anyone canoe tripping in Algonquin Park knew better than to fall asleep with their food anywhere near their campsite. Some campers tied their food pack to a rope and hoisted it up a tree, securing it about forty feet up in the air, dangling over a branch. Sure, bears could climb, but if the branch the pack was hanging from was barely strong enough to hold up the pack, but not strong enough to support a bear, well, the food would stay safe and the bear would wander off the campsite looking for a different convenience store.

Some trippers lashed their food packs to the thwart of a canoe, covered it with a tarp, and then towed the canoe out to the middle of the lake. There they anchored it, leaving it to bob in the water for the night while everyone slept peacefully in their tents. Most bears, especially those in Algonquin, weren't ambitious enough to swim out to a canoe and try to get the pack. Word got around the bear community that the packs were hard to get, and at the end of the day, the effort wasn't worth the reward. Bears weren't natural hunters while swimming. They preferred their feet on the ground.

So, I didn't understand what had gone on here. Why might a bear have attacked this man? It didn't make any sense.

"Did you find any tin foil or wax paper or plastic wrap while you were looking for the guy's ... pieces?" I asked Cindy over my shoulder as we walked.

"No, why?"

"I wondered if the guy was carrying some food in a pocket or something."

"No, I didn't find anything like that. Not a crumb."

"Because bears don't attack someone for no reason."

"They don't?"

"No. I can't believe you don't know that from your forester days."

"I only *wanted* to be a forester. I never was one." Cindy was a trifle defensive.

"I mean, there are some rumours, sort of underground

drumbeats, about some bears going nutso because they've eaten poison in people's garbage. Batteries. Cleaning fluids. The mercury and chemicals make their brains scramble. Those bears will attack."

"Poor bears." She didn't mean it.

"Maybe my brother ate a battery." I said half-heartedly, trying to lighten up. But I was being unkind. "Just joking."

"No, you're not."

She was right.

"So anyway, I'm wondering why this guy got attacked."

"He got attacked because he was an asshole."

"How do you know that?"

"All men are assholes."

"Cindy, you know that's not true. Most gay women are gay for other reasons."

"Not this one."

"Okay, but why do you think this particular guy was a dipstick?"

"Other than the fact that all men are stupid?"

I sighed. "Oh, okay, I'll play. Other than that."

"He was carrying a clipboard."

"First of all, how do you know that?"

"There was a clipboard underneath his, um, torso."

"I didn't see that."

"You were busy with other things. Like throwing up the delicious lunch I made for you."

"I helped make it."

"Oh, slapping already made tuna salad and already washed lettuce on bread is helping?'

The truth was coming out. I'd have to make dinner if I wanted to eat again.

"Lots of guys have clipboards. That doesn't make him stupid. Maybe it makes him smart."

"Bears hate clipboards."

"Cindy. Now who's being stupid?"

"Okay, but he had a pencil attached to the clipboard. With an elastic."

"So?"

"What kind of nerdy person does that?" She started singing Donovan's "Hurdy Gurdy Man," only changing the lyrics to "Nerdy Nerdy Man."

"That song's from the late sixties. You were what, ten?"

Cindy huffed, "I wasn't born yet."

"Nice try. Besides, I'd attach my pencil to my clipboard with an elastic. If I had a clipboard. Personally, I use my recording phone app. But if I did use a clipboard, I'd use an elastic. You don't want to lose your pencil."

"My point. Who uses a clipboard? Only assholes. Plus, it was an HB yellow pencil, the kind with an eraser. He'd chewed the eraser and the metal band holding it in place had bite marks in it."

"Maybe the bear did that."

"Robin. Now who's being stupid?"

"I can't believe we're arguing about this when there's a dead body in the woods."

"A carc*ass*. And most people use those clicky pencils now, the ones with the long leads. HB pencils went out with the dodo bird, right after clipboards. Speaking of birds, why are there no vultures swooping around?"

"I saw three large black birds over the forest earlier. Maybe they were turkey vultures."

"Are we almost back at the cottage yet?"

We'd been walking for some time. I was shivering, even though the day had warmed up. "Two more steps." I parted the last branches and walked into the clearing.

Cindy dusted herself off and pulled her bug hat off her head, shaking out her red frizz. "It's unbelievable how thick the woods are. It's like night and day. One minute you're in complete shade and the next, *ta-dah*," she twirled, "out in the open."

I marched on ahead, my shoes leaving behind damp imprints

in the yellowed grass. The ground was still sodden with winter melt. I pulled my phone out of my pocket and cupped my hand over it to create shade so I could see if I had a signal. "Three bars! Pretty good. Do I call nine-one-one or the station?" Cindy was the expert on matters like this.

"The station. This is hardly an emergency where time is of the essence."

The image of the headless torso floated across my retina and I thought I was going to gag again. "You call."

"Do you have the station number?"

I had the number because some yahoos across the lake had been singing at the top of their lungs well into the night last summer. It was me who wrecked their fun. The number was saved into my contacts under "police/yahoos," in the event I had to call again. I read it out to her.

We stood in the sunshine and brushed away flies while she talked to an officer at the station, her phone pressed against the edge of her chin. I heard her say "body parts" and felt bile flooding my mouth. Then she said she was sure it was human. And then she huffed and said that coyotes don't wear jackets. She looked at me to check her accuracy as she gave the address to the cottage and told them we'd be waiting inside. I could tell that they wanted directions straight to the body because she was insisting that the trail was complicated or non-existent and she would have to take them. She looked pretty satisfied as she tucked her phone into her back pocket.

"Why didn't you tell them how to get to the body? All they would have to do is follow the orange tape tied around the trees."

"Robin, Robin, Robin. How am I ever going to make a crime reporter out of you? If I told them where the body was, then I wouldn't be able to go with them. I am a crime reporter and the opportunity to get inside a crime scene is a rare and happy event."

The flies were beginning to bother me. I grabbed her arm.

"Anyway, let's get inside and wait. I'm going to go too, so I can show them exactly where I puked." I dragged her a few steps. "Hey, wait a minute, you said 'crime scene.' Have you changed your mind?"

She shrugged. "It will make them come faster. But I think the guy got attacked because he was an idiot."

"I don't. Bears don't do that. They are scared of people. So, who knows why he attacked."

"He? Maybe it was a she-bear and the guy got between her and her cubs. I hear that can be a big no-no."

She was right. Maybe that was all it was. A mother protecting her babies. It was spring, bear breeding season, after all. Or maybe not. I still couldn't understand it. "I wonder who the man was."

"Oh, don't worry about that, just another asshole with a clipboard."

I rolled my eyes. She was so jaded.

As we neared the cottage, I could see Lucky standing at the screen door, wagging his little tail madly, his whole body wriggling back and forth. I opened the door carefully so he wouldn't get out and grabbed his collar as Cindy was coming in behind me.

"Here, you go sit down. I'll make some tea." She put on the kettle. "We can drink the water here, right? You look like you need some peppermint tea to settle your stomach."

I walked through the kitchen but not before taking the plastic spray bottle that I had found in the woods out of my pocket. It had a little repellent left, maybe a spray worth, so I put it on the windowsill next to the other one.

"Yes, we have a good well. We aren't drinking lake water here. And yes, I could use some tea. Thanks, Cindy." The taste of vomit lingered in my mouth. The room tilted to one side.

"I'd make a good husband."

I tried my best to laugh. Suddenly I wasn't feeling very well. This was all too much for me, a mild Home and Garden reporter. I wrote about decorating, not death. Was this a normal death? It didn't feel right to me. Maybe no death did. But I wondered if I should call Ralph. No, I didn't need a big strong man to save me. I perched against the door frame and closed my eyes, waiting for the room to stop spinning.

7.

I WATCHED CINDY SCOOP OUT some peppermint tea from a mason jar into a pot. The water in the kettle seemed to rustle like dead leaves as it began to simmer. I held on to the counter with my right hand, trying to steady myself. I felt as if a deep freeze had entered my soul, turning it into a block of ice. There was a buzzing in my ears and my eyesight seemed to be blotchy one minute and then super clear the next. It was so weird. At first, I saw everything in high definition. The edges of objects were so distinct, almost as if outlined in black marker. And then, broad swaths of what I was looking at would vanish. I staggered into the family room, leaving Cindy to make the tea.

The cottage living room swayed and tilted like a boat on choppy seas. I pitched myself onto the corduroy-covered couch under the window and sank like a leaking vessel into the pillows. Lucky leapt up onto the couch beside me and leaned his warm body against mine, putting his nose into my neck. How did dogs always know? I absent-mindedly scratched his soft head, swirling the fur under my fingertips.

The images I had seen in the forest flickered across the movie screen of my retina. I couldn't believe what I had seen. This was nothing like the other dead body I'd been up close and personal with. That one was a piece of cake compared to this guy. My very first dead body was lying on a bed. No blood. No gore. No severed limbs. He was neatly dressed, looking like he'd settled down for a nap after work. Most importantly, his head was attached to his body. He still had skin. I felt my stomach constrict.

Would I puke all over the newly laundered couch cover? Andrew would have a fit.

Maybe I shouldn't have anything to drink. I could see myself, hurling my mint tea all over the police officers when they arrived. What would I say? "After-dinner mint, anyone?" My chest shuddered and I felt colder and colder. I looked down and it felt like my entire body belonged to someone else. Then, Lucky licked my face and I came back.

Cindy came into the living room carrying two cups of tea. Mine, I guessed, was the heavy clay mug, glazed with a picture of a moose. Hers, I deduced, was the rainbow-festooned porcelain cup. She looked at me, one eyebrow arched. "You okay?"

"I feel kind of funny, like I'm dreaming, only I'm very cold."

"Oh, *that*. Don't worry. You're in shock. It will go away. Here's a blanket."

She picked up one of the quilts that Andrew had neatly folded over the arm of the couch and shook it out. "Drink your tea. You'll feel better in a minute."

Her brisk words belied her gentle approach as she gently lay the quilt over my shaking body, covering me all the way up to my chin. This side of Cindy was a rare sight to behold. The Cindy I knew was relentless in her aggressive search for a story. She was determined and persistent. She was a hard-nosed reporter. Nothing got in her way when she was on the scent. She muscled her way through crowds to get up front and centre to any disaster. Crime scene tape was invisible thread to her. But now, she was patting a blanket around me, tucking me in as if I were a newborn, stroking my arms and rubbing my shoulders softly. Kindness flowed from her like warm water over my cold, trembling body.

"Don't get any ideas," she said.

The old Cindy was back.

I smiled at her and nodded, acknowledging her tenderness. A "thank you" would have made her uncomfortable. "When will the police get here?" My voice sounded tinny.

"I think I can hear them now." Her brief indulgence into affection had completely evapourated and she paced around the room like a coiled spring, ready to pounce. Her tightened muscles almost vibrated with tension, her sparking energy finding release in straightening up objects that had already been straightened by Andrew.

Sure enough, I heard the remote whine of sirens in the distance. Soon their high-pitched wails pierced through the surrounding forest, rising and falling as they covered the miles from town. How many were coming? I could hear three different sirens weaving together. Exactly what were they racing to? The guy was dead. Being a small-town police force, maybe they had to try out their sirens for the first time this year to make sure they still worked. The mile-long dirt road to the cottage clearing would slow them down.

I had maybe five minutes to pull myself together. I took three large gulps of the mint tea. It was sweet. Cindy must have put honey in it. I willed myself to breathe deeply and mumbled a Nichiren Buddhist chant under my breath to calm myself. I sat perfectly still, trying to clear my mind of all thoughts, but the headless torso was firmly wedged into my neurons and refused to budge. Nonetheless, the inner shaking was slowly subsiding, and the tea was warming me up from the inside out. Just in time.

Car doors smacked shut in the yard, and the spongy ground thudded with heavy boots. A large man with a boulder for a head on top of a Greek column of a body stood at the screen door. I was guessing that he couldn't see me in the depths of the house, or perhaps he could make out my silhouetted outline. I was sitting on the couch in front of the large picture window. But I, on the other hand, had the great advantage of clearly being able to see him. He had a small black baseball cap incongruously perched over one large bushy eyebrow, with the letters O.P.P. embroidered in shiny gold above the brim. Ontario Provincial Police. I could see there was a gun at his hip, holstered in black leather. I had never actually seen a gun in my life, even holstered. My eyes kept darting to it as if it were a magnet. I guessed it was better to stare there than the other pistol where my eyes tended to wander at will. Not that he could see where I was looking, being a silhouette and all. I snuck a glance at his crotch.

He raised a beefy arm and with a hand the size of a dinner plate knocked surprisingly delicately on the screen door. *Tap, tap, tap*. Lucky launched himself from the couch like a missile and yapped his head off while turning tight circles in front of the screen door. Cindy walked nonchalantly through the kitchen, swinging her hips and tossing coils of red hair off her face. The power in her body was palpable. She talked through the screen, putting the cop at a disadvantage because she would be able to see him clearly while she would be in shadow.

"Yes?" She was so controlled.

A look of puzzlement flickered across his fleshy features. He took off his hat. "Detective Kowalchuk. You called the police about a dismembered body?"

It was a statement. Not a question. Almost accusatory and certainly challenging. In two seconds, they were already engaged in a power play. It was so stupid, I knew. The police had the power. They always won. Even against the mighty media, the journalists, whose pens were swords. But Cindy never gave up trying.

Several uniformed officers loomed behind him, swatting at their heads and looking longingly through the screen door. Kowalchuk stood as still as a statue, immune, it seemed, to the swarm of blackflies circling his head.

"Identification?"

Cindy was such a badass.

Kowalchuk, his face completely blank, reached into his back

pocket and tugged out his ID. Unsmiling, he pressed it against the screen, holding it close to her face.

"Thank you, Detective Kowalchuk. Please, come in." Now, she was all sweetness and light. I knew her act. She wanted them to know that she was not to be trifled with. She knew her rights, yes, sir, but she could be civil. Silly girl. A waste of time, really. The police were, well, the police, and they would always win in a scrimmage with the public.

As each cop filed past her she said, "Cindy," and shook their hand. No last name and no explanation of who she was.

From my vantage point on the couch, I could see the kitchen filling up with the bulky figures of what looked like four or five policemen, all wearing black. Must be the whole force, I thought. The spotless floor was taking a beating from all the mud they dragged in on the bottom of their buffed boots. Steel-toed, no doubt. Andrew's frown danced across my mind. Lucky was sniffing around their knees and gracefully allowing pats on his back. I took a slow sip of my tea and decided that the time to be social was upon me. I could do it.

"Come in," I shouted from the couch. It was, after all, my cottage, and although I didn't trust my knees to support my body, my voice worked. I could at least be polite and invite them into the living room.

They filed into the room and found themselves seats on the couch opposite to the one I was on. I was wrong. I thought there were four or five of them, but there were only three. Two guys and one female. Each cop must have driven their own vehicle. I was certain I had heard three sirens. So that meant they weren't partnered up. Was that safe? Or were things different in the north? In Toronto, the cops seemed to always be partnered up. Except for Ralph. Maybe he wasn't the partnering kind.

Was he? Where was this relationship going? I had to make a decision about him and our direction. I wasn't sure about us, but I couldn't put my finger on the problem. Was it the drinking? My mind drifted over the past few months. He had always been kind and fun to be with. Always tender. And no doubt about it, the sex was great.

Cindy coughed softly to bring me down to earth. Geezus, Robin, grow up. What was wrong with me? There were cops in my living room and I was thinking about sex. C'mon Robin. You're not a teenager in love. But then, maybe, this was the way I coped with trauma.

Cindy sat in an overstuffed chair a little off from the group. My father's reading chair. I yanked my mind into the here and now. She was just as bad. Her gaze kept sidling over to the female officer. What a time to flirt. Although I had to admit, a quick peek showed me that the cop looked interesting. Muscles roped down her neck and wrapped around her forearms. The sharp point of a tattoo peeked over her starched collar. Her broad and firm shoulders fought against her bulletproof Kevlar vest. This woman was ripped and tough. No ring. Clear and intelligent brown eyes under sleek eyebrows. And when I looked back at Kowalchuk, I could see in my peripheral vision that the female officer was stealing glances at Cindy. Well, well, well.

Kowalchuk leaned his hefty bulk toward me, legs spread wide, his gun pushing into the spare tire around his waist. He had sunk so low into the couch that the cushions had risen up and cocooned his body. I was looking forward to watching him fight his way out of that. I wasn't good at guessing people's weight, but he looked as if he were at least two of me. His boots had left little indents in the braided rug between the two couches. Although it was a cool day, he was sweating and wiping his forehead with a clean handkerchief. I hadn't seen one of those in years. I wondered who pressed it. Right. I was the press. I had to get with it if I wanted to write a story about all this. Shirley, my boss back at the office would be salivating about this turn of events.

His arrogant gaze settled upon me. "You must be Robin MacFarland. You're a journalist, right? And Duncan's daughter."

I was shocked. He knew me? "Yes, I am. You know my father?"

"My father went to Huntsville High with him. Said he was a dynamite lacrosse player. Always doing sports when he wasn't going out with Janice what's-her-name?" He snapped his fingers. "Templeton?"

My father played lacrosse? "That's my mother. They got married and moved to Toronto."

"Isn't that nice. High-school sweethearts." He showed his teeth. Maybe it was a smile. "And your brother?" He snapped his fingers again, as if that would summon up his name. The other male officer shifted in his seat. Was he impatient with this ritual of establishing who was who in the north? "Andrew. Yes, Andrew."

"That's right. Andrew." A germophobe who'd go berserk if he saw you inside with your boots on.

"And you and your friend..." he snapped his fingers yet again while he looked to the right above Cindy's head, "Cindy, right? You found a dismembered body in the woods." He said it as if he didn't believe it.

"Yes. We think a bear got him."

"A bear." His mouth formed a thin line and his huge head gave a small waggle as he politely considered what was obviously an outlandish idea. He smiled, again showing all his teeth. So. He was a patronizing prick. Great. That would go over well with Cindy. I could hear her breathing getting a little fast all the way over from her corner chair. "Not likely. I have never heard tell of a bear attacking a person in these parts. Although they can get pretty territorial in the spring. If they've had their babies and you get between them and the mother, well, you're just asking for it."

Oh dear. There was that line. *Just asking for it.* You might as well put some TNT under Cindy. She flared from the corner, "No one asks for a crime to be committed against them." Her eyes flashed around the room, daring anyone to challenge her.

The female cop looked down, her face reddening. The tense silence in the room was punctuated with a *thump, thump, thump*. Lucky's tail.

Detective Kowalchuk pretended to look sheepish. "Of course not. It was a slip of the tongue. An idiom. My mistake. Proper language is so important. I really must try and rid myself of these old sayings."

Imperious idiot.

But the point was made and Cindy settled back in her chair. Out of her sight, the male officer rolled his eyes. I shot him a dagger. He had the good grace to look contrite. Sure he was.

Kowalchuk continued his questioning. "And why do you think it was a bear that killed this person?"

Cindy's eyes met the female cop's. Something passed between them. Cindy blew out her cheeks as if she had been slogging through wet clay. The guy was so dim. Whatever. "Claw marks."

"I see. And pardon my rudeness." He gestured to his right. "This is Officer Niemchuk. And this..." he shifted his massive girth the other way towards the female, "...is Officer Andrechuk."

Cindy cocked her head. "Huntsville has a large Polish population?"

Kowalchuk, proud of his heritage, sat up straight. "Of course. Huntsville was originally settled by Poles. The Ravenscliffe Cemetery has many graves ending in c-y-z-k. Now of course, we all spell it c-h-u-c-k, or c-h-u-k. So much easier to pronounce. And yes, my officers and I have all heard the silly joke, 'How much wood would a woodchuck chuck if a woodchuck could chuck wood?' We also know our names all rhyme with the words 'buck,' 'luck,' 'suck,' 'duck,' 'puck,' and so on. We've heard them all. We've even heard the term 'cluster chuck' mumbled as we are leaving a scene." Kowalchuk laughed good-naturedly. "But we Poles are a forgiving people. Now, tell me about this body."

Cindy and Officer Andrechuk, were now making googly eyes at each other. I was guessing something like "pole" dancing was on their minds.

8.

KOWALCHUK CROSSED HIS LEGS neatly at the ankle, probably because he couldn't manage to put one muscular thigh over the other. The officer was enormous—a man mountain. But I could tell he wasn't soft; every time he moved an inch, his muscles undulated under his skin. He settled his arms across his giant girth, waiting patiently as if he were going to be told a great story.

"Tell me. This body, you found it in the woods. You were on a hike. You had arrived from Toronto and were going out to stretch your legs?" He stretched out his own two telephone poles as if to illustrate his point.

"Actually, no, I was..."

Cindy interrupted me with a hiss. "Yes, that's right. Just a walk in the lovely woods at the beginning of the season."

Kowalchuk looked from Cindy to me, his eyes searching for the truth in the conflicting answers, her 'yes,' my 'no.' And maybe wondering what our relationship was. Two women at a cabin by themselves? Did he care? If he did, that didn't bode well for Officer Andrechuk's future in the force. "You were going to say, Robin? Why were you in the forest?"

For some reason, Cindy wanted to keep the real reason for our walk secret although I couldn't for the life of me figure out why. What did it matter? We were simply checking out the land that someone had recently bought. Surely, he wouldn't charge us with trespassing? Nonetheless, Cindy was the crime reporter. She had experience with cops and knew the ropes, whereas I knew about curtain rods. So, I followed her lead.

"I was going to say that I was looking for ramps. You know, those oniony plants that taste so good in soups? There are a few patches of them about and I wanted to see if there were still any around. They're usually gone by now, but you never know."

He didn't believe me. I could see it in his eyes. "And you stumbled upon a body." It was a statement.

"Actually, it was *body parts*. We stumbled upon body parts." I touched my throat to calm the rising acid as the image of the neck stump spiked up into my vision.

Kowalchuk, perhaps sensing my discomfort, turned his massive form toward Cindy. The couch groaned and heaved as the tugboat changed course. "What parts did you find?"

Cindy rattled off a list of the bones that she had discovered in the woods. "A leg and an arm, a head, a torso."

"Did you touch them?"

"Are you kidding me?"

"A 'yes' or 'no' will do."

"So would a reasonable question."

One of these days Cindy was going to get into real trouble for her smart mouth.

Kowalchuk smiled and let it go. "Did you see anything suspicious?"

Cindy paused and then lowered her voice, her electric green eyes fixing him with an icy stare. "He had a clipboard." She said this as if she had found a shiny black Glock under his body. It was hard to read whether or not she was poking fun at him.

Andrechuk choked down a snigger while Kowalchuk looked uncomfortable, perhaps thinking he was being laughed at. He studiously made a note on his phone, his sausage fingers tapping quickly. He probably relied heavily on autocorrect. "I see. A clipboard." He looked up, only this time his head was cocked like a mighty mastodon facing me. "Anything else?"

I hemmed and hawed. All I could remember was the neck stump. The shard of white bone poking through dried ligaments.

He examined his nails, giving me time to collect myself. When there was still no answer forthcoming, he tried to jog my memory. "How did you discover the location of the dead body? How did you actually find it? Did you really 'stumble' upon it? Was it directly on the path you were walking on?"

I looked down at the floor and retraced my steps in the forest that led up to that horrible moment. I saw the yellow rock that wasn't a rock. "There was a jacket."

He creaked his head back towards Cindy. "So, now we have a clipboard *and* a jacket." He was accusing her of withholding information.

She grinned sassily. "But the jacket wasn't suspicious, which I believe was your question to me. Did I see anything *suspicious*? Jackets are not suspicious. Clipboards..." She shook her head, the meaning clear.

Kowalchuk drew his head into his neck, creating a thick woolly turtleneck. He gamely entered the sparring match. "And why is a clipboard suspicious?"

Cindy looked at him disbelievingly. Andrechuk leaned forward, her hands on her knees, waiting to hear what this smarty-pants would say next. Cindy merely spread her hands, as if she were saying "Duh" to a dim-wit. And then she gave her head a dismissive waggle. Kowalchuk was so stupid.

He was not to be bullied. "Enlighten me."

Cindy scoffed, "Who on earth uses a clipboard these days?" She looked around the room as if to prove her point. Everyone was holding a phone. "Even you"—the word "you" was sniffed with mocking disbelief—"even you make notes on your phone. I think a clipboard is very suspicious. No electronic footprint. A paper one. And paper can be burned and flushed. Data on the other hand..."

"Was there any paper on the suspicious clipboard?"

"The clipboard was turned over, upside down, under the body, so I can't tell you."

"It was under the body? You implied you didn't touch the body. How did you see under it? With your X-ray vision?"

Although this facetious question was directed at Cindy, given her answer to the last time he asked about touching the body, I thought I'd step in. "Nobody touched the body or anything that belonged to the torso, like the arms or the legs. But we tried to lift the jacket up out of the leaves so we could hang it on a tree branch. We thought someone had dropped it, and we were going to hang it up for them so if and when they walked on the path again, they would see it. Cindy tried to lift it up herself but couldn't. We thought it was stuck in the mud, so I offered to help. We both tugged on it, and then the torso half rolled out." I shut my eyes at the grisly memory. "So, although we didn't touch the body, it was moved, somewhat. The torso sort of shifted. Rolled out. Oh, I said that. I think one arm was still inside the jacket. So that's how she saw the clipboard. It was under the body. I didn't see the clipboard." I knew I was babbling.

Kowalchuk shifted forward in his seat. The springs in the couch below him *boinged* in protest. "And, I'm guessing here, that that's how you saw the claw marks?"

Cindy nodded. "Yes, they were down the front of his torso. Maybe teeth marks too. At first, we thought all we'd found was a jacket. We could only see the back of it."

Kowalchuk looked at me. "Did you see the claw marks?"

No, I was puking my guts out. "No, once I caught a glimpse of the torso I averted my eyes." And screamed my head off.

Kowalchuk settled into the back of the couch. "The scene has been disturbed, then. Good thing it was only a bear, if it was a bear, that got the guy. If it wasn't, I'd be pretty angry that you messed with the scene."

If only he knew. I pictured Cindy's foot scattering leaves

left right and centre while she dug with her toe in the earth for bones. I pictured how I was sick, not once but twice, okay three times, if you count the drool, right near the discovery, my vomit spewing over any DNA. If bears had DNA. Of course they did. They had bear DNA. That's why they were bears and not people. I suddenly saw in my mind's eye the reality of the bear attacking that the poor man. How frightening to be mauled to death by a bear. If it had been a man. Suddenly, I thought about the head, the skull really, with its remaining wisps of hair. Was it a man or a woman?

As if Kowalchuk were reading my mind, he asked, "Was the dead person a man or a woman?"

Cindy volunteered an answer. "I asked myself the same question, and I'm pretty sure it was a man." She looked out the window as if she were considering a list of facts. "Yes, it was a man."

"How can you be so sure?"

"Well, first of all, the jacket was a Carhartt. Not many women wear Carhartt jackets. There are only a few styles made for women. It's basically a man's company. This was a Berwick. Cotton duck in Carhartt Brown. A man's style. Perfect for this time of year."

"How do you know about the style of jacket? You a fashion queen?" He was being sarcastic.

Cindy was still wearing her hiking boots, rolled-up ratty old blue jeans, and her ancient hoodie with the bits of towel fluff all over it. "At one time I wanted to work in a rodeo."

I looked at her in astonishment. She glanced at me and a corner of her mouth twitched.

Kowalchuk seized her faux pas. "But if you wanted to wear this kind of jacket, then maybe the person who was wearing it in the woods was female. I mean, you considered it."

"Better not to make assumptions about me, officer. Who says I ever considered wearing it?" This from the woman who didn't want to look like a biker chick, if I recalled the conversation we'd had about the jacket in the woods. "I was a little ticked off, shall we say, that the company was sexist in its design department. They have about eighty jacket styles for men and only a few for women. That great jacket is made to fit men and men only. The bottom snaps do not do up on a woman. So, yes, it was a man inside that jacket."

Kowalchuk said, "'Detective.' Not 'officer.' And secondly?"

She looked at him questioningly. "Secondly?"

"You said 'first of all' it was a man because he was wearing the Carhartt jacket. So, secondly...?"

"It was a man." She tossed her head like a proud but cornered filly. There was no second point.

"I see." He seemed overly cheerful that he had scored a point. Andrechuk took a deep breath. Men.

I was getting tired of all this bullshitting around. The deep shaking at my core had settled down completely and I was feeling more myself, as if my legs would actually support my body if I happened to engage them. I felt ready to see the dead guy again. Time was ticking. The shadows were getting longer and if we didn't all head out soon it would be dusk. So much for the Town Hall trip. But Kowalchuk wasn't quite done with his questions. He directed the next one at me.

"Nice place you have. How long has your family owned it?"

Now why would he want to know that? "Well, as long as I can remember. A long time. Years and years. My great-grandfather was the original owner."

"It's a beaut, that's for sure." Kowalchuk looked around with admiration in his gaze. I could see him taking in the old pine hutch, the scarred harvest table, the pressback chairs. He squinted his eyes against the sun reflecting off the lake as he looked over my head out the window. "It sure is a beaut," he repeated. "One would do anything to protect it. How much land have you got here?"

I really didn't know. "I'm not sure. A few hundred acres, probably." What was he after?

"Did you know the land beside you was recently sold?"

I looked over at Cindy and saw that she had kept her face completely neutral. Great, she was no help. I didn't have a clue whether I should admit I knew this tidbit, or if I should act as if it were startling news. He was watching me carefully. And so was the other male officer. What was his name? Something 'chuck.' Woodchuck? Right, I would call him 'Woodchuck.' Andrechuk was still stealing surreptitious glances at Cindy. I went for the truth because I'm a goody two-shoes. Most of the time.

"Yes. My brother Andrew told me at a family dinner over the weekend." For some reason, I wanted to get Kowalchuk away from his line of thought, whatever it was. "My father and mother were there as well."

Kowalchuk appeared to be diverted, although I was beginning to wonder if he was way shrewder than I had thought at first. "And how are they doing? They must be getting on by now."

Cindy was tapping her toes and her leg was bouncing. She wanted to move on. I sat back and acted very relaxed. "They're around the eighty mark, so they are as well as can be expected. My father has some memory challenges and my mother's vision is failing. Dementia and macular degeneration."

"That's tough. Well, the next time you see them, give them my regards." He put his hands on his tree trunk thighs and made to get up.

"Thanks, I will."

He heaved himself out of the cushions with surprising ease. "Time for me and my officers to take a look at the body."

Cindy said, "Parts. Body parts." She stood up with him.

"Right. Body parts."

"And we will show you where it is. Where they are."

He waved his hand dismissively. "Thanks, but no. You girls stay here. We'll find it, I'm sure."

Uh-oh. Two boo-boos. He shouldn't have said, *girls*. He

might as well have raised a red flag in front of Cindy. Plus, she would not be left out. He was done for.

She said, "No problem at all. It's this way."

With that Cindy grabbed her bug hat off the kitchen counter and marched out the door, allowing it to slam in his face.

I looked at Andrechuk, raised my eyebrows, and mouthed the word, "*girls.*"

She knew what I meant.

9.

I JUMPED OFF THE COUCH, zipped to the kitchen, and scooped my bug hat off the counter as I galloped outside. Geez. I wished Cindy hadn't taken off like that. That *girl* would be the death of me!

The screen door clacked loudly behind me as I hollered in the direction of the woods, "Cindy, c'mon, wait up. There's a bear out there. Cindy!" Of course, there was no reply, although I could hear her crashing through the woods. At least, I hoped it was her.

I was torn. On one hand, I wanted to quickly follow her into the woods as I was frightened about the bear getting her. On the other, I felt an obligation to show the cops the way to the torso. What to do? The bear was probably still full from his last meal. I decided to remain behind.

I hung around outside and slapped at my head while I waited for the troops to gather themselves together. Through the screen door I could see Kowalchuk adjusting his baseball cap on his mammoth head and Andrechuk patting her pockets, looking for something or another. Oh, her bug hat. Woodchuck—no, his name came to me in a blinding flash, *Niemchuk*—was standing in the kitchen and I watched as he picked up one of the spray bottles of insect repellent off the windowsill. He held it up so I could see it through the screen and gave it a small shake, his eyebrows enquiring. It was the almost empty bottle Cindy and I had found in the woods.

He called out to me, "Do you mind if I finish this up?"

"Not at all, but I'm warning you, bug spray stinks. The bugs won't go near you, but then nobody else will either. Please spray it on yourself outside so the reek doesn't get into the house."

Niemchuk obliged and came outside with the little bottle in his hand. He stood about ten feet away from me and doused himself all over, rubbing it in with his hands. A cloud of putrid stench drifted over to me and I walked quickly away from it. No way did I want any of that stuff on my skin. It stunk. He flapped his arms to dry it off and looked a little regretful. He peered through the haze at the label on the spray bottle before tossing it into the plastic garbage can beside the steps leading up to the porch. He snapped the two handles over the lid and made sure the garbage can was good and shut.

"I warned you it stank," I said, laughing. "But it does work. No flies on you." I chuckled again.

Andrechuk, bug hat in hand, burst through the screen door, followed by Kowalchuk's hulk of a body. He fanned his face. "God, what on earth is that smell?"

Niemchuk snickered, "That's super-duper bug spray. Contains DEET. I am not going to get bitten."

Andrechuk put on her bug hat. "And neither am I. No way would I spray that poison on my body." Her voice was low and melodious. Hard to reconcile with her muscular physique.

"Me neither," I chorused as I put mine on.

Niemchuk was defensive. "They bite through bug hats you know. If the mesh is touching skin, they poke their little stingers through the holes and suck your blood." He was looking smug.

Andrechuk sighed. "And that's why I wear it over my cap. The bill holds the mesh away from my face."

Kowalchuk followed suit and stretched his bug hat over his cap, making sure it wasn't touching his skin. "Okay, let's go. Robin, you might as well lead the way."

So, I was in.

The four of us marched across the muddy yard to the orange piece of tape wrapped around the trunk of the tree at the edge of the forest that marked the beginning of the trail. Within seconds, we were surrounded by clouds of blackflies looking for a place to bite. We made speed, trying to keep ahead of the bugs. I could see Cindy's blue hoodie in the distance, heading up a small incline.

"Wait up, Cindy," I shouted. She didn't.

We crackled through the leaves on the forest floor, over hill and dale, following the orange bits of tape around trees. Our feet squelched through the swamp and we slapped at the air, trying to keep the sudden influx of flies from landing on us. The wind had picked up a bit, now that it was later in the afternoon, and the tops of the trees swayed, their branches rustling in the breeze. The forest smelled like damp leaves disintegrating into rich loam and there was still a scent of winter lingering in the air. We trudged along in single file, each person reaching behind to stop long branches from snapping in the face of the person following them. Our boots sunk in the soggy soil and new maple shoots bent under their weight. No one spoke. Finally, we reached our destination.

Cindy was lounging near the Carhartt jacket, pretending to buff her nails, feigning nonchalance. But I, who knew her well, could see the lines of tension around the edges of her mouth. Perhaps the gruesome scene reminded her of the power of nature, of the force that we mortals tried to contend with but rarely surpassed. The spirit of the universe could be felt in this place, and maybe she was simply in awe of its generous pervasiveness. Or maybe she was just plain scared of the bear.

The scene looked pretty much like we had left it. Highly disturbed. I glanced around and noticed with dismay that it was definitely obvious that we had been here, interfering with the evidence. Leaves had clearly been scattered, leaving brown arcs of damp dirt where Cindy's toe had scraped through them to the ground in her quest for bones. My stomach contents were visible in the undergrowth; wilted lettuce and soggy pieces of bread dripped from the twigs of a small bush. We would have to answer for this, I knew.

Off to the right, the blank eye sockets in the dead man's severed head stared blankly at the bits of sky visible through the canopy of budding branches. The arm bone with the fragments of reddish-black tissue still leaned against a tree. I looked up and saw the long, white leg bone was still way up high. How had it come to rest up there? Had the bear tossed it over his shoulder after picking it clean, like knights did at medieval banquets? Or maybe a wild cat had come along and dragged it up into the tree to keep the booty safe from other predators. I doubted I would ever know.

Kowalchuk and his merry band stood stock-still in a small group, their eyes busily surveying the scene. I watched them absorb the details: The numerous arcs of scraped earth, the drool and puke on the bushes, the far-flung body parts. Kowalchuk cleared his throat and took charge.

"Andrechuk, I am not sure what we have here, but I want you to document the scene. Start taking pictures here." He pointed at the jacket.

Andrechuk dutifully walked over to the jacket and took numerous photographs from a variety of angles with her phone, her lithe body bending this way and that. I watched Cindy watching her. Yup. Definite interest. When Cindy caught me looking at her, she smiled impishly and looked away, pretending to be a professional journalist assessing the scene.

"Don't forget this piece of evidence." She pointed up one of the trees to the leg bone wedged in the branches and their eyes followed. Andrechuk took a picture of it with her cellphone and then walked around the tree and took another. Then Cindy pointed at the head off to the right that was partially buried in some dried-up leaves. It's a wonder she hadn't kicked those away as well. Andrechuk aimed her phone at the head and

I could see her activating its camera's zoom function as she walked closer to the skull.

Kowalchuk growled at Cindy and me, "Looks like the two of you had a field day in here, checking out the body and the surrounding area. I'm surprised. Everyone knows not to do this. Even TV makes it very clear that scenes around a dead body are not to be touched. I don't understand you two. It's very important to not disturb any scene around a dead body, whether or not you think the death was caused by an act of nature and not a murder. There are unusual things about this scene and I don't quite know what to make of it yet. It doesn't help that you interfered. Now I have to figure out what mess was caused by the attack and what mess the two of you made." He looked around, clearly puzzled by what must have been a frenzied assault. "Bears don't usually leave quite this amount of chaos behind. But I don't think anything here is suspicious, in fact, I'm almost a hundred percent sure it isn't, but nonetheless, you should have called us right away. Immediately. Before you did anything. All sudden deaths must be investigated."

Cindy and I, chastised, both looked at the ground.

Andrechuk held her phone up high. "They couldn't call. No service here, Sir."

So, she had Cindy's back. And mine too, because that was exactly what I was about to say. I piped up, "We really didn't do much. I lost my lunch on that bush over there."

Kowalchuk didn't have to follow my pointing finger. "Yes, I noticed that."

"And Cindy was looking for bones with her foot. That's what all those scrapes in the earth are. We are really sorry. She's a journalist as well and our curiosity got the better of us."

"You're both journalists? Well, that explains a lot."

I didn't like the way he said that.

"What media do you work for?"

Cindy and I both said, "*The Toronto Express*," simultaneously.

The detective harrumphed and pulled a latex glove out of his left front pocket. He snapped it on to his right hand with more vigour than was needed. I could guess what he thought of journalists. He bent down and with his thick thumb and forefinger lifted up a corner of the jacket and peered underneath. Cindy and I had struggled unsuccessfully with our combined strength to get the jacket completely out of the mud and I marvelled at his strength. Two of his beefy fingers would easily match the strength of two very fit women. Okay, one fit woman and another woman having a fit. I watched his face as he took in the gore under the jacket. His features betrayed nothing at all.

"Andrechuk, hand me a twig or something. Maybe a pen. I want to get this clipboard out," he grunted as he balanced on his hefty haunches, still holding the jacket containing the torso slightly off the ground.

"Here, Sir." She handed him a weathered branch that had been whitened by time. It was thin and fairly short, but strong.

Cindy's eyebrows raised approvingly. Andrechuk caught her eye and shrugged modestly. I felt a bit left out in this exchange of inside forest knowledge. I knew it was a good stick, too. Sure I did. Then I reminded myself that there were much more important things at hand. Like a dead man. Get over yourself, Robin. This isn't the time to be jealous of your friend.

Kowalchuk prodded the clipboard out from under the torso with the stick, careful not to touch it with his ungloved hand. When it was finally lying on the ground away from the torso, he hooked the stick into the metal hoop at the top of the board. He lowered the jacket to its resting place and stood up, the clipboard's muddied hook hanging on the twig. The clipboard dangled in the air for all to see, it's sodden pages, shredded in places, sticking together and blackened by blood, earth, and mould. Whatever had been written on that paper was long gone. Still, Kowalchuk squinted at the top sheet, trying to discern anything that would give him a clue as to why the man was in the bush.

"Here, Niemchuk, you have better eyesight than I have. Can you read anything?"

The young man walked over from where he was standing about ten feet away from the torso. He didn't look at the clawed jacket as he walked gingerly around it, and I felt a wave of sympathy for the young cop. He was about twenty years old, fresh-faced and eager, and I wondered if he had ever seen a dead person. He put his nose about a foot away from the gory pages and peered intently. "Not a thing, Sir. There's a lot of blood and mud. I can't see any writing through the dirt."

"I'll send this to the lab. We'll see if he was an unlucky bird-watcher who got mauled to death by a bear." With his right hand he pulled a large plastic bag out of another pocket and gingerly lowered the clipboard into it. Once it was protected, he pressed the ziplock closure shut and then placed it carefully on an old tree stump.

"Niemchuk, how are you at climbing trees?" Kowlachuk pointed up high. "I need you to bring that leg bone down. Andrechuk can gather the bones on the ground."

Niemchuk looked doubtfully up at the tall pine. "I'm not that good with heights, Sir."

"Me neither," I volunteered so he wouldn't feel too ashamed of himself.

Cindy preened. "Well I, on the other hand, can scale a pine in seconds flat." She looked at Kowalchuk. "I'd be happy to go get that leg bone, Sir, unless, of course, you want to. Sir." She faked subservience.

Kowalchuk manufactured a lame excuse. "No, no, that's fine. I need to coordinate activity here on the ground and I would appreciate you getting the bone. Niemchuk, you help Andrechuk look for body parts and bag them."

He handed Cindy a very large bag and a latex glove. "Try not to touch it too much and hold it very gently. If the bone has fingerprints on it, I don't want them smudged. We'll take your prints for elimination purposes later in any event, but a clean bone would be better than one that has been handled even ever so carefully."

Cindy took the glove and bag and tucked them into her back pocket. "I have no intention of handling a long, hard bone with a careful hand," she said innocently as she walked to the base of the tree.

I stifled a giggle.

Andrechuk poked her in the ribs as she sauntered past. There were definite sparks happening between the two of them. If Kowalchuk were aware of it, he gave no sign.

Niemchuk collected the arm bone from the base of the tree and then stood off to one side, the bag dangling from his hand while he looked up and watched with admiration as Cindy shimmied up the trunk and then swung her leg over the lowest branch. From there, she hoisted herself up and began the long climb. I could barely watch, my stomach dancing in my throat, and turned away from the group, trying to divert my attention from her acrobatics. I breathed slowly and deeply, looking as far as I could into the expanse of forest.

Kowalchuk said, "You two, back to work. You'd think you'd never seen someone climb a tree."

Andrechuk and Niemchuk quickly bent over and sifted through the earth, lifting leaves carefully with their gloved hands and rummaging around for bones in the dirt. Kowalchuk was absorbed in the torso and had rolled it over, staring at the front of the jacket and taking some measurements. Yes, I thought, it must have been a very big bear. There was hardly a sound as everyone engaged in their tasks.

I drifted off to the right, deep in thought, wondering what on earth I was doing here in the middle of the woods trying not to step on a dead person's bones. I looked down as I walked away, making sure nothing other than leaves crunched under my feet. I was meant to be investigating the development of land, not the death of a person. I'd been given a list of angles for a story from my editor and "dead body" wasn't on my list.

I looked at my watch. It was past three-thirty and now there was no way that Cindy and I would be able to get to Huntsville and check out the Town Hall for information about the land ownership. Was it a shady deal? I wasn't sure. On one hand, Kowalchuk had acted as if it were a bona fide sale. But I simply didn't know and I wanted to confirm my facts. I had to check it out. Was it Crown land or did it truly belong to a Rosedale fat cat who'd sold it to another fat cat?

I sighed. A full day was gone. I wondered if Shirley, my sexpot editor at *The Toronto Express*, would want a complete report on the story's progress today. Well, I guess I could tell her the truth about stumbling over a dead body. I brightened at the thought. Maybe she would be happier with a dead body than a shady real estate deal. I would emphasize the long, hard bones. She'd like that.

God, I had such a weird job. The death of a human being trumped pieces of paper acknowledging land ownership. Did anyone really own land? Now there was a question. Oh well, papers had to be sold, stories had to be clicked open in apps. Every click counted so advertisers would be happy about their reach.

I didn't dare look at how high Cindy had climbed. The view from up there would be stunning. I cast my eyes around the forest. I loved it here. Tiny atoms of rage against the developer multiplied like hot fire in my chest. In that moment, I understood why someone would want to murder anybody associated with destroying a forest. Maybe that's what had happened here. Maybe this dead person was a land surveyor. And maybe someone had murdered the land surveyor and left his body to the wildlife. I laughed to myself; if you try to destroy the forest, the forest will destroy you. So ironic. *Ugh.* I was mocking what was maybe a murder. Not good, Robin. You should do a Buddhist chant to protect yourself from uncharitable thoughts.

10.

LOST IN THOUGHT about the loosey-goosey framework of my moral compass, I kept wandering away from the group, shuffling through the brittle leaves on the ground and looking down, immersed in the concepts of right and wrong. Who owned land? Was it ownable? That's not a word, Robin. Possessable? That's not a word either. I kicked at the leaves with my foot, partly because I didn't want to step on a small bone, and partly because I liked the sound of my foot brushing against them. It was such a soothing whisper. It felt as if my foot was caressing the skin of the earth. The low rustle reminded me that the planet was always there, always solid. My moral compass had a good foundation, even if it danced around, sometimes a bit drunkenly. Okay, more than a bit. One day I would stop that hand to mouth thing I did every night. I breathed the rich loamy smell deep into my lungs. No, land could not be owned. Not really. Of this I was certain. But could it fight back? I thought so.

People might think they owned land. There were tons of industries set up to divide it into plots. There were real estate companies, lawyers, surveyors, even whole departments in governments, all doing their best to chop the forests up. But, at the end of the day, the land remained. Nonetheless, I was perturbed that someone had bought the very land I was standing on and were going to change it, building something or another. And all for the sake of civilization. Why couldn't people leave the land alone? Why did they have to destroy the wilderness?

It made me so sad. And so fucking angry. Oh, let it go Robin. Getting angry wasn't going to solve anything. I looked around to make sure I was alone and did a quick Buddhist chant under my breath to calm myself down. To hope for protection for the land. *Chant, chant, chant.* I was whispering. Wouldn't want the cops to think I was a little cuckoo. I wasn't worried about Cindy. She knew the score.

I had meandered quite far away from the group and felt better after chanting and being away from the blood and gore. I didn't want to be near that dead body. It was so gruesome. My nervous system couldn't cope with the shock of it all. I was full up with shocks. Done with them. Trevor's death from being hit by a drunk driver. Bringing up four feisty kids alone. Things that had happened in my own childhood. I was *done.* No more shocks for me. I was hypersensitive to every curveball that life threw at me. Maybe that's why I drank.

Oh geez, now I was back to the moral compass thing. I kicked at the leaves and resolved to call Sally Josper, my naturopath, as soon as I got back to the city to get a better handle on my drinking. It had to go. With that resolution in place, I looked up from the rich earth to see where I was.

I could hear the low hum of the group's chatter, but they were out of sight, beyond the knoll I had just clambered over. I looked around to get my bearings. It really was a beautiful forest, full of old-growth trees standing tall and swaying gently in the breeze. I took a deep breath and felt gratitude for witnessing such grace and let it fill my being. My heart ached to think that someone was going to destroy all this loveliness and build a golf course or a resort or a bunch of trails for ATVs. A paintball enterprise. A condominium resort for seniors. Who knew what would happen. The sun was shining through the small green leaves, casting a soft green light into the pine-sweetened air. Yes, I understood why someone could kill anyone who was determined to destroy such beauty.

Out of the corner of my left eye, I spotted a large shadow moving swiftly through the forest, weaving around trees and seemingly floating over small bushes. As it got closer, the form took shape. It was a huge bear, running straight for the hill the group was behind. I stood frozen as it charged about a hundred feet away from me through the undergrowth. I could hear twigs snapping and felt the earth vibrating under my feet. It was massive and it was heading right for them. Thank God it hadn't seen me. I stood perfectly still and held my breath, hopefully praying that bears have poor eyesight but an excellent sense of smell.

Once it raced past me, I opened my mouth to shout but no sound came out. I frantically patted my pockets, searching for my air horn. Fuck, I had put it on the living-room sideboard when I got back from discovering the body. I flapped my arms, warning of danger, but of course, the group couldn't see me. I frantically looked around for a solution. I had to warn them! And then I looked up and saw Cindy, perched aloft and looking down at me, a look of puzzlement on her face. Why was I flapping my arms? I pointed numbly at the retreating bear as he scrambled up the small hill toward the cops. I watched her head turn as she followed where I was indicating from her vantage point high in the air. Suddenly, she could see the bear.

She yelled at the top of her lungs, "A bear. Watch out!"

I raced after the bear—not too close, I'm not stupid—to the top of the hillock I had just climbed over until, like Cindy, I had a bird's-eye view of the scene. It was terrifying. I was watching an enormous bear charging at a group of unsuspecting people.

All of the cops' heads lifted in unison to look questioningly at Cindy sitting high in the tree and then followed her pointing finger, like a well-orchestrated dance. They stood mesmerized, staring at the charging hulk. It seemed to be heading straight for Niemchuk who was standing stock-still off to the right, halfway up a small rise in the ground by the dead man's head.

He still held in his hand the plastic bag containing the arm bone and there was a small piece of bone in his gloved left. Probably a bit of neck. A vertebrae. Amazing how miniscule details zip through a mind in the face of impending danger.

I yelled, "Niemchuk. Stand tall. Wave your arms. Shout. Jump up and down."

He looked at me dumbly. The bear was now fifty yards away from the group and growling, mouth open, fangs shining white.

I repeated my instructions. "Niemchuk, jump up and down. Drop the bag and the bones. Shout."

He looked at the objects in his hands, then at the bear. He was welded to the ground.

A shot pierced the air. Then another. And another. Where had they come from? Oh. Andrechuk. The bear took as much notice of the bullets as it did of mosquitoes and rushed non-stop at the group.

Niemchuk, his brown eyes wide with fear and his mouth a red slash against his pale face, was jolted out of his stupor and finally moved. Like an out of control puppet, he waved his arms spasmodically while his feet danced jerkily. The bear was now about twenty yards away from him. It had been slowed down slightly by the vexing onslaught of bullets from Andrechuk's gun, but even that had not deterred the bear from its certain intention to get Niemchuk.

By now, the bear was moving so quickly it was hard to get a good shot at it. I saw a new difficulty looming. The closer the bear got to Niemchuk, the more likely Niemchuk would be hit by a slug. I watched from a distance, helpless as the tragedy unfolded, my heart pounding so hard in my chest I wondered if it was going to break a rib. I could hear my blood thundering in my ears like an approaching tornado.

I glanced up into the tree and saw Cindy watching the scene intently from her aerial view. As my eyes focused on her way up high in the branches, I could see she was reaching into her back pocket with one hand, while curling the other around the tree trunk so she wouldn't fall. She pulled out her phone and started shooting pictures of the bear charging Niemchuk. I couldn't believe it. Here we were, on the edge of witnessing a man being mauled to death by a bear, and she was taking photos. Always a journalist, our Cindy. She was risking her life for the sake of capturing some newsworthy images? She leaned forward and balanced precariously on the branch so that she could follow the bear's movement. Paralyzing fear crept up my spine. I couldn't watch Cindy's balancing act any longer and looked back down at the drama.

Andrechuk's weapon was now empty and she was busy reloading. Her face was red with exertion and panic, but her fingers looked steady and sure. It dawned on me that she had been shooting to frighten, not to kill. I admired her morals, being the animal lover that I was. But the bear was closing in on Niemchuk.

My moral compass shook as it shimmied around to point in a different direction. Now the story was different. The bear had to be killed. Despite Andrechuk's efforts to scare the bear away, it had not turned tail and taken off into the woods. If anything, it was more focused on Niemchuk, more determined in its attack, more frenzied as it crashed through the bush toward him. I was convinced that this was the same bear that had attacked Jacket Man. Not many bears behaved with such madness, such crazed focus to kill. This had to be the same bear. The air throbbed with frenetic energy. If the massive beast wasn't stopped quickly and now, it would certainly kill Niemchuk.

From the top of the hill that had previously hidden me from the group, I could see that Kowalchuk, slightly lower than everyone else as he stood by the jacket, was pulling his gun. His gargantuan body was moving with coordinated precision and skill. He planted his elephant-sized legs wide apart as he raised his police-issued pistol to eye level. This was the first good close look I've ever had of a gun in my life. Details flew in and out of my brain like frightened birds. Long. Black. Shining. Metal.

Niemchuk was sandwiched between Kowalchuk and the bear, which was now about five yards away from his victim. Niemchuk's horrible screams pierced the forest and the air felt like it was swirling around me. Birds shrieked wildly and scattered high to the treetops. Could Kowalchuk make the shot without wounding Niemchuk? The situation looked impossible to me.

Kowalchuk was standing below Niemchuk, which meant that a bullet from his gun would have to travel through Niemchuk to hit the bear. Plus, Niemchuk was jumping up and down, in constant movement. It would be extremely difficult for Kowalchuk to time his shot so that it would hit the bear when Niemchuk was on his way down, and would thus be lower than the bear's head. It would be a risky shot, but Kowalchuk had no choice but to try.

I watched the detective steady one hand with the other as he sighted down the barrel. In the chaos of the moment, my ability to distinguish left from right had flown out the window. Why was I even thinking about this? Niemchuk had only moments to live. I was witnessing terrible violence. Again, I marvelled at how the mind got stuck in a loop of tiny details when coping with enormous fear. Maybe it was a survival instinct, a distraction so the brain would shy away from trauma. I could see that Niemchuk was going to be killed. It would either be by the bear, or by a bullet. I was certain Niemchuk was dead meat. He was waving his arms frantically and leaping up and down to make himself appear bigger. The bear was not frightened off.

Kowalchuk fired a shot just as Niemchuk's feet were heading back down to the ground. The bullet whistled not even an inch over his head and then hit the bear between the eyes. I had never seen anything like this in my life. Not even on TV. The timing and marksmanship were superlative. I couldn't believe the bullet had hit its target. The animal staggered two steps forward and then crashed face-first to the ground, only a few feet from where Niemchuk had stood. He too had fallen, his body a collapsed heap lying motionless in the leaves. Had he been hit? No, of course not. The bear had been hit. There had only been one gunshot. I could still hear it reverberating through the forest.

And then, suddenly, the air was deathly quiet. I felt like I was in a vacuum. There was no air, just a hollow absence of where it had been. Everything moved in slow motion. A bird soared soundlessly into the sky, its beak open. Was it cawing? It must have been a crow. A low hum reverberated in my eardrums underneath the sound of my pulsing heart. A leaf rustled in the silence, sounding as loud as a motorcycle on a summer's night. A shout echoed roundly in the air. Kowalchuk. I had no idea what he'd said; the words swam by in an alien language. Niemchuk lifted his head and yelled back in the same bizarre gibberish. I watched dumbly as figures moved as if in a silent movie.

And then I felt like I was floating in an underwater nightmare. Bursting bubbles of air snapped and zapped at my skin. I slowly dove down to the bottom of the sea around me. The trees at the edges of my vision dissolved into waving seaweed as darkness rolled in from the deep. The last thing I heard was a shout in barely audible acoustics. Perhaps it was my name.

11.

I SWAM UP FROM MY underwater nightmare. Where was I? On the ground? I could smell earth. So, on the ground. I slowly took stock of my body. Was I okay? Were all my bits functioning? Whatever had happened, at least I was alive. I was alive and breathing. I moved my head a fraction and a leaf crackled by my ear. It sounded like a gunshot. Something very bad had happened, but I didn't know what. I was paralyzed into a stillness, curled in a fetal position. I scanned my body for problems from the head down.

Eyes were shut. Ears could hear. A small stick was jutting into my rib cage. My feet felt tingly yet very hot. I cautiously moved my fingers and toes. Nothing broken. Nervous system intact. But I was on the ground. How had that happened? I gathered together all my courage and opened my eyes.

Copper-coloured leaves. Dark, damp earth. A small, light-green shoot. Was it a budding maple key? Cindy's hiking boots. About a foot away from my face. Beige suede trim. Blue breathable uppers. Frayed laces with the plastic thingies on both ends missing. I turned my head slowly, registering the feel of dirt on my skin. Smelling it. My eyes followed Cindy's very long legs up her body. She was holding a plastic zipper bag containing a long white bone in her hand. My eyes climbed over her blue hoodie until they reached the red halo of her head. She was staring down at me, a look of concern playing around her eyes.

"Hey, Robin. How you doing?"

Her voice sounded far-off, as if it were bouncing around in a distant steel tunnel.

"You fainted. You've been out about five minutes, maybe less. Barely long enough for me to get down from the tree."

The tree. What tree? Right. On our walk. She had climbed up a tree and I couldn't find her. Then I was worried she'd fall out of the tree. But wait. *I* was the one lying on the ground. She wasn't. Had I fallen out of a tree? No, she meant a different tree. She had a bone in her hand. I didn't want to remember. I couldn't seem to find my voice and looked dumbly up at my friend. I shifted one leg and my foot dug into the wet earth. The smell of earth filled my mouth and I swallowed its rich nutrients. It was time to stand up. The dampness of the loam was seeping through my clothes.

"Can you stand up? Do you think you can do that?"

She extended a hand wearing a ripped latex glove. A *glove*? She had a glove on her hand and was carrying a bone. She had scrambled down a tree to get to me. What was going on? My upper body wouldn't bend. It was impossible to move. Suddenly, a kaleidoscope of sepia-coloured images jerked and jumped across the screen behind my eyes. It was all coming back to me like an old-fashioned movie that had been slowed down by an unseen hand on the reel. A bear had attacked a police officer. I whispered, "Niemchuk?"

"He's fine and so are you. The bear was shot by a cop. They are helping Niemchuk now. And taking pictures of the dead bear. Time for us to move on. Get over ourselves. The bear is dead. C'mon. Get up." She held out her hand, waiting for me to take it. She shook her fingers impatiently. Shredded latex flapped.

Cindy had lots of practice dealing with terrible events. Shootings, knifings, bombs, suicides. She was a crime reporter, after all. I wrote about bamboo-filled pillows. What had happened was, way above my pay grade. I shut my eyes, trying to block out where I was and why I was lying on the ground. But my mind's eye began replaying the bear barging at Niemchuk, its shiny brown fur undulating with every step. A dark veil crept up from the back of my brain and floated over my eyes. Curtains. Room darkening. Fuck. I felt giddy.

"Don't do that rolling your eyes into the back of your head thing with me." I could hear Cindy's discombobulated voice piercing the dark recesses of my brain. "Open your eyes. Let's go. It's time to split this pop stand."

When I opened my eyes again the world seemed to shimmer. I wondered if I'd hit my head on the way down to the ground. I felt my stomach contract and bile filled my mouth. Not this again. I took a few deep breaths and willed myself to not throw up. I had to sit up. No way was I going to pull on Cindy's hand and stagger to my feet. Way too embarrassing for her to know how heavy I was.

Funny what we think of when the chips were down. Chips. I could use a bowl of chips. And a drink. Or ten. That's why I was so heavy. Whatever. Ralph didn't seem to care. Ralph liked to drink too. Wait. Why was I realizing this just now? Or was it old news? I repeated it in my mind. Ralph drank. This was not good. The two of us had to quit. But wait. *Ralph.* I should call Ralph. No, we were in a fight. No, we weren't. He was working. Was he? I had to call him. I needed him. Shit. What was that about? I didn't need anyone.

Cindy got down on her haunches and stared into my eyes, her green ones worried. "Look, it's time to go. You're getting eaten alive by blackflies. You have to get up now. You okay to do that?"

I lugged myself out of my twilight zone. "I think so. Look, I'm sitting up." I brushed a leaf off my sleeve and ventured a smile. My mouth felt a little quivery, but I knew I would be up on my feet in a minute or two. Cindy bent over me and picked a twig out of my hair.

"You're not cut out for this," she said.

"No guff."

"No one says 'no guff' anymore," she said, making fun of how I had corrected her earlier. "But, if you still want to be a crime reporter, you'll catch on. It takes a little practice."

"Let's go home," I said. All the Buddhist practice in the world wouldn't have prepared me for this kind of stuff.

"I'm not sure the police will let us leave. We were witnesses to a police shooting, and now there'll be all kind of paperwork."

I eased myself up, got my legs under me, and brushed off the bits of dirt the best I could. Fragments of leaves were embedded in the fabric of my socks. I picked at them. Bending over was always a challenge. I would diet after dinner. "Not my problem," I said.

"No, you're right," said Kowalchuk. Where had he come from? "It's my problem, along with many other problems. Let me take that bone from you, Cindy." He gave her a fixed, cold stare. Daring her.

I hadn't seen or heard him approach and wondered how such a huge man could move so silently over dried leaves.

She handed him the bag and slowly rolled the ripped latex glove off her hand like she was peeling off a condom, staring right back. "Sometimes these things break, especially when they come in contact with long, hard bones," she said as she held Kowalchuk's eye.

His eyebrow twitched. I wondered if this was his version of a belly laugh. I could see Andrechuk about twenty feet behind him, clamping her lips together to stop her from guffawing. The release of fear was turning us into comedians.

Suddenly, Cindy spun on her heel and took off into the forest, hips swaying, long legs striding. "Come on, Robin. Let's hoof it."

She was right. I felt an energy surge through my body. Must have been an adrenalin dump. There was nothing I wanted more than to get away from this crime scene. Did I say crime scene? Really? Is that what it was? Or was it a random bear having a random attack of insanity? Something felt way off to me.

I gave Kowalchuk an apologetic smile and carefully lifted one foot and then the other in the direction Cindy was flying. Well, look at that, I could move. My legs stomped robotically as I tramped through the woods in Cindy's wake. She was making tracks. I guess she wanted to get her story written and submitted while it was still fresh in her mind. Time was of the essence; the afternoon was drawing to a close and the next issue's deadline loomed large. But she wasn't about to tap it out with one finger on her phone here in the woods and her iPad was back at the cottage.

I could hear Kowalchuk calling out to us, "Girls, wait." Cindy's back froze. She would not be called a "girl."

Kowalchuk, as if sensing his politically incorrect statement, amended it to, "Ladies, wait. We will need statements from you."

Of course, "ladies" was worse than "girls" to Cindy. She raised her right hand and flipped him the bird.

"Okay, no problem...," Kowalchuk's voice drifted off. "We'll meet you back at the cottage."

I hurried through the leaves and new undergrowth, trying to catch up to Cindy. I scanned the forest for dark beasts bashing through the trees. The whole bear incident was completely unbelievable, so unusual. I had never ever heard of a bear with the single-minded purpose of attacking one person. Sharks, maybe. I had heard of sharks going exclusively after women who were on their monthly period, but Niemchuk was not female and a bear was not a shark. That bear was definitely going straight for him. All the other people were ignored. The bear wanted Niemchuk and Niemchuk alone. Poor guy. He must have been terrified, seeing that huge animal charging at him, fangs gleaming. He'd probably have night terrors for years. I was now on top of the knoll I had clambered over before I saw the bear crashing through the bush and stopped to look over my shoulder. In the distance, the police formed a desolate crowd, gathered around two brownish lumps on the ground, a headless torso and a dead bear.

Yes, they would have paperwork.

I briefly wondered what my editor, Shirley Hay Hair, would say about all of this. Should I call her? This was about as far away from a real estate deal as one could get. I plodded along and imagined myself in a face-to-face with her. I could see her, stubbing out her cigarette against the metal rim of her garbage can, bending over deeply so that her cleavage was visible for all to see and saying, "Oh-h-h-h, it sure is hot in here." And I would, once again, grab her coffee mug and splash it on smouldering bits of paper. Sometimes it was hard to permeate through Shirley's steaming sexuality. But I thought the dead bear and the headless torso might catch her attention before she flounced off to rub up against Doug, Cindy's editor, to confer about what the two of us had stumbled into. No, I didn't think I'd tell Shirley a thing. Not yet. I had to sort this out in my mind.

I was breathless as I chased after Cindy in the woods. She was practically skipping through the forest. That girl, okay, not a *girl*, loved a story. "Cindy," I called. "Cindy! Wait up. Slow down. You'll hurt yourself. Trip or something." I was gasping. She glanced briefly over her shoulder and waved, smiled gaily, and continued on her mission. She reached the densest part of the woods, right at the beginning of the trail, and parted branches with hurried abandon, trying to get into the clearing, to a cell signal. Maybe she had been scared as well and couldn't wait to get into the light. Naw, she just loved a story. I concentrated on where I was putting my feet, looking down, so I didn't trip on a rock or root.

"Ow," she yelled.

I looked up and saw her through the thick bush, holding her hand against the side of her face, her eyes scrunched up. Now what?

"That fucking branch snapped into my face."

I didn't laugh, which I felt was kind of me.

She swiped away a bit of bark. "Good thing it didn't get my eye."

I finally caught up to her and peered at her face. Her cheek by her ear was bleeding. "Cindy, your cheek is bleeding," I looked at it more closely. "It's actually a bad cut."

She looked at her hand and saw a streak of red blood over her palm. "It's nothing. I've had worse."

And indeed she had. Cindy had been shot, knifed, and strangled within an inch of her life. A brick had been thrown through her living-room window. Her staid neighbours hadn't thought much of that. A few months ago, she had nearly been blown to bits by a car bomb, placed there by some drug gang or another. Their response to her poking about gangs in Toronto. It had detonated when she clicked the locks open with her remote, about twenty feet away. A miraculous malfunction caused by an uneducated bomb-maker. Bye-bye Honda Accord. Now, every time she got into her new car, another Honda Accord, she checked underneath for a bomb. Every time. Maybe that's why she wanted to come in my jalopy for this little sojourn into peaceful northern country. Peaceful my ass.

I followed her through the clearing and marvelled how she could tap away on her phone while beetling across uneven ground. I would certainly be flat on my face, my lard oozing over the flattened grass. "Finally I have service. I have to send a text to Doug," she tossed over her shoulder, "to let him know that there's a story coming through shortly and to hold up the deadline for ten minutes."

He'd be happy about that. Not. But he would do it. Cindy was one of their top crime reporters. She let the screen door slam behind her as she bounced up the stairs to get on her iPad. I stood in the living room, uncertain, as usual, about what to do. Lucky danced around me, sniffing at my clothes and rubbing against my leg where I had probably lain in deer poo or something else lovely.

I checked my phone. Service. I should call Shirley to let her know what had happened. If nothing else, this would slow down my week of researching a real estate deal and she should know I would be late on that. In any event, she would shortly hear the news about the bear from Doug, second-hand, and then I would be in hot water, again, for not telling her about it. But how to phrase it? "Hi Shirley, Cindy and I…"?

She would screech, "Cindy? What the hell is she doing with you? You're writing a nice little story about real estate in the north. You were taking your dog, not Cindy." I would have to phrase the Cindy connection carefully. There were about a hundred barriers to get through before I could even tell her the whole story. How I had kept from her that there was a massive sale of wilderness right next to my very own cottage, for starters.

I might as well face the music. Before Doug got to her. I pulled out my phone.

"Shirley Payne." Throaty chimney voice. Pain in the ass, I thought. No, that was uncharitable.

"Hi Shirley, checking in to let you know that things have escalated here a bit in the north." An understatement. I imagined her silk, or maybe it was polyester, blouse rustling as it tugged against her rather large battleship of a chest. I heard her ever-present costume jewellery beads clatter. And then there was silence. Good, I had her attention. "I've been pretty relieved, actually, that Cindy had time off and could come with me." Good job Robin. No screech. More clattering. "We were walking on the huge plot of land next to my cottage because I'd heard a rumour that it had been sold." So far so good, a cigarette was being lit. "I thought we should check it out. As we were walking through the woods, we happened to stumble across a body. Probably someone surveying the land. He had a clipboard. Attacked by a bear." A sharp intake of breath. Did she clock the irony? Or was that a drag on her smoke? And then there was a ping.

"Hang on," she said. She'd received a text. I was put on speaker. I strained to hear what was happening. Her nails, probably painted vermillion were tapping. Doug. She was texting Doug. I knew it. I head the *swoosh*. I heard his reply. She took another drag.

"What did Doug say?" I asked innocently.

An exhale. Smoke was probably coming out of her nose. "Doug doesn't control this. You're my reporter and you are there at my request. So, the question, Robin.... The question is, what do I say?'"

Geezus. Who would have guessed that Shirley was currently in a power play with Doug? Probably over salaries or some benefit. Or even column inches. But I acquiesced. "What..." I paused. "*Shirley*, what do *you* say to all this." I paused again. "*Shirley*."

"I say, *Robin*," she was matching my tone, mimicking me, "I say, *Robin*, it sounds like you've fallen into the shit again, so be very careful. This is your story, not Cindy's, so do not let her boss you around. She may try to submit a story to Doug. Perhaps she is doing so right now."

I could hear Cindy reading her story aloud upstairs. She always did that right before she submitted to make sure it sounded okay. So cute.

"Her story is going to be rejected by Doug, because, as I just said to him, or texted rather, to be accurate, that this is *your* story. You were sent there by me. Your story can have Cindy's name below yours, you can work that out with her, but I repeat, this is your story. You answer to me on this, not Doug. Got it? This is probably a real estate story. It's about how real estate can get people killed. Greed. Money. You know the regular stuff. No, give me a second. It can't be that." Another puff off her cigarette. She was thinking. "You say it was a bear attack? Hmmm. More likely it's a story about the dangers of walking in the woods in the spring. Yes, I like that better."

I didn't think so. But I'd play along. "Sounds good."

"*You* get to the bottom of this. Not Cindy. Got it?"
"Got it."
"Good."
The phone went dead.
I hated office politics.

12.

FIRST THINGS FIRST. I had to tell Cindy not to bother sending off her story. She hated rejection, and I knew that Doug, in order to keep the peace with Shirley, was going to have to turn it down, no matter how good it was.

I called up the stairs, "Hey, Cindy?"

"Hold on a minute, I'm almost finished here." I could hear her reading what sounded like a closing paragraph.

"Cindy? Wait."

"Okay, I'm finished." I heard a *whoosh*. She'd sent it. Damn. It's in. "What? Wait for what?"

Shit's going to hit the fan in about two minutes. "Nothing. Just wondered where you were."

She came down the stairs, scraping her hand through her wild hair, joggling her iPad in one hand, smiling as pleased as punch. "There. That's in. Doug will be so happy!"

No, he won't. "So, you got it in on time for the deadline."

"Yuppers. That old tightwad'll be thrilled that he wrangled a story out of me while I was on holiday. Great photos, too."

Lucky picked up on her good mood and jumped on and off the couch in rapid succession. Cindy looked at him and shook her head, an indulgent smile on her face. "That's one untrained dog, if you ask me."

"But loveable." I patted Lucky and covered his ears. "Don't you listen to that red-headed weirdo. You're the best."

"So, where are the cops? They want our statements or what?"

"They said they'd be by shortly."

I heard gravel scrunching in the driveway and looked out the window behind the dining-room table. Cindy peered over my shoulder. Not the cops. An ambulance. Too late for that, I thought.

"Oh look, they sent a full-length ambulance."

She was so disgusting sometimes.

"I'll go out and show them the beginning of the trail through the woods."

And where was that rejection text from Doug?

I met the two young guys on the path to the cottage, intercepting them and saving them from Cindy's "Stop while you're *a head*" comments. One carried a body board under his arm and the other had a zippered body bag. They looked about sixteen years old. "The trail begins over there, where that orange tape is. See it?"

The younger one, who was perhaps fourteen, shaded his eyes with his hands and looked where I was pointing. "Yes, Ma'am."

Oh God, save me. I was a "Ma'am." I said, "I'm Robin, Robin MacFarland." Now that I'd set that straight, I thought I'd better warn them. "It's pretty gruesome in the woods, only a torso, really, and scattered bones."

The older one opened his mouth and let out a deep hoot. "Cool. Sounds like a bear got him. Shouldn't go in the woods in the early spring. Those mother bears can sure act crazy."

I guess they hadn't heard it was politically incorrect to say "crazy." Nonetheless, they didn't know from crazy. This was a completely frenzied attack. And that big dead bear in there was no female. Its young were nowhere to be seen. But the guy's hoot somehow reassured me that they would be okay with a torso and some bones, so I said, "The police are still with the body, probably waiting for you."

"Thanks, Ma'am," said the younger one as they turned tail and headed off to the woods.

"Robin," I said to their retreating backs. "Robin MacFarland." Not that they heard me, but it made me feel better. "Ma'am" indeed.

When I got back into the cottage, Cindy was sitting on the couch, smiling away while patting Lucky. "His ears are so silky soft."

"I know. Listen, would you like a snack or something before the police return?" I had to eat. Then again, I always had to eat.

"No, I'm good, thanks."

I foraged in the fridge and while hiding behind the door, bit off a hunk of cheese. Dead bodies sure built up an appetite. Where was that text from Doug, spiking Cindy's story? I wanted to get this sorted out before the police returned. And I really wanted this story. It felt so off. I wanted to get my teeth into it. Clearly, I liked getting my teeth into lots of things. I took another bite of cheese and then tried to smooth out the bite marks so Cindy wouldn't know how uncouth I was. This story wasn't what it looked like. No bear attacks like that, ever, for no reason. Should I call Shirley? There'd been no text from Doug to Cindy. I smacked my lips and tried to clear out the cheese slime from my throat while I dialled my editor's number from behind the fridge door.

"Shirley Payne." Still a pain in the ass.

I looked over the door into the living area to see if Cindy was listening. No, she was whispering to Lucky. "Hi, Shirley. So, about that story? Cindy's heard nothing from Doug."

Her gravelly voice boomed into my ear. I hastily turned the volume down. "She will. Doug's licking his wounds. He read it, liked it, said the pictures were terrific, and he wants to print it. I said no, it was your story. He said it would sell papers. I said it was your story. He said it would go on the front above the fold. I said it was your story. He said he would do it in colour. I said it was your story. And so on. And then I said a few other things and now it's your story."

She laughed a dirty laugh and I didn't want to know. Cindy's phone *pinged* in the living room. "Thanks, gotta go."

I watched my friend from behind the open fridge door. I scooped some hummus out of the container with my fingers and stuffed them into my mouth. Cindy's hand was poised in mid-air over Lucky's head while she read her phone. Then one leg crossed the other. A faint blush crept up her neck. Then her hand fiddled with an earring. Touched the raw wound from the branch. Her lips pressed together. She put the phone down, turned her head and looked out the window behind her. She did not do rejection very well. Me? I was great at it. I had so much practice.

So now I had a dilemma. Did I pretend that I didn't know what the text said, or did I meet this issue head-on? On one hand, it would look as if I'd been talking behind her back if I let on that I already knew her story had been rejected. Well, I *had* been talking about it behind her back, and that didn't look good. On the other hand, if I came out and acknowledged it right away, like now, then my prior knowledge might get buried in her rejection angst.

I bit off a hunk cheese. Dipped a corner of the hunk into the hummus and ate that too. I was out of control, oh yeah.

I was ashamed by how much I wanted a story on the front page. I took a fingerful of hummus. It had been months since the last big story and I hungered for it. But not at my friend's expense. Well, okay, maybe a little at her expense. She wouldn't even be in the vicinity of Huntsville if it weren't for me. I was the one who was here working. She was the one on holiday. It was next to my family's land and had nothing to do with her. By rights, it should be my story. I ate more cheese as I talked myself into being honest with her. But I did feel badly. She wanted the story. She'd no doubt written a good one.

I walked into the living room, nervous as all get out, wiping my mouth.

Cindy looked back at me. "Don't worry so much. I'm not going to take my toys and go home. We can play together. I'll even lend you my great photographs."

Well. That was easy.

"Thanks, Cindy. I feel badly that you won't get the story and I will, but..."

"Don't give it another thought. I'm on the front page all the time. You haven't been on the front page since the water mess. It'll be good for your career. Doug explained it all to me. It really is your story. You're working, I'm on holiday. I wouldn't be here if it weren't for you. You will be more passionate about the story because it's next to your family's land. So, don't worry, I'm cool with it. I'll be in a mentor/small contributor role. But I want some credit for that."

What she meant was her name on the piece below mine. Maybe even "With files from Cynthia Dale."

"Of course." I sat down on the couch beside her and started patting Lucky as well.

She frowned. "Well, aren't you going to write it now? Get it in?" She looked at her watch. "You still have twenty minutes before the late, late breaking news deadline."

"Naw." I played with Lucky's ear. "I'm not sure what the story is yet. I need to think about it."

She pulled herself up straight. "What's to think about? It's a simple plot. A big bad bear killed a dumb guy who ventured into the woods in the spring with no bear spray. Probably he was a land surveyor, what with the clipboard and all. Pretty ironic that, don't you think? Him being killed by a bear. I mean, the bear's habitat gets threatened by development so it attacks the person who's responsible for dividing the land into small little plots. Next thing you know, he's in his cemetery plot. I think that's ironic, don't you?"

"Well, yes, but you know..."

"And then the big bad bear, who has now been put on high alert and has tasted human blood, is antsy, which is how bears get after being threatened, so it charges a police officer. I got great photos of this to prove it wasn't a frivolous shooting. You know how the public gets about cops shooting bears."

"I'm sure Andrechuk and Kowalchuk will appreciate it."

"So, there's your story, Robin. Write it down, it'll only take a minute, and get it in!"

She'd leaned over Lucky and literally put her face right in front of mine. "You have time, right now." I leaned back and held up my hand as if I were pushing her away.

"You have to get out of my face, Cindy." She was bugging me. Her sense of urgency wasn't mine. Her drive and her aggression toward work wasn't mine. I needed to *think*. There was something not quite right about all this. Bears simply didn't do what that bear did. And this wasn't a mother bear. I had seen no baby cubs around anywhere. This was a great big daddy bear.

Cindy's eyes widened as she pulled back her head. She wasn't used to me being assertive. "Sorry. I just think that if you..."

"No, this is *my* story and I am not happy with the facts. I am not going to post anything until I am. Nothing. So back off." Wow. I had never spoken to Cindy like that. Maybe this wasn't such a good idea, inviting her to my cottage for a whole week. At this rate, we'd be in a cat fight.

She turned her head and looked out the window behind the couch again. Now I felt badly. She really didn't do rejection very well, and here I was, right after her story had been tossed out, telling her to back away from me. I tried to make it better.

"How many pictures did you take?"

She mumbled, "Fifteen, four usable."

Great. I'd hurt her feelings. "So ... can I see them?"

She handed me her phone, head still turned. Lucky sniffed it as she passed it to me over his head. The dog probably was confused by a phone that didn't smell of wine and cheese. I tapped on the photo icon and scrolled through her last pictures. "Holy smoke, Cindy. These are fantastic." And they were. She had a series of aerial shots of the bear charging ever closer to the group of officers. Her finger must have been quickly tapping the button. "They could be laid out like small freeze-frames.

They're all usable. What an angle! You should get danger pay for taking these while up in a tree. The progression is striking." Had I overdone it? Was I being obvious?

"Look," she said, "it's not your job to make me feel better about losing the article. And I'm sorry I get so rabid." She was still looking out the window. I didn't like this Cindy, the one where she lost her mojo.

I poked her in the arm. "Hey, girlie." That should do it.

She turned her head and looked at me, a glint in her eyes. "Don't."

"Don't what?" I poked her again.

"Don't call me 'girlie.' And don't poke me."

I imitated her. "Don't poke me." I punctuated each word with a poke.

"Fuck off." She got up from the couch and said, "It looks like we're good." She walked over to me, arms wide to give me a hug, and leaned forward, lips puckered to give me a kiss. At the last moment, she stuck out her tongue and slurped all over my face. Then she ran up the stairs to get away, laughing her head off.

"I'll get you for that," I yelled. "You're not getting away with that, no way."

I hated germs and she knew it. I was not quite a germophobe like my brother Andrew, but pretty close, and flew into the kitchen to scrub my face. When I looked up, I saw through the kitchen window the two EMS workers carrying the body board out of the woods and over to the ambulance. On it lay a zipped-up body bag, the two ends lying completely flat and a hump in the middle.

"Hey Cindy, the ambulance guys are bringing the body out of the woods."

"Nice try," she called back.

"No, really, I mean it, quick! You're the photographer with the better phone. Get some pictures."

I heard her window open. "I'll take some from up here." A

minute later, she ran down the stairs and out the porch door, phone in hand.

I grabbed a tea towel to dry my face and then held it up. Ironed. Who on earth did that? Probably Andrew. He probably ironed his underwear too. He was so pompous. Keeping up with the Joneses even at the cottage.

I watched through the kitchen window as a scene unfolded in front of me. Cindy trotted up to the EMS guys while behind them the branches around the bright orange piece of tape marking the trail started to shake. Out stumbled Andrechuk, carrying four or five plastic bags filled with the detritus surrounding the body. Dirt. Leaves. A few shiny things. The female officer hurried over to the running ambulance and gave the bags to the younger fellow, who in turn put them carefully into the back of the ambulance. He slammed the passenger door as the wheels spun out of the drive, kicking up gravel behind it. Boys.

And then the rest of the police burst out of the woods. Niemchuk, looking pale, and Kowalchuk, looking large, trudged to the cottage, swatting at their heads to keep the bugs at bay.

I sat back down on the couch and held Lucky by his collar so he wouldn't turn into an attack dog when they came into the kitchen. I decided then and there I would keep my suspicions about the bear attack to myself. Lucky started licking the front of my shirt. Cheese.

13.

THERE WAS A PERFUNCTORY knock at the screen door and then a slam. They just barged in? How rude. I tried not to look accusatorily at Kowalchuk as he entered the living room, followed by a shaken and pale Niemchuk.

"Sorry to be so brash as to waltz right in," said Kowalchuk, seeing my look, "but time is of the essence."

No, no it wasn't. The guy who'd lost his head wasn't in a hurry. "No problem. Make yourself at home." I plastered a pseudo-smile on my face so he would know I was displeased.

There was another slam and Andrechuk entered the room, followed by a giggling Cindy. I hadn't seen Cindy giggle in years. In fact, in at least a decade. If ever. No, I don't think I'd ever seen her giggle. She wasn't the giggling kind. I looked at her quizzically. Yup, she was smitten. I didn't know many women who giggled. None of my daughters did, I hoped. But my boss Shirley giggled. Shirley also tilted her head and looked through eyelashes manufactured in a sweatshop. But both Cindy and Shirley were tough as nails and could switch in and out of the helpless female role, it seemed, on a whim.

Everyone took a seat. Cindy parked next to me and beside a restrained Lucky on the couch. I liked sitting there, particularly in this situation. As long as I was positioned in front of the large picture window, I knew they wouldn't be able to read my expressions clearly. I would be a black silhouette lit up from behind, especially now that the sun was beaming through on its slow descent toward the horizon. This was a small advantage considering that they had guns.

Andrechuk plopped into my father's reading chair, slightly off in a corner, and the two other cops took a load off on the couch opposite Cindy and me. The settee looked like a teeter-totter, with Kowalchuk weighing down one end and bouncing thin Niemchuk high in the air. I didn't laugh. But my stomach growled. Dinner should be soon, I thought and glanced at my watch. Four-thirty. Not soon enough. But the minute these yahoos were gone, I'd have some wine to go with some more sneakily wolfed down cheese.

Kowalchuk had caught my glance at my watch. "In a hurry? Going somewhere?"

He could see me better than I thought. But I wasn't going to be bullied. "I understand you want statements from us? How would you like that to work?"

He heaved one gigantic leg over the other, trying to look casual. Niemchuk held on to the arm of the couch as the cushions rippled towards him. "Well." It came out like a tornado blowing through town. "You tell us what happened, Andrechuk here writes it down, and then you sign what she's written."

He was being patronizing but it washed right over me. That Buddhist thing was working. For now.

I acted surprised. "No tape recording?"

Cindy held up her phone. "I'll tape it, nonetheless."

Kowalchuk exhaled, feigning patience. "Sure, go ahead." He waved his hand in the air.

"I actually don't need your permission," she snapped.

One day she was going to land in hot water. Andrechuk cocked her head and gave it a tiny shake. Cindy didn't see it, but I sure had. Had Cindy gone too far and jeopardized her chances with Andrechuk?

Andrechuk said, "I take very thorough notes, don't worry."

I had trouble reconciling her musical, tinkling voice with the woman who had stood her ground and shot rounds into a charging bear, feet spread. But now I knew what was behind that tiny shake of a head. She'd been insulted by Cindy. It wasn't a warning to show more respect to her boss as I had first thought. I had better leap into the fray before anyone dug themselves into any deeper holes.

"I'll begin. We were going for a walk in the woods..."

Kowalchuk interrupted. "Back up. Why were you up here in the first place?"

I lied. "It's my cottage. I came up for a short holiday from my job."

He smelled a rat. "You're a journalist, right? Always after a story? Why are you really there?"

"To find ramps. As I told you earlier." I didn't like where he was going. And I didn't like his attitude. He uncrossed his legs and spread them wide, leaning forward. Men are so transparent. Showing me his junk? What an asshole. But I wasn't going to be intimidated. "We were going for a walk in the woods before doing our shopping for the week and literally stumbled across a jacket that was lying on the ground."

He growled, "I'll let it go for now, but we will revisit, yet again, why you just happen to be here later."

I plowed on. "We looked at the jacket and decided to leave it there, in case whoever had left it was coming back. The bugs were pretty bad so we decided to head towards the lake and get out into the open."

"It would have been faster to turn around and head back to your cottage."

He was so suspicious.

I continued. "We also wanted to see if there was any ice left on the lake and what temperature the water was." I made that up. "So, as I was saying, we headed for the lake with the plan that if the jacket was still lying on the ground on our way back, we would pick it up and hang it on a branch or something. That way, whoever lost it would be able to see it."

Andrechuk sat forward. "So, you got to the lake, saw there

was no ice, and felt the water. What temperature was it?" What was she doing? Trying to undermine my honesty?

Cindy and I said in unison, "Freezing."

Kowalchuk looked over his shoulder at Andrechuk. "Kimberley, it's best if you don't interrupt."

Her name was *Kimberley*? You would have thought with a name like Andrechuk her first name would have been Katya, or Natalia, or something that was in keeping with her background. But no, she was a Kimberley. From the corner of my eye, I could see Cindy taking this all in. I could also see that Kimberley wasn't happy. First of all, she'd been disciplined in front of civilians, which was boorish, and secondly, those said civilians now knew her first name, which was so unprofessional.

I watched Andrechuk as she recovered from these little jibes at her self-confidence. Her interest in Cindy seemed to be ebbing like a retreating tide. Or maybe she felt her interest should subside because Cindy would no longer be interested in her. She'd been told off by her superior, diminished somehow. If this was the case, she didn't know Cindy very well. To her, mistreating an employee was a red cape to a charging bull. But Cindy was sitting beside Lucky, acting as cool as a cucumber, her latent energy and power being, well, latent. She was taking in all the little missteps and warping of power. I knew there'd be reaction of some kind eventually.

Cindy shattered Kowalchuk's attempt at decorum with, "Good question though, Kim. Shows you were questioning our story."

"Kim" was it now?

Andrechuk's face transformed as her generous lips stretched into a wide smile. All was not lost. But I worried. Maybe she was a bit young for Cindy. Kim's foundation wasn't that of a woman in her prime, unwavering and authentic, it was the formulating foundation of a forty-year-old, still flexible and yielding with the years of remaining youth. Cindy needed a wrecking ball of a gal to reach her inner workings. Was I a wrecking ball? I knew her really well. I'd think about that later. Not that Cindy ever had a flexible personality. Even at the age of three, I'm sure she was strong-willed and outspoken.

Kowalchuk's head bounced like a ricocheting pinball from Andrechuk to Cindy to me. He rebounded from Cindy to me a couple of times. "You go on holidays much together?" he asked.

"Cindy and me?" I ventured innocently. "What does that have to do with a dead person in the woods?" I was getting feisty.

"Just *fleshing* out all the details, trying to picture the whole story here."

Cindy answered by standing up. If anything even hinted at homophobia, she was gone. "Nice to meet you. Thanks for coming by." It was a dismissal.

Kowalchuk didn't move. "We can do this at the station," he said.

He was right. He could easily ask us all to get in a squad car and go downtown to Huntsville's police station. Cindy knew it and sat down, lips curled against her teeth, her smile resembling the fangs of a bobcat ready to pounce on a mouse. Andrechuk straightened the notebook on her lap and I continued the story. "After feeling the water, we walked back the way we had come. The jacket was still there. Cindy tried to pick it up out of the dirt, but it was lodged in the mud. So, I offered to help and we pulled on the collar together. There was this sort of sucking noise and then..." The white severed neck bone skittered across my mind. I could feel my eyes losing muscle control and rolling back into my head.

"We saw that there was a torso inside the jacket." Cindy finished the sentence for me.

My phone, which had been clamped in my hand, suddenly vibrated and rang. I yelped. Electric shocks were coursing up my arm to zap my heart. I looked at the screen. Ralph. He said he'd check in when he was done his paperwork. "I have to take this," I said to no one in particular. I stood up and walked into the kitchen and faced the screen door. I didn't dare go outside with all the bugs, and there were no other rooms on the first floor. Hopefully, no one would listen in. Good luck with that. The cottage's open-plan concept had its disadvantages.

"Hi Ralph," I whispered. "I thought you were snowed under. You're done early. How are you doing?"

"Yeah, done early for today. Just finished the last bits of today's paperwork. I'm great. Lived through another shift." He always joked about that. I didn't think it was funny, him being a cop and all. "But you sound funny. Why are you whispering?"

"There are a bunch of police in my living room."

"Police? Why? Are you okay?"

His concern was heartwarming, although for some reason my heart wasn't warmed. We'd only been going out for about six months, okay eight, but he still had so much baggage. I couldn't unpack it to reach who he was. Frankly, I was tired of trying. He had to either dump the little fortress he'd erected around himself or I was gone. *Erected.* Hmmm. He had his good points. Points. Hmmm. So to speak. Maybe I'd wait a little longer for him to be emotionally available.

"Yeah, I'm fine. Just peachy. Found a dead guy in the woods today."

"Ugh. That must have been pretty disgusting. Was the body still intact? Or had the animals got to him?"

"You might say that. An animal."

"Pardon? You're breaking up. I'm losing you."

How perceptive. Maybe he was losing me. I walked closer to the window to get a better signal. The living room was silent. Were they listening in? "A bear. He was attacked."

"I know. I can't bear spotty cell coverage either. It is so tacky."

"No," I hissed. "Cindy and I found a guy who had been killed by a bear."

"Cindy is unbearable? I could have told you that." Cindy, being a crime reporter, was shunned by cops all over Toronto.

"Why did you invite her up?"

"Creston!" I hissed again. "We found a guy who'd been killed by a bear."

There was silence.

"I don't think I heard you right. Did you say you'd found a guy who'd been killed by a bear?"

"Yes." Finally, the news had been delivered.

"Naw. That's impossible. Bears don't kill. Not in Ontario anyway. Not those little brown bears."

The image of that huge bear crashing through the undergrowth, his fur shiny in the sunlight, crossed my mind. "Little" was not the adjective I would have used. "That's what I'm thinking. But it happened. And then Niemchuk got attacked."

"I'm not a tacky numbskull." He laughed, knowing he'd heard me wrong.

"Look, the cell service is impossible and I have to give a statement to the police here. I gotta go."

"Who's in charge up there?"

"Kowalchuk."

"Bless you."

"Kowalchuk." I said louder.

"Oh him. Big guy, right?"

"Yeah, that's him."

"I went to school with that guy. We trained together."

"Ralph?"

"Yes, honey?"

"Can you come up?"

Now why the hell did I say that? Two seconds ago I was thinking of breaking up with him, wasn't I? God, I was so weak. A few hours away plus one dead guy and I needed my boyfriend like some pathetic damsel. So dependent.

"Oh sweetie, no, I'm so sorry. I can't come up right now. Maybe in a few days I could take a long weekend."

He sounded truly sorry. He really was sweet. Maybe I'd get through his crap to his centre after all.

"What are you working on?" I asked Ralph, ever the journalist.

"You know I can't tell you that. But it's almost over, and when it is, I'll come right up. Okay?"

"Thanks. I'm a little freaked out by all this."

"Kowalchuk is a good cop, if not a tad gruff. He'll figure it out. Go give your statement and then have a drink."

You betcha. Wait, was he enabling me? Were we codependent? I'd have to think about that, too. How much did he drink anyway? I was so busy hiding my sneaky little gulps that I hadn't noticed what he was doing. "Okay. Good plan. It will settle my nerves. I feel jangly all over my body."

"It'll be okay. Bye. Love you."

I nearly fell over. *Love you*? Where had that come from? The L-word. Fuck. Did I have to say "love you" back? My throat did a funny gurgle thing and I hung up. I could blame it on the poor cell service. I stood in the kitchen for a second gathering my thoughts. Right. Focus. Statement. Police. Headless torso. Nothing to do with love.

I walked back into the living room. They'd found magazines and were leafing through them. Kimberley was paging through a *Mechanix Illustrated* from 1974. Interesting choice. Kowalchuk put down a *Good Housekeeping* from the eighties, and Niemchuk, whose colour had returned, was chuckling at the jokes in a *Reader's Digest*.

"Sorry about that," I said.

"Were you talking to Ralph Creston? I thought I heard you say "Creston."

Kowalchuk *had* been eavesdropping. "Yes, he said he knew you, that you'd trained together."

"Yeah, the Police Academy. Years and years ago. He's a good cop. He's your partner?"

"No." God, no. No. No. No. Despite the L-word. "Just a casual boyfriend."

He looked at Cindy and then back at me. I saw the wheels turn as he ascertained that we were not an item. He must be blind not to notice the frisky eyes she was making at Andrechuk. "Okay, let's finish this up."

I went through the whole story. The scattered bones. The barf in the bushes. The clipboard. The ring.

He went ballistic. "Wait, you found a ring? What ring? Where is it?"

Cindy stretched her legs out and leaned back so she could squeeze her hand into the front pocket of her very tight jeans. She wiggled her hand down to the bottom of the pocket and pulled out the ruby ring, leaned forward, and handed it to Kowalchuk. He took it from her and held it up to the light, inspecting the surface.

"No fingerprints left on this smooth surface," he said glaring at Cindy. Nonetheless, he held it by the edges and carefully dropped it into a plastic evidence bag that he had taken out from the pocket of his Kevlar vest.

She shrugged. "It was buried in the earth. There'd be no fingerprints on it anyway. Plus, chances are good you would never have found it."

She was right. That Cindy could dance rings around anyone.

14.

WITH SIGNED STATEMENTS held tightly in hand, Kowalchuk got up and moved through the kitchen to the screen door, followed by Niemchuk and Andrechuk. I watched amazed as Kimberley, her hand slightly cupped, gave Cindy a hidden scrap of paper as she walked by. What was this, grade school? Cindy palmed the note and casually put it in her back pocket. No expression registered on her face.

"Thanks for answering our call, you guys," I said. "But listen, I'm going to be writing a story about the dangers of entering the woods in the spring and was wondering if I could see the autopsy results, you know, to flesh out the story." Bad choice of words. Ugh, "flesh." It made me think of those bones in the woods that had no flesh. On second thought, it also made me think of Ralph.

Kowalchuk looked at me blankly for a second or two. Then, "Sure, sure, no problem. I'll email it." I wondered why he'd had to think about it. And I also wondered if he was happily saying the words and had no intention of sending me the information. If so, why not? I knew he wasn't just being polite.

I rooted through my purse and handed him a fairly unstained business card with my email address on it. I brushed off the crumbs on its journey towards his baseball mitt of a hand. Those damn peanut butter Ritz crackers I'd thrown into my bag a year ago kept surfacing. The gift that kept giving.

He took the card, while saying, "I already have your contact information Robin, you gave it to me in your statement a minute ago." He looked behind me to Cindy. "And I have yours too, Cindy, in case Andrechuk here should need it."

Huh? So, he had noticed. The guy didn't miss a trick.

The screen door *thunked* shut behind them. What an ordeal that was. But I wanted to know what the note said. "So, what did she write you?"

"Who?" Cindy did innocence with aplomb.

"Don't play that game with me, missy. Read me the note that Kimberley gave you."

She frowned at my "missy" and took the note out of her back pocket, slowly unfolded it while looking at me, slowly read it, and then slowly read it aloud, "Meet me at the town dock for pizza tonight. I'm off at six."

I high-fived her. "A date! You have a date!"

Cindy looked doubtful. "Should I go?"

"What? Of course you should go. She's so cute. And what a fabulous voice. I wonder if she sings? You know, in a band or something, as a hobby."

"Do you mind? It would mean you'll be here alone."

I hadn't thought of that.

"It's been a pretty rough day, Robin. I can always go another time."

I wasn't sure about that. I thought Andrechuk was a little skittish, and if rejected on the first go around, she might not be receptive to an alternative plan. But Cindy was right. I didn't want to be alone. Maybe there was a compromise. "You're right, I don't want to be here alone in the dark. Maybe you could have some pizza with her, get to know her a bit, and then come back before it's pitch-black out."

"Yeah, that's better for me anyway. I'm not too sure it would work out between us. She's a lot younger than I am, although I am pretty attracted to her."

"Really?"

"Was it obvious?"

"Duh. Your tongue was hanging out a foot."

"My tongue wasn't hanging out."

"Yes, it was."

"I'm a sophisticated North Toronto matron. My tongue never hangs out."

My phone rang again. I retorted, "Saved by the bell."

I read the screen. Ralph again. What did he want? "Hi, sweetie," I said. He did say he loved me. I had to give him *something* back, if only a term of endearment.

"I finished up," he sounded excited. "Sooner than I expected! If I left now, I could be there before dark. What do you say?"

I hesitated, perhaps a bit too long. Did I want him to come? I was over my damsel-in-distress act.

He was hurt. "If you don't want me to come, that's okay. I have plenty to do here."

"No, I want you to come. Right now. It would be great if you came now. Way better than tomorrow morning. Or in a few days. That's the only reason why I had to think about it. It took a minute for my mind to adjust to the change in plans."

When did I learn how to lie? Cindy warned me months ago that if I became a crime reporter I would learn how to lie. It was not a skill I coveted. The truth was way better. I enjoyed Ralph, he was a good friend with benefits, and I was happy to benefit from them, but I would have to talk to him about his emotional availability. I wasn't going to put up with a shallow relationship.

"Great. I'll leave in about half an hour, so I should be there by seven-thirty. Maybe we could have dinner together. I'll pick something up on my way through town. Some of that chicken that we had before."

"And fries," I said, my mouth already watering. Ralph didn't seem to mind my few extra pounds. A few? Oh, how I loved a euphemism.

"Sounds good," he laughed. "And I'll bring some wine."

"No whining here," I said, keeping up with his mood. "But

you don't need to bring any. Andrew had a cocktail party here about a month ago and there's quite a lot of alcohol left over. He may be many things, but stingy is not one of them. Plus, I brought some." Yeah, a steamer trunk full. I had told Ralph a bit about my entitled brother and how I felt about him.

He laughed again, his good humour completely restored. "See you soon. Bye."

He hung up without waiting for my reply. Really? I looked at my phone and tapped the end button. That was one of the problems with the relationship. It was all about him. Was I right about that? Probably not. Was I too picky? I was too something, that's for sure. Robin, figure it out.

I thought back to my excitement eight months ago when our relationship had started. My husband Trevor had been killed by a drunk driver, and it had been a while, a long while, since I'd been with anyone. The first few months of dating Ralph had been thrilling, right down to the you-know-what. It was such an exhilarating time after being so heavily burdened with bringing up the kids, taking care of the pets, and paying off the mortgage. During those months after Trevor's death, I had become an old and fat alcoholic. I felt I was a failure in my career, plus I was all alone. I remembered the day, somewhat over half a year ago, when I had had an epiphany: I had become old, fat, an alcoholic, a failure, and all alone. The problem was, out of the five issues, only two were gone. I was still old. Nothing I could do about that oh so attractive crepe paper skin. I was still fat, which I could do something about but hadn't, and I still drank, which I also could do something about, but hadn't. I was no longer alone, though, Ralph had been a good antidote to that. And I wasn't such a failure. I had been on the front page of the paper. And now I still wasn't such a failure as it looked like I was heading that way again. But really, my score was just two out of five.

"Who was that?" Cindy batted her eyelashes at me and jolted me out of my daydream She knew who it was.

"Ralph. He says he's going to come up tonight. In fact, he'll be here by dinner time. Before dark. He's leaving Toronto about now. So, you're off the hook. You can stay out as late as you want with Kimberley."

"Thanks, Mom."

I ignored her. "It's perfect, isn't it? You can go have fun and Ralph and I can have fun." I wasn't sure about that for either of us.

Cindy picked up on my mood. "I know you've been having some doubts about Ralph, and I really don't know about this Kimberley, but let's see how it all unfolds. You never know. Maybe we'll both have a great time."

"Yeah, right."

"No, be positive. Maybe we will."

"Listen, I thought Ralph was camera shy, you know, after that ugly divorce. And I thought that he was reserved. An introvert. But now I'm wondering if it isn't emotional baggage that keeps him unavailable. Or maybe he's just shallow."

"Most men are." Cindy really didn't like guys.

"No, Cindy, they're not all like that."

"Okay, maybe not shallow. Maybe they're just predictable. Plus, they're all mama's boys."

"No, they're not."

"Okay, maybe not they're not all mama's boys. Maybe they're all stupid."

"No, they're not."

With a stalemate hovering between us, Cindy changed tack. "Do you think Kowalchuk will actually give us the autopsy report?"

"I sensed he had no intention of emailing it to me. But it doesn't matter now if he does or doesn't. Ralph will get it for me."

"See, men do have some uses."

"Be fair, Cindy. He has plenty of uses."

"Right, he can take care of your plumbing and headlights."

With that, she flounced upstairs. "I'm going to get ready for my datelette on the town dock."

I supposed I had better change into something that didn't have squashed blackfly juice on it and followed her up the stairs. I needed a shower badly. I was covered in dirt.

An hour later, Cindy left for her date and I waited on the couch with Lucky for Ralph to arrive, running my fingers through my damp hair, trying to give it more volume. I wondered where our relationship was going. Was Cindy right? That men were shallow mama's boys who were somewhat stupid? Or was he a really smart guy who had hidden depths? Was he a stepping stone? Was he my toy boy? No, I meant boy toy. Or did that apply to much younger men? I'd have to ask one of my kids. No, I had better not. Then they would know. I had kept most of the details of my relationship with Ralph secret from them. They knew I was dating, and they knew the guy's name was Ralph, but they didn't know he was a cop, that he'd saved my life, and that I really liked him. Wait. Did I actually think that?

There it was. I really liked him. Maybe I was frustrated because I couldn't decide if he was a keeper. I was out of practise when it came to dating. He had told me he loved me. But did he? Or was that a long-ago habit of saying "I love you" at the end of a phone call? Did I love him? I guess that was the question. Not that he was shallow or stupid or a toy boy. Boy toy. Whatever. I wish he'd get here so I could have a drink. Maybe I'd have one anyway. Now there was a plan.

I cracked open a cold bottle of white and took a shining glass out of the very clean cupboard. I should have Andrew come clean my house. As I was pouring the wine I heard a scrunch of gravel. A car was coming up the driveway. Ralph? That was fast. He must have driven like a maniac. Or maybe he had called me while on the road, assuming his arrival was going to be fine. Yes, that was it. He should have said so. I really didn't like subterfuge. But I was a fine one to talk. I watched through the dining-room window, wineglass in hand, as he walked up the driveway, suitcase in one hand and a bag of takeout chicken in the other. God, he was so handsome. Tall, mostly dark hair, and he moved like a dancer. My eyes strayed over his lean form, took in the ropey chest muscles bulging through his T-shirt and landed squarely at his crotch. Oops. But I kept looking. My heart built up speed and I knew, in that moment, that no matter what else was going on between us, some things about the relationship were great. I made it into the kitchen when Lucky started barking at the door, tail wagging. What a litmus test that dog was. If Ralph was okay by Lucky, he was okay by me. The screen door squeaked as he pulled it open.

He planted a big kiss on my lips and then started unpacking the goodies. "It's so good to see you. Let's eat before we do anything interesting.

"You must have called me from the road. You knew I wanted to see you. All of you." I patted his bum.

"Yup. I'm famished. As hungry as a bear. I could eat you all up." He laughed, but looking at my face he knew he'd hit a sore spot. "Sorry. Driving makes me so hungry."

Everything made me hungry. "Me too." The idea of him eating me presented a tough choice. Dinner for two, or dinner for him only. "We have a lot in common, big boy. Driving makes me hungry too." I put a hand on his crotch. "But after what I saw today, I'm not sure the bear analogy would put me in the mood." Although, strangely, it did. All that shining fur. That strong and fluid movement. How sick was that? I needed therapy. No, maybe I was normal. Wasn't it Marian Engel who wrote a famous book that won some literary award about a woman making love to a bear? No one said she needed therapy.

"Later. Let's eat. I see you've started on a bottle of wine. I brought more, in case." He started divvying up the chicken onto two plates. Such a chef.

The bottle of white was pretty much a third gone. There

were really big glasses at the cottage. Small jugs, if I had to be specific. "Here, let me pour you a glass."

"Thanks."

He carried the plates and I took the two glasses of wine with the bottle tucked under my arm to the table.

"Where's Cindy?"

"She fell in love with one of the cops today and they've got a pizza date on the town dock."

"So, she's not here? Perfect."

Sometimes she really bugged him.

I had stuffed some deliciously moist chicken into my mouth. "Hey, this is really good, where did you get it?"

"Wing and a Prayer. In town."

"That chicken place run by the ex-minister?"

"Yup." He swallowed. "I also called Kowalchuk from the car after I called you to let him know I was coming. You know, foreign cop on local territory and all that. A courtesy call. He's a nice enough guy. Huge, if I recall."

"Still is. Seems shrewd. A pretty good cop." Plus an arrogant prick. But the fries were crispy and steaming.

"Don't cross him. He can be ruthless."

"I got the sense of that."

"Anyway, he gave me the preliminary autopsy results and told me to tell you."

"Already? I can't believe it. They must have a good budget for things to happen that quickly. The body must have just been delivered, and in the last hour of the day as well."

"It's only a preliminary report. It's easy to tell right off the bat if a body is male or female. Pelvis measurements. I know you thought it was a male, but the body belongs to a woman." He looked at me to gauge my reaction.

"A female?" The chicken got lodged in my throat. I croaked, "But that couldn't be right. The coroner is wrong. There was a Carhartt jacket. Brown. A style that doesn't do up around the hips of a woman. It's a man's jacket. And there was no long hair anywhere. Not on the skull, not lying around the head. Plus, there was a clipboard."

"Women carry clipboards."

He was right.

"And they can have short hair."

He was right about that, too.

"And many women wear men's clothing, you know, to be funky. And thin women can wear men's jackets."

Funky? Now there was a word I hadn't heard in several decades. I think I was wearing baggy plaid pants the last time someone used the word *funky*. But he was right about all of that.

"You're right. Sometimes I wear a man's dress shirt to bed."

The lines around his eyes deepened as he smiled. "After you take it off me."

My thoughts wandered to taking a shirt off Ralph and then, with heroic effort, I tugged them back to this odd news. "A female." I let that sink in. "Any idea who?" I didn't expect an answer. It was too early for an identification.

"Darlene Gibson."

I was surprised he knew the answer to this. The name sounded familiar. I forked in a serving of coleslaw. It was tangy and sweet. "Why does that name sound so familiar? And how did they identify the person so quickly? The bones were scattered all over the place."

Ralph gulped some wine. "The ring. There was an inscription that read 'For Darlene.' That plus her father had reported her missing about a month ago. That tallied with the condition of the body. They're going to do some dental matching to confirm the identity."

"But why does the name ring a bell?" I put the emphasis on the word "ring." It was my attempt to make Ralph smile again. He didn't. Was that because it wasn't about him? Or maybe the thought of "rings" made him nervous.

"She was in the news about six months ago. *The Toronto Express* did a piece on her. I think Cindy wrote it. Sexual assault case against that Toronto actor, David Sparling. Not guilty. Remember?"

Did I ever. It was a fiasco. The guy had clearly been guilty. "Did I read something about a lawsuit?"

"Yes, I think she was suing him."

Ralph picked up a chicken leg and was gnawing away, giving it a good once-over. He put the bone in his mouth and pulled it out slowly, his eyebrows raised. That guy.

15.

AFTER DINNER, while I was washing the dishes and Ralph was beside me drying, I brought up the subject of the bear again. "Ralph," I asked, "have you ever heard of a bear attacking a person for no reason?"

"Not really, but I think it does happen." He wiped a dish slowly, thinking, "Well, there's probably a statistic on that. Once these dishes are done, let's look it up." He nuzzled the back of my neck.

I nudged my elbow into his ribs. "Stop it, I'm working here."

"And I'm a hungry bear and I'm going to attack you," he growled. I could feel his breath on my cheek and something on my lower cheek as he shuffled his feet so that his body was closer to mine. He put his arms around my waist. I could feel all his benefits pressing against my body.

"Hmmm," I said. "I don't think we have to look anything up. Feels like things are looking up already." I laughed. My, wasn't I bold. He knocked my elbow and my hands splashed in the sudsy water.

He laughed, "Oh look, you're getting all wet."

Enough of the innuendo. I shook the water off my hands, turned around, slipped out of his arms, and sprinted up the stairs. He chased me and was closing the distance. "What time is Cindy getting back?"

"Late, late. We won't be interrupted." And we weren't.

Around ten o'clock we were sitting in the living room, quietly reading, when Cindy waltzed in. Not so "late, late" after all.

"How was your date?" I asked. It couldn't have been good if she was home already.

"Hi Ralph," she answered, ignoring my question. Wasn't good at all.

He grunted. And didn't look up. He turned the page he was reading with exaggerated care.

"Fuck you, too," she sang.

He smiled a little.

"Do you like her?" I asked.

"She's great, in a lesbian 'I-want-to-go-to-the-arctic-while-wearing-my-Birkenstocks' kind of way."

"A bit young for you, then?"

"If sprouted broccoli had been a topping, her pizza would have been covered with it."

"Are you going to see her again?"

"Not unless another dead body shows up. Specifically mine."

"Okay-y-y-y. Speaking of dead bodies, that body we found was Darlene Gibson."

Cindy's mouth dropped. She knew right away who that was. "Darlene Gibson? The woman who brought charges against David Sparling? The guy who got off on strangling her and then got off for strangling her?"

Ralph spoke up. "Impossible to prove. It was his word against hers and his meant more. He was a famous actor and she was a lowly government employee."

Cindy said, "Well, no. She had a different job." She leaned against the kitchen door frame, crossed her arms, and put her hand under her chin. "I remember now. She was a set designer for the show he starred in. A true abuse of power. But still lowly I guess, compared to him. I gave the trial some coverage. I don't believe it. A woman? She must have had really skinny hips to wear that Carhartt jacket." She thought for a minute. "And she must have cut her hair. It was long when I interviewed her." She poured herself a glass of wine and sat down on the couch beside me and Lucky. "And what was she doing in the woods up here anyway, carrying a clipboard?"

Ralph replied, "That's what I meant about lowly government employee. She was likely eyeballing possible lot lines for the next-door property. The new purchaser was going to sell lots of plots. She got a job up here in Huntsville so she could live with her parents after the court case. Apparently, she was vey upset with the result of that case."

Cindy's eyes narrowed. "How do you know all this?"

"Kowalchuk." He went back to reading.

I was listening to this interchange with interest. A government employee? Plots? Probably worked for the Town of Huntsville. The planning department. "She worked for the planning department?"

Ralph looked up, "Yup. That's what Kowalchuk said. Her job was to measure lots in undeveloped land. Location of structures. Distance from lakes. That sort of thing."

Cindy put her finger on her mouth, thinking, "Right. That makes sense. I remember now. She got a Master's Degree in Urban Planning from Dalhousie, couldn't find work in her field, and became a set designer. I guess that didn't work out for her." She laughed.

I could feel anger bubbling around in my chest. How could the two of them be so cavalier? Here was a young woman, dead for God's sake, and they were discussing her like nothing had happened to her. I tamped down my reaction. "Couldn't have been the most popular position here in the north. I mean, there's so many groups that oppose development. And she was on the front lines."

Cindy started counting on her fingers, bending each one back as she stated the people who would oppose a developer: "Environmentalists, animal rights groups, cottager's associations, water protectors, light pollution people, native bands. The list is endless." She thought for a moment. "And you, Robin. And your family."

I let it go. "If her death were a murder, there could be lots of suspects, lots of plots against her."

Ralph looked up. "But her death wasn't a murder, Robin. She was simply attacked by a bear. There was no murder weapon but fangs and claws. It was pretty obvious, according to Kowalchuk."

But I wasn't so sure. "I'm not so sure. Maybe someone killed her and left her in the woods, hoping that animals would destroy signs of a stabbing, or a strangling, or a clubbing on the head. Or however people die."

Ralph stopped reading. "The full autopsy report will reveal any or all of those things. You saw the skull. Did it look crushed in any way?" He was challenging me.

Cindy stepped in. "I didn't take a really good up-close look, but from what I saw, it seemed pretty intact."

My stomach lurched as I pictured the skull half-buried in the leaves, black holes for eyes.

Ralph continued. "The coroner will inspect the bones carefully for signs of a knife nick or a strangling. But with all the tooth marks? I don't know. Pretty impossible to tease it all apart. Anyway, Kowalchuk will let us know the verdict."

Cindy put her wine down on a table and picked up a magazine. The subject was closed as far as she was concerned. But I had my doubts. There were so many people who despised development of any kind. They became so angry. Their passion was heated. And here was a beautiful piece of property that had been sold to a developer. Not to a conservancy group, or a philanthropist, but to a greedy developer who would slice it up into little plots and destroy the forest and habitat for hundreds of species, both for plants and animals. Even though I was incensed, I wouldn't murder the person who was measuring the lots. No, I'd go for the developer. Legally. Or maybe key his car. Late at night.

But maybe the developer was unavailable, was off in some foreign land. Foreign investors were buying up plots of land

and houses left right and centre in Canada. Maybe that's what the story was, not the sale of one piece of property, but the sale of the whole country. Foreign investment had become so rampant that Toronto and Vancouver had both implemented foreign investment taxes. But I didn't blame foreigners for wanting a piece of Canada. Who wouldn't want to invest in a stable government, a fairly tolerant society, and safe cities? At any rate, I would tie on my patience hat and wait for the coroner to examine the body under a microscope and give a verdict as to cause of death. In the meantime, time was of the essence and I had a story to write. I would stick with Shirley's suggestion of not going into the woods in the spring or you might get eaten by a bear. That would placate her while I got to the truth of what had happened.

My phone rang. Who'd be calling me so late? I took a quick glance at my watch as I reached into my back pocket. Ten-thirty. The screen said it was Andrew. What did he want?

"Hi Andrew. What's up?"

"I read the online news a minute ago. About the body in the woods near Huntsville. The article said that two women found it while hiking. Are you up north? Was that you?"

How did that story get out? He had to know everything. "Yes, and yes. I'm at the cottage. I'm here with Cindy. We were walking through the woods on the property next door and found some remains. Called the cops, they came, took the body away. End of story."

"Don't be like that, Robin. I was pretty sure it was you. No one else walks in those woods but members of our family and it is the largest tract of land around. Except for that Dick Worthington. I called to make sure you were okay."

"Sure you did." He was just plain nosey and controlling. But I relented a tad. I had to be a good Buddhist and not contribute to bad feelings in the universe. It was hard to do with a butt plug of a brother like Andrew. "Thanks for asking, We are both fine."

"I'm not worried about Cindy, she's used to dead bodies. I'm more worried about you."

God. He thought I was a weakling. My family had such an inaccurate perception of who I was. And then I remembered how I had barfed, fainted, could hardly walk. If the shoe fit, I had to wear it. "Thank you, Andrew. It was a bit rough at first, but I'm okay now. Kind of you to ask." See, I could be open-hearted. That Buddhist thing was sinking in. After all, it was kind of him to call.

"How did you find the cottage?"

At the end of the driveway, stupid. Oops. Old habits die hard. I reset my compass. "Great. You must have been cleaning for hours, both before your cocktail party and after. It was spotless."

"It was the least I could do. Not that the crowd was full of yahoos."

He rhymed off a short list of some his guests. He was hobnobbing with bank presidents and the CEOs of multinational companies. They didn't sound like the kind of people who would trash a place. My parties, not that I had any, but if I did, would be peopled by a completely different set. "Nice friends," was all I said.

"On the whole, they're pretty cool. But I have to say, those people in the entertainment sector, they can get pretty wild."

Of course he had to say that. He wanted me to know he was rubbing shoulders with stars. "They like to play, do they?"

I could see him puffing out his chest, looking important, as he gossiped about people he knew. What a little boy. Maybe Cindy was right. Bunch of mama's boys. Now, now, Robin, be charitable. He's just insecure. Maybe. Maybe he's just an asshole. "They got a little smashed?"

"More than a little. That David Sparling? You know, the guy who starred in *Cruising Away*, the musical? Some of the cast were there. But Sparling? He was really tying one on. Tossing off his clothes, knocking back the shots, and going after various women. Wives even. He had no discretion. And when I asked him to cool it, he asked me if I knew who he was, he was that high. Of course, I knew who he was. I'd invited him. I manage his money. We are friends. But right then I wanted him to cruise away."

"Sounds like a boor, Andrew. My friend Cindy wrote a piece about him and his court case in *The Toronto Express*."

"I know all about that." Naturally he did. "He got off, didn't he? I can't believe that a friend of mine would be involved in something like that. To make matters worse, Darlene's parents were at the party. So awkward. They're friends of mine up there."

"It was her body that was found."

"You're kidding me. Darlene's?"

"Yes. Completely dismembered."

"That's terrible." Andrew continued as if her death were nothing. "Anyway, her parents are clients as well."

"You sure do get around." *Blah, blah, blah.*

"Her father Harry was in precious metals. I think he's about fifty-five and took early retirement last year. I handle his money," he said by way of explanation. "It was pretty difficult. They knew who he was, but he had no idea who they were."

"If he's about fifty-five, that puts Darlene in her late twenties." I was thinking she'd still be thin at that age and able to wear a man's jacket. "And how old is David Sparling?"

"He looks about fifty, but he could be older. His face looked a little tight."

A little tight? What did that mean? Oh, a facelift. I lived in the wrong demographic, was part of the wrong class. He must be pretty successful. Considering I was having trouble scraping the money together for a crown on my crumbling back molar, I guessed a facelift was out of the question. Or liposuction. "He preys on younger women then."

"I finally got him to go upstairs to bed by telling him I'd invited some officers to the cocktail party and they would be arriving soon, after their shift at midnight."

I was curious. "Why did that make him hightail it out of there?"

Andrew coughed, "Blow."

"Blow?" I blew into the phone.

"No Robin. I mean blow, blow. Cocaine. He was ripped."

I really ran in the wrong circles. Or maybe the right ones. But I'd had enough of my conversation with Andrew. It was taxing trying to be kind to him. I would have to chant for inner strength. "Anyway, I'm glad it worked out. The cottage looks great. And thank you for calling to check up on your little sister."

"One last thing. Why are you at the cottage anyway? It's during the week. Are you up to something?" He knew me too well.

At that moment, my eyes met Ralph's. He was looking at me quizzically. I pointed at the phone and mouthed "Andrew." He angled his head toward the stairs and faked a yawn. He was tired and wanted to go to bed. Cindy was getting up off the couch and lumbering into the kitchen. I watched her as she reached for the kettle. Tea, I guessed, to drink in bed. I'd stick with wine. Oh yeah.

"No, I'm not up to anything weird. My editor wanted me to do a story in cottage country, that's all."

"So, you're not investigating whether or not the property next door is Crown land. I already looked that up. I told you. At the Town Hall. It's not. I told you this at dinner, that it was owned by a neighbour of mine in Rosedale."

His voice had taken on that fake English accent that people in Rosedale use when they're feeling under fire. As if it gave them credibility. The old Andrew was back. Still an arrogant fat cat. I despised him. I really had to chant more.

"I know you did, Andrew." Why did I have to please him? "And I'm not doing a story about real estate. It's going to be on the dangers of walking in the woods in the spring when mother bears are protective of their young. Cindy got some great shots."

"Shots of what?"

"Of a bear charging through the woods on its way to attack someone."

He was horrified. "Robin? How did that happen? I thought you only stumbled onto a dead body? What's going on? A charging bear? Charging whom? Are you really okay? Should I come up?"

"Charging 'whom' Andrew? Language is fluid. No one uses the dative case like that anymore."

"Don't change the subject. Charging who?"

Ha. I'd won that little skirmish. "A police officer. But don't worry. I was miles away when it happened. No need to come." Please don't. But I was a little touched by his concern. I wondered if now that Dad was becoming infirm if Andrew was stepping up to the plate. Whether he was or not, I was getting the sense that the direction of our relationship was changing. Slowly, like a car with no snow tires in a blizzard. It would be so easy to slide into a ditch.

"I've never heard of a bear charging a person like that, not our bears."

As if our bears didn't shit in the woods. "Listen Andrew, all bears will protect their young if threatened."

"I don't like it. I really don't, Robin. I don't want you in the woods if there's a bear like that around. They get into people's garbage and eat things that make them crazy. Mercury in batteries. Paint. Chemicals."

"Andrew, trust me. It's taken care of. The bear is dead. It was shot by the police. I guess that didn't make the news. But I'm sure it was the same bear that attacked Darlene. There can only be one loose cannon of a bear out there."

"This doesn't make any sense, Robin. A bear attacked Darlene? And then attacked a police officer? That bear could have been around when I had my party. Oh God. Someone could have been killed."

Thinking about himself again. Cindy was right. Narcissistic.

Guys. "But nobody was so it's okay, Andrew."

"I really don't like this, Robin. I know it's late, but it's not that long a drive. I think I should come. I'm up for it. What if there's another crazy bear out there?"

"I said don't worry Andrew. Ralph, my boyfriend, is here as well."

"You have a boyfriend? I thought you said Cindy was there."

He was practically shrieking. What on earth was going through his mind?

I said in my calmest voice, "Yes, I have a boyfriend. I've been keeping it private. Cindy is here. So is Ralph. I am not alone. I am safe. We can talk later. Thank you for offering to come at this late hour, but please, don't come. Everything is okay. Goodbye." I poked the end button before he could object.

I looked over at Ralph on the couch. He was so cute with his eyes half-closed. I wondered if he was up for coming upstairs. Again.

16.

I WOKE UP WEDNESDAY morning with Ralph curled up beside me, breathing soft puffs of air scented with stale toothpaste and the sickly-sweet undercurrent of alcohol. I blew into my hand and sniffed. Yup. The same. So alluring. It was definitely time to stop. Boy oh boy, did I ever need to follow Sally Josper's directions every day. I lay there and reviewed her concise instructions. In the morning, I was to log three things I was grateful for.

I had to follow her instructions if I wanted to stop drinking, and I did, because most of the time I did not want to be an old homeless person pushing a shopping cart full of cheap bottles of wine tucked into my possessions. I had to weigh this visual against the picture of me lounging in a beach chair, a chilled glass of white in my hand, licking the condensation dripping down the side, deliciously cold on my tongue. Sometimes it was hard to make choices.

I wouldn't put Ralph on my grateful list of three today because I had written him down every day this week. But still. I looked at him, his face relaxed and his mouth slightly open. I looked closer. His nose hair was undulating softly on every out breath. Maybe that wasn't so cute. But his lips were so plump and pretty. But wait. Was that drool on the pillow? I peered at the corner of his mouth. Yes, there was a very thin transparent filament stretching from his mouth to the yellow daisy on the pillowcase. I actually thought it was kind of cute. Big strong man, drooling on the daisies.

He was a cop and, in general, I was grateful for cops. That could be my first thing I was grateful for. Yesterday was a terrible day, and thank heavens there were cops to call. It was very comforting to know we had that safety net. My mind wandered. It always did. Was I losing it? No, I consoled myself, stress does a number on a brain. It was just stress. I tugged my thoughts back from the swirling drain in the dark chamber of my brain. Yesterday. What a fuck of a day.

I had a feeling that Kowalchuk and I would be seeing each other again. I wondered why only Niemchuk had been attacked. What was so special about him? Maybe it was young male testosterone. Perhaps that threatened the bear. If he hadn't been there, would someone else have been the object of the bear's frenzy? I didn't think so. The bear had burst through the forest directly for Niemchuk. Not a sideways glance at anyone else. I wasn't sure if bears did sideways glances, but this bear did not. Is that what had happened to Darlene? No sideways glance? Had the bear sniffed the air and aimed for her like a homing missile? What did Niemchuk and Darlene have in common? We all know that bears can't see worth a damn. I had read somewhere that if you stand perfectly still, a bear will not be able to see you. I probably got that off the internet, and we know how reliable that is. Bears sniff air. Their noses can smell a squirrel a mile away. Niemchuk and Darlene must have given off the same odour or something. On the other hand, my breath this morning could be used as bear spray.

Focus. Where was I? No more drinking. Gratitude. I was also grateful for Cindy. Sure, she drove me bananas, what with all that tree climbing business and her bad manners, but she had been very kind to me after finding the body and then when I fell down in a faint. I couldn't remember my own mother ever touching me so gently. Cindy was a good friend. I was sorry that her date hadn't gone well. It was hard to be gay in a predominately hetero world. She was having such a difficult time finding someone who was on her wavelength. In the meantime, I'd try to be a better friend to her.

And I was thankful for my Buddhist practice. Sure, I would be a little self-conscious later, chanting with other people in the cottage, rubbing my beads together, *clackity clack*, making noise. I mean, how weird is that? But it made me feel good. And I could sense my life was changing, which was the point. Human revolution began with one's self. World peace would result. I thought about my relationship with my brother. I'd been chanting for his happiness, with great difficulty I might add because I didn't like him. But surely, he was miserable behaving the way he did, and low and behold, *chant chant chant,* and he was actually nice to me. And I think I was pretty civil to him. Outwardly anyway. It was a start towards world peace.

So that was my three things. Cops. Cindy. Buddhism. Maybe I would stop drinking soon. Maybe not. I would see Sally Josper when I got back from the cottage. So far I wasn't having much luck, but she had said not to worry about it. So, I I decided not to worry about it for the rest of the week. I simply loved my wine. I was already looking forward to a glass, okay, a jug, of it in, oh let's see, only ten hours.

I slowly slid out of bed, being careful not to jiggle the mattress and wake Ralph, which was no small feat considering I was manoeuvering a whale out to sea from a comfortable harbour. I padded into the bathroom across the hall. Lucky, who'd been sleeping on the floor, followed me, his nails clicking on the wooden floors. I guess he thought if I could watch him pee, he could watch me. I turned on the bathroom light and yelped when I looked in the mirror. I hastily averted my eyes. My hair was bunched up on the left side of my head and salad was caught in my teeth. Good thing I got up before anyone saw me and I could make some adjustments.

What was I going to do today?

Research. I formulated my plan as I brushed my teeth and combed my hair. First of all, I was going to talk to Darlene's parents. I hoped they would talk to me, despite my being a reporter, because they knew Andrew. Imagine how painful it would have been for them, being at the same party as that awful David Sparling, knowing what he did to their daughter, getting off scot-free, and him not knowing who they were. God. It must have been infuriating. What was Andrew thinking, inviting them both? Nit-wit. I'd ask them all sorts of questions. Delicately. They would have likely just found out their daughter was dead. I wanted to know if she had ever been in the bush before, if she knew how to deal with bears. Did she even have bear spray? I was pretty sure they'd talk to me.

And I would read up on all the things a person should and shouldn't do in the woods in the spring. Cindy could help me with this. She had wanted to be a forester. There was probably a bear book that she'd read, somewhere in her youth. Plus, I'd ask her to google stuff. And then the article could legitimately say, "with files from Cynthia Dale." I left the bathroom and bumped into her in the hall, just as she was coming out of the bathroom she had cornered for herself.

"Hi. You hungry for breakfast? A little coffee?" she asked me.

"Ralph's still asleep, but he may saw logs for hours, so let's go ahead and get going on the day. I'm starving."

"You're always starving." Cindy scratched her rib cage and yawned. "Sounds good. But I'm always starving, too. I was thinking we should do some research on forest etiquette. I could do that, if you like, given it's your story."

What the hell was "forest etiquette?" Maybe if you bumped into a tree, but no one was around, you would still have to say you were sorry?

But at least I didn't have to ask her to help. She volunteered. That was a relief. I could tell though that she was still a little bitter that I had gotten the story. I thought I could smell the smouldering ashes of anger wafting through her voice. I grovelled a bit to put the fire out. "That's so nice of you, Cindy. What a good idea. You're always thinking ahead. I mean, we know some basics, given that we are Canadians," I flexed my right arm, "and have some familiarity with forests, but I'm sure there are facts we don't know. Like what colours to wear and not wear, what perfumes to use or not use. That sort of thing." I could tell my soothing platitudes hadn't taken the edge off her frustration.

"Bacon and eggs sounds perfect." Her green eyes were flashing.

I hadn't fooled her. And she didn't like being an underling. Yes, as bitter as day's old coffee in a corner café. Didn't like being told what to do. My mistake. It was only eight in the morning. Great start to the day. "Let's get dressed and make a feast."

We made breakfast and I told her my plans for the day. "I thought I'd try and get an interview with Darlene's parents, you know, to get some insights into what happened to her daughter. I am really puzzled by this bear's behaviour and want to ask them why they thought the bear went after her the way it did. Whether or not she knew about bears and how to avoid an attack."

Cindy broke off a piece of her toast, thinking, and was mopping up bacon grease and egg yolk off her plate. She shoved it in her mouth. Chewed a bit too hard. "I think the better approach..."

"Don't talk with your mouth full. I don't want to see your food half-chewed." Cindy's manners were terrible.

She swallowed quickly and stuck out her tongue at me. I think she meant it. "If you approach it like that, they will think you're blaming the victim. I think they will be very sensitive to that, given her court case with Sparling." Her movements were a little jerky.

"I didn't think of that." Cindy had a point.

"It might be better," she said, being uncharacteristically diplomatic, or perhaps holding back a roaring tide of anger, "if you let them know you were writing an article to warn people about the terrible things that can happen if you enter the woods in the spring, and that Darlene's example will save lives."

I threw back some coffee. Delicious. Made by Cindy, not me. "That makes sense."

But Cindy wasn't done. No, she was just beginning. It *was* a tidal wave of anger, now unleashed. Riptides. I braced myself. "A lot of women won't report sexual assault now because of what happened to Darlene in her case against David Sparling. She was shredded by the judge, *shredded*, called a liar, an unreliable witness, had a faulty memory, behaved like she asked for it and had consented, given her begging emails and texts to him. Which all came after the alleged assault. And so on. The case was so high profile that the public even turned his name into a verb. 'Don't report that assault, little miss, or you'll be *Sparlinged*.'"

"I'd heard of that. But I didn't really connect with what it meant."

Cindy pointed her fork at me while she chewed. Luckily, this time, she waited until her mouth was empty before she began spewing her fury. "It means," she shook her fork, crumbs of toast flying over the table like missiles of indignation, "that the effects of sexual assault are not recognized for what they are, a mixture of the Stockholm Syndrome and Post-Traumatic Stress Disorder. It means that prosecutors do such a fuck-up of a job for the victims, such a slipshod asswipe of a job," Cindy was getting really wound up, "they don't even put on the stand a psychiatrist that specializes in assault as an expert witness to explain the victims' actions. It means," she sucked on her glass of juice like a Shop-Vac on high, "that judges are completely uneducated about sexual assault. About what it does to a woman." She thumped down her glass. I leaned back, staying out of the line of fire. There was more; she wasn't half done. "It means..." she paused and ripped a piece of toast in two, scrubbing her plate with it, "...that fuckheads like Sparling, arrogant little pricks who abuse their power, doctors and teachers and priests, with their fancy-schmancy defense lawyers, get off, because they have evidence of lovey-dovey emails and texts and photos before and after the assault, which all, ostensibly, illuminate the consenting behaviour of the victim." She shouted, "That's what being *Sparlinged* means." Her eyes flashed with flaming spikes of hot green fire as she looked at me, daring me. To do what, I didn't know.

I waited for the air to stop vibrating with her outrage. The morning sunshine that had floated through the window ten minutes ago was now glinting like shards of glass. I looked down and finished off my bacon and eggs, chewing slowly. Once her breathing returned to normal, I ventured into the minefield, and not that meekly to give myself credit. "So, best if I don't insinuate, in any way, that she was responsible, somehow, for a bear attacking her."

"Right. That's what I fucking mean." She slapped her palms on the table and got up. Breakfast was over.

"Okay, then." I followed her stiff back into the kitchen with my plate. I would need to smooth this over. "I'd really like you to come with me. That is, if they will agree to see me. You seem to have a good handle on her case and it might be pretty awkward, you know..." I couldn't imagine what it was like to lose a daughter.

She turned to face me. The storm had passed. "I think you'd be surprised at how well they are doing. Don't forget, Darlene had been missing for weeks. This is the north. Women go missing in the north and they end up dead. Period. It's a given. Don't get me going on *that*. Her parents probably came to terms with her being dead weeks ago."

"I hadn't thought of that," I said, though I wondered if Cindy wasn't maybe making a huge assumption. Nevertheless, I really wasn't on my game. I'd been so focused on the puzzle of a bear attacking someone for seemingly no reason that I had missed the reality of the here and now. "I really want them to talk to me, but they are probably pretty wary of the press. But maybe Andrew will introduce me to them."

"Andrew? Your brother?" She said this the same way she had said "asswipe" a minute ago.

"Yeah, they're clients of his."

"Of course they are." She didn't like him either. "And they live locally?"

"The next lake over."

"I think you need to mention his name. That'll be enough to get you in the door. You don't need to ask him to call them or anything extreme like that."

"Ask who?" Ralph.

He was leaning against the door frame and gazing into the kitchen. He looked handsome in his faded pajama bottoms. He had a towel draped over his arm so it fell in front of his body. I looked at his crotch and then met his eyes. He winked and I think Cindy noticed.

"Cindy and I are going to the next lake over to talk to Darlene's parents this morning. I was wondering if I should ask Andrew to introduce us first, you know, by phone, to make sure I could get an interview."

"Good idea. They'll never see you."

Cindy bristled. She didn't like being contradicted. "Sure they will. She needs to say she's Andrew's sister. No need to make a big hairy deal about it." She looked at the towel pointedly. Yup, she'd noticed his wink.

He shrugged his strong right shoulder. He didn't give a shit what Cindy thought and turned to walk away. The sun bounced off his smooth skin. "I'm taking a shower. And then I think I'll go to the station and meet up with the local gang. Say hi to Kowalchuk. Catch up on old times. Meet you back here for lunch." He did a Queen Elizabeth wave over his shoulder as he went back upstairs.

I unplugged my phone from its charger and googled 411.ca to find Darlene's parent's number. Gibson. Right, there it was, on Lake of Bays. "I found their number, and now I'll call." Well, duh. I looked at Cindy. For what? Moral support?

"You don't sound too certain about that. Want me to do it?" She looked up from putting the butter in the fridge.

I kept my butter out of the fridge. That way it would be nice and soft, ready to dip a cracker into. Ready to spread on soft bread. I loved butter. Almost as much as wine. "Thanks, you're right, I don't want to, but no, you don't have Andrew as your brother. That'll be our ticket into their house." I deliberately used the word "our." I tentatively tapped their number and put the phone on speaker. Cindy and I passed each other as she walked into the living room and I went into the kitchen. She bent over to pat Lucky and I opened the fridge door with my free hand to take the butter out. The phone was ringing, its buzz filling the air with a staccato jangle.

"Hello?"

Darlene's mother's voice was timid and sounded bruised. This was not a good idea. It was too soon. I felt like I was invading a small bird's nest with a bazooka gun. "Mrs. Gibson?" I tried to keep my voice soft. "This is Robin MacFarland."

Her voice found some strength. "Oh, Duncan's daughter. Andrew's sister. How nice of you to call. I understand you found Darlene." Her words shook in the air. "Thank you so much for handling that terrible situation the best you could. Officer Kowalchuk let me know that you and your friend came across her body in the woods next to your house and called them in. I'm so sorry you had to find her." Mrs. Gibson's voice cracked.

Oh God. This was terrible. Her daughter had died and she was worried about me? Sincere. I'd try to do sincere. Not that I'd have to try. I was feeling sincere. Actually, I was feeling terrible about doing this. All for a stupid story. Sometimes I hated my job. "My friend Cindy and I would like to come over this morning, if that's okay with you. We are very sorry for your loss." I had to come up with an idea for why we had to go over. There was a gourmet store on the way to her house. Hopefully, they sold frozen lasagna or something, "We'd like to bring you a casserole," I said. "We could be there in half an hour."

"Oh, you are so kind, of course. I'd love to see you. It would be a good distraction. Bring your friend. Do you know how to get here?"

"You're not too far along Highway 60 and then the first right turn? I take it to the end?" If they had enough money to be Andrew's client, they probably had waterfront at the end of the road.

"That's right. We're the pale yellow house on the right, at the very end of the road. We're the last building on the point that juts into the lake. Is Andrew there with you, too? Such a nice fellow. If he's there, he's more than welcome to come over as well."

Nice fellow? "No, he's in Toronto. It'll just be Cindy and me. Will your husband be home?"

"Harry? Yes, he's around here somewhere. Probably working on that old boat of his. It's his project this year. Needs a complete refit. And I'm Sandra, by the way."

"Thanks, Sandra. See you about eleven, then."

"The pale yellow house, at the very end of the road. The name of the cottage, "Moot Point," is over the front door."

"Right. I won't forget." How could I ever forget a house the colour of butter? Now that was a moot point.

17.

MY RUSTY OLD SENTRA bumped through the green tunnel of bushes leading to the Gibson's house. Dried grass tickled the underside of the car as we lurched slowly down the lane to the pale yellow abode by the water's edge. Every time a branch snapped against the car, Cindy gasped and jerked her head back, instinctively shying away from the noise. I, on the other hand, didn't bat an eyelash.

"Will you relax?"

"I am relaxed." Another branch slapped at the car and she twitched involuntarily.

"No, you're not. The branches are outside the car. You're inside. And I really don't care about the paint job."

"Well, I guess there are advantages to having a shitbox for a car."

"Low blow." I patted the dash. "Don't you listen to that big, bad Cindy. You are a beautiful car."

Cindy rolled her eyes.

As we approached the bungalow, I could see dappled sun shimmering over the freshly painted wooden siding. Small buds graced the trees around the house with that slightly pink tinge of new growth that only occurs for a few days in the early spring. Being further north, the trees in Muskoka were a week or two behind Toronto's. In the back seat perched a frozen lasagna, frosty with condensation. It was going to be a warm day for May.

Mrs. Gibson, Sandra, strode toward us on long strong legs, head held high, a brave chin jutting forward, her arms held out, ready for an embrace. She was wearing capris and sandals, not one to waste a day of elusive warm weather. Blackflies hovered around her short-cropped hairstyle, an Audrey Hepburn pixie cut that only tall and beautiful women can pull off with aplomb. I could tell this woman was usually very well put together, right down to matching lipstick and nails. But not today. There were signs. Today, her jersey knit T-shirt was inside out. Price tags at her wrist were flapping morosely as she walked. There was a small stain on her capris. Butter. Believe me, I knew. I had experience with this kind of oily blotch. These two things, plus a tissue crumpled tightly in her hand, a corner escaping from her clenched fist, were indications that something very bad had happened in her world.

Cindy whispered, not moving her lips, "She's not waving the blackflies away."

Four small signs.

"You grab the lasagna and give it to her while I give her a hug. Looks like she's gunning for one."

Cindy wasn't the hugging type. At all. "Roger that."

We shouldered the car doors open and went about our jobs. I was bashed by Sandra in mid-stride. She stopped walking only when she clanged into me, her arms flinging around me like loose strands of rope. I had to reach up, being only five-foot-two to her almost six feet, to hug her in return. "I'm so sorry about Darlene," I muttered into her chest. "What a terrible loss."

Sandra's arms clutched me harder, trapping me in a viselike grip. I didn't like it, not one bit. This was not your usual hug between two strangers who only knew each other through a third party. Where was the peck on the cheek? She was grasping onto me like a cobra. Bending over, even her head was trapping mine. Panic surged up from my belly. I had to get away from this woman.

Cindy must have sensed my discomfort and knocked Sandra's rib cage from the side with the lasagna. "Oops. Sorry. My mistake. We are so sorry for your loss. Where should we put this?" She bumped her again and Sandra looked at the lasagna with surprised eyes.

She suddenly released me and air sucked into my lungs. What was wrong with this woman? She turned her back to me and took a step over to Cindy, arms open. Cindy took a step back. She held the lasagna in front of her like kryptonite. As Sandra took another step forward, missing her cue, Cindy used the lasagna like a battering ram, pushing it into the air between them. She simply would not be hugged by a stranger.

Sensing that she had lost this battle, Sandra held out her hands, palms up. "Thank you so much. Harry loves this lasagna. It's from that gourmet place on the highway, right?" She reluctantly took the gift, as if to touch it would harm her.

Cindy gave me a quick glance with slightly widened eyes, a glance that only a good friend could interpret. Harry liked it, but not her? But she said, "You're welcome. It was the least we could do. What happened was awful." Cindy was trying to figure out this mother. Something was not right. For a second, her eyes turned into slits as she watched her.

"Yes, it was." Sandra said it like she was asking someone to pass her the salt. Maybe she was drugged.

Off in the distance, I could see a man working at the side of a wooden boat with a paint scraper. Harry. Sandra followed my gaze. "That's Darlene's father. He's hardly spoken a word since she went missing over about a month ago. And now, this news." She unravelled her tissue and dabbed at her eyes. I wanted to tell her to stop, don't touch your eyes with a snotty tissue, you'll get a sty. Guaranteed.

Her shoulders sagged as she abruptly turned on her heel and strode back to her butter-coloured house. I followed, well back, with Cindy a few steps behind me. I had so badly wanted to like this woman who was grieving in her peculiar way for her dead daughter, or maybe it was for something else. But I did not. There was a weird air of something floating under her grief, an unleashed emotion that I couldn't put my finger on. A little of it had seeped upwards through her sadness in that hug. I could smell it wafting on the air. My old familiar snake friend that slithered through my veins was rattling away, its tongue shooting in and out, tasting the vibrations in Sandra's wake.

Cindy caught up and nudged me with her elbow, whispering under her breath, "There is something weird going on here. That woman is weird. I mean, really weird."

I didn't want Sandra to hear us talking about her, literally behind her back, and shook my head, not even daring to whisper, "*Shush.*" I made a circle with a forefinger around my ear and pointed at Sandra, eyebrows raised. Crazy? Cindy nodded in agreement while pushing my hand down, and admonishing my grade-school gesture. "Be compassionate" she whispered. "She might have a mental illness."

We would need to be on our toes and find out what was going on in this house. As we got closer, Harry, who was off to the side of the garage, looked up and gave us a defeated wave. I wondered briefly if he'd seen my sign language. From his blank stare, it didn't look like it. He slowly rubbed his hands down the front of his plaid shirt, knocking off curling bits of wood shavings and lumbered over to us, stooped and broken, his feet scuffing the ground.

"Hi, I'm Harry. You must be Robin," he said to me. "You look like your brother." Harry didn't hold out his hand for us to shake. He realized his social gaffe, and apologized, looking at his grubby nails. "Dirty." He slid his hands down the sides of his pants, wiping them off. "Sorry about that. Andrew is a great guy." Harry's voice was flat and guarded. "He's really helped us with our investments. We should be able to survive on what we have for the rest of our lives."

Harry didn't look pleased about this, in fact, he sounded like Andrew had given him a death sentence. I pretended not to notice. I also pretended to like my brother. He was, after all, our ticket to be here. "Yes, he's good at his job and I'm glad he's made you feel secure about your future." Did I say the right thing? Harry was looking at the ducks swimming on the lake like he wanted to murder them.

Sandra opened the screen door and ushered us inside. "Come in, come in. We can have some lemonade."

Said the spider to the fly.

I took in my surroundings. Rusty-brown shag carpet. Flowered wallpaper on one wall, plastic wood panelling on the others. Fake velvet, patterned upholstery, stiffened with age, on a couch with wooden arms. Blue mountain china. A cabinet full of teacups with gold rims. Molded globes of green glass for ashtrays on water-marked side tables. A painted rocking chair. I was in a Salvation Army Thrift Store. I sensed rather than saw Sandra watching me. The hairs on the back of my neck stood up. Definitely bad energy.

"This was my mother's house," she said by way of an explanation, sweeping her long arm around the decrepit living room. "She loved it and hated change. Unfortunately, she died late this winter of a heart attack. Overweight," she said, eying me up and down. Warning given and received. "She left it to Harry and me. We talked to Andrew about the best thing to do. We are both sixty, Harry and me, and want to retire. I worked in retail, women's clothing, and Harry was in a bank. What with everything going on and Darlene moving in, we just haven't had the time to renovate. We sold our Toronto house and moved here. Andrew told us it was the wisest thing to do."

Was I being blamed for the loss of their Toronto house? Was that what the odd vibe was about? I took in the warped wood panelling and the aluminum windowsills, spotted with grey. The worn linoleum on the kitchen floor. "I understand."

"Have a seat." Harry gestured at the couch while Sandra went out to get a pitcher of lemonade. He leaned over to me, a glint in his eye. Predatory? "And how's Duncan's little girl?"

Fuck off. I was fifty-six. This couple was giving me the creeps. I couldn't get a read on them. What the hell was going on? "Did you know my father well?"

"Ever since I was a boy. We had a cottage on Peninsula Lake near yours and your Dad and I used to build forts by the rock face when we were kids."

"So that's how you knew Andrew?"

"Your father's pride and joy."

Didn't I know it.

Sandra came in bearing a heavy tray laden with an enormous glass pitcher covered in drops of water and four large tumblers. No cookies. Cindy jumped up and took it from her, laying it on the coffee table in front of the couch, murmuring her appreciation. I politely took a glass and a small sip. The lemonade had way too much sugar in it and my fillings sang an opera. I was convinced something was really off about these people. I wanted to find out more. I wanted to search their house. But how could I do that without actually doing it? How could I manoeuvre these two weirdos into showing me around? My job! I could say I was an interior design reporter and was interested in antiques.

"I'm working for a paper now, *The Toronto Express*," I said, feeling coy.

Darlene's father raised his eyebrows. "Oh, that's what you ended up doing?" He made it sound like I was mucking out manure. "Spying on people and digging up crap?"

Oh dear. "Oh no, not at all. It's a great job," I said, undampened by his insinuations. "I work in the Home and Garden section. Interior decoration. Flowers. Antiques. Cooking. Domestic stuff." Domestic murder. Domestic abuse. Cooked-up stories.

"That sounds very interesting," said Sandra. "Maybe you'd like to look around a bit here? My mother had lots of antiques. There's an old Singer sewing machine on the landing upstairs. A treadmill."

Upstairs. Fantastic. "If it's not too much trouble." I stood up and hoped she wouldn't follow me. She did. Shit.

We climbed the thin staircase one after another. When we reached the top, Sandra said, "Three bedrooms up here. It was hard for Mom to deal with the stairs, but she managed." Sandra paused outside a door in the hallway. "This was Darlene's room."

I looked around her through the door and saw a sea of pink. What? It was a kid's room?

"When we moved here, Darlene had already moved out from our Toronto home into an apartment. But we wanted her to live with us after ... well, you know. Harry and I thought it best to unpack her old bedroom into this room. We thought she would find it consoling being surrounded by her childhood memories while she stayed with us, given what had happened with that man. Sparling."

Not likely, I thought. She probably found it creepy. I danced around Sandra, *oohing* away, pretending to be interested in a faded print in a cracked frame on the opposite wall. "Oh look, this might be valuable. Do you ever think about selling some of the antiques?" I turned around and looked at her innocently, meanwhile scanning the room for anything at all that might be revealing. What, I didn't know. It was a typical little girl's bedroom with a chest of drawers, a desk with a chair, all painted white. In the top right corner of the desk, Darlene had scratched her name, "Darlene Olive Gibson." I ran my finger over it, feeling the bumps of the chipped paint. Darlene had been determined to carve her name, that was for sure. It seemed there were no clues here to help me figure out what made this family tick.

Sandra sat down on the desk chair and looked sadly around her. "I couldn't bear to change a thing while she was missing. What if she came home?" This seemed practiced somehow. Rehearsed. The widened eyes and frowning eyebrows looked pasted on. "The police looked in here for any clues about where she might have gone. I told them she wouldn't have taken off. That something had happened to her. They didn't seem to believe me."

"The police can be very persistent sometimes in their beliefs, right or wrong. Where did they look? Did they take her computer?" I was going to look where they hadn't.

"It was awful. They pawed through her desk. I watched them. And they started fingering her clothes in the closet. I was furious. My little girl was missing and they were *fondling* her clothes. They didn't find her computer. And her personal phone was never found. Neither was her work phone. She had two, you know. Work and personal. It's probably in the woods somewhere. I told them to leave and get on with their job." She was sitting up very straight, remembering, anger flitting across her face.

Not a thorough search then. And what an odd adjective to use, describing the way a police officer checked clothing for clues. "Fondling." The police were probably checking the seams for hidden bits of paper or an object of some kind. I sat down on the twin bed covered neatly with a satiny duvet, pink with lace around the edges. A little girl's room. On the pillow was a stuffed bear, one eye dangling from a black thread.

"Spooky."

"Pardon?"

"The bear. She named him Spooky. She kept special objects inside him, in that little pouch on his seat. She thought if she named him after a ghost he would be able to scare away all the other nighttime ghosts. She'd had him all her life."

I could tell. His fur was rubbed off in spots, leaving behind worn, beige fabric. I gave him a squeeze to see if he squeaked. Nope. But I felt something hard. I made sure my face gave nothing away as I squeezed some more. There was definitely something hard inside the bear. Sandra stood up and walked around the room, touching things and giving me a history lesson. Her china horse collection. A ukulele. A jewellery box with a dancing ballerina that spun to music when you lifted the lid.

I slowly slipped my hand into the slit in the bottom of the little bear and fished around. At the very end of the pouch my fingers bumped against something hard, flat, and plastic. I was betting it was a phone. My heart raced. From the size of it, it felt like an iPhone 6. Maybe a 5. Before the phones got really big. But a new, flat screen one, not a flip-top phone.

While Sandra gave me a tour of Darlene's bedroom, yattering away, I tried to slide the phone out of the Spooky's soft butt. She picked up some miniature glass figurines that Darlene had placed on a mirror, probably when she was ten, and stroked them lovingly. Meanwhile, I was making progress. The phone was descending down its furry birth canal, helped by my forcep-like fingers. I hadn't yet figured out what I was going to do with it once I got it out. But then, the phone's case snagged on a loose thread. Shit. I wiggled it around and tugged it, feeling the way a vet must feel when pulling a baby foal out of a mare. I hoped against hope that Sandra didn't turn around, seeing me with my hand jammed up the bear's ass.

But, of course, she did, looking right at me. I sat perfectly still on the bed, a smile frozen on my face. My hand trapped up the bear's colon. I wasn't going to let go of that phone for love nor money. No way on earth. I held the bear to my chest with my right hand up its bum and patted it gently on the head with my left, hoping that my right hand looked as if it were holding the bear and not creating hemorrhoids.

Sandra said, "Patting Spooky like that reminds me of how much Darlene loved that bear." Sandra took a step toward me as if to take the bear and I thought I would be caught red-handed. Panic skittered through my veins. My vision vibrated. But no, she was on her way to the photographs stuck in the edge of the mirror over Darlene's dressing table. As she talked about this one and that, who was related to whom, this dance, that boyfriend, I safely extricated the phone from the bear and stuffed it in my back pocket. For a horrible moment,

I thought Sandra might have been able to see me reflected in the mirror, kidnapping the bear's baby. I raised my eyes and looked at the mirror. No, I couldn't see her, so she couldn't see me, right? That's what truck bumper signs said: "If you can't see me in the mirror, I can't see you."

I stood up, the phone burning a hole in my back pocket, "Thank you so much for showing me Darlene's room. I'm so sorry she's gone." I had to get out of there.

"Thank you. Let me show you her brother's room."

God. I followed meekly as Sandra led the way down the hall and flung open what was clearly a little boy's room, all in blue with hockey equipment and footballs, trucks and insect jars containing a carcass or two. Luckily, there were no antiques that I could pretend to be interested in and we could look at the room from the doorway. I had had enough of this weirdness, this Miss Havisham frozen-in-time concept. A time warp that was repellent and confusing at the same time. Who were these people? Sandra then marched determinedly past the third bedroom, which I presumed was hers and her husband's, and thankfully headed down the stairs to the living room.

Cindy and Harry were talking about fabrics. Or rather, she was talking about fabrics, giving some bullshit about dying wool, and he was sitting there, face blank. I caught her eye and gestured madly at the door with my head. Time to go. I didn't want to catch cooties from these strange people. Plus, guilt was probably written all over my face. I could feel my eyes bugging out and red blotches bursting all over my neck. I had stolen a phone. Evidence. Me: Miss Goody Two-Shoes. I felt like laughing my head off. What a find. A phone! Whole lives are stored on phones. And this one had been hidden. Who knew what was on it?

Cindy took one look at me and stood up immediately. She had a good nose for urgency, being a crime reporter who'd had to duck bullets. "Thank you so much for the lemonade, it's been lovely meeting you."

Harry stood up and shook her hand. "You too, and good luck with your wool dying and rug hooking."

Geezus. Rug hooking? Couldn't she have come up with something better than that? "Yes," I said. "Cindy's got a real talent for spinning her own yarn. And hooking."

She shot me a look. We hugged Sandra goodbye and I tried not to dash out of the door.

I ran-walked to my car like a stiff-legged penguin, propelling Cindy forward by the elbow. "What's the fucking hurry?" Cindy whispered, her mouth not moving.

When we were both in the car, I threw it into reverse and roared backwards up the lane. Cindy's head kept jerking, getting out of the way of snapping branches, just like it had done on our way down the lane, only much faster. "Slow down, idiot. You'll wreck your car."

"Too late," I trilled.

When we got to the main road, I pulled over, put my head back, and howled with laughter. Cindy was not amused. "What are you laughing about? You didn't ask a single question. We know nothing about that Darlene. Who she was. Why she got attacked. Not even if she was familiar with bears and how to avoid them. I was stuck with Harry and you were upstairs, mollifying that kooky woman. What the fuck were you thinking? I was warming him up. In another minute, I would be able to ask him some real questions."

I lifted a bum cheek, reached into my back pocket, and pulled out the phone. With a flourish I presented it to Cindy. "*Ta-dah!*"

18.

"WHOA. YOU FOUND HER phone? Amazing! Why didn't the police find it? Surely, they searched her room when she went missing. Where was it?" Cindy took the phone from me and turned it over in her hand. "An iPhone 6. Where exactly did you find this?" She fixed her green eyes on my face.

"It was up the bear's ass." I laughed and laughed. It was hysterical. Killed by a bear. And then this.

Cindy stared at me. Her head was tilted and puzzlement scooted around her eyes. She didn't find this funny. "What? I don't understand. Did they stuff the bear that killed her? They were certainly eccentric. Something is really off-kilter about them. They seem capable of anything. Was there really a stuffed bear upstairs? Sort of like a testimony or something? An altar? And then you put your hand up its butt? Was the bear all stiff?" She made a face at the image. "But wait a sec. I thought the bear was alive and well and attacked Niemchuk."

"Not *that* bear. It was a stuffed bear, for sure, but it was Spooky." I was having so much fun, laughing away, the adrenalin from my theft bubbling out.

"I know her parents were spooky, but spooky enough to stuff a bear? Were there crosses and candles around it? Was it like a religious sacrifice? No wonder you were gone so long. How bizarre is that? A stuffed bear. How did they get it upstairs? I knew those people were strange."

Okay, enough was enough. Time to come clean. I swallowed my roars and said, "Darlene had a stuffed *teddy* bear. She named it Spooky. It was the kind of bear that had a pouch in its seat for hidden objects. Remember those? I hid cigarettes in mine."

"Oh-h-h. It was a stuffed *toy* bear named Spooky. I get it." Cindy nodded with dawning comprehension. "And the phone was up its ass?" She started to laugh. "Like where toys are meant to stuffed? It's not an eye phone. It's a bum phone. A bum phone 6."

I grabbed it back from her. "Here, let me see it. Maybe it turns on. I held down the two buttons to turn the phone on, but the screen remained dark. It needed a charger. If we had a phone that matched this one, we could power it up. We needed an iPhone 6, according to Cindy. "We need a charger. What kind of phone do you have?"

"I recently got an iPhone X Plus. Mine's too new, won't work."

I took out my phone from my purse and compared the two. "Looks like I have the right one." I held it out to her for confirmation. I wasn't really into technology.

Cindy glanced at my phone for less than a second. "Yup, yours is an iPhone 6. So, do you have a charger?"

I slid the phone back into the side pocket of my purse. "Duh. Of course I do. I know a phone needs to be charged every day. It's at the cottage."

"You charge your phone once a day?"

I was confused. "Yes. Why not? Is that too much? Have I harmed my phone by overcharging it?"

"I can't believe it. Most people have to charge their phones at least twice a day. Don't you ever use yours?" She was looking down her nose at me.

Shit. I was tired of her judgment. So what if I was a techno dud? I snapped the key in the ignition on and stormed away, kicking up loose gravel from the shoulder of the road. I wasn't going to defend myself, especially after my great find. I snipped,

"Let's get this baby charged up."

We drove along in silence for a few minutes. The air was a little thick with tension. Cindy had figured out she had crossed a line. She warily said, "I think it's best that we don't tell the police we have the phone. Not right away. Let's see what's on it."

"I agree."

We drove along in silence for another few minutes.

"You agree?"

I looked at her.

"Watch where you're driving."

"I have eyes out the back of my head. Ask my kids." I kept my eyes on her.

"You agree?" she asked again, not breaking the stare.

"I know we're withholding evidence. And I know my boyfriend is a cop. And I know the right thing to do is to hand it in. But I also know something very odd is going on here. And I want to know what it is. So," I took a deep breath, "I agree. Let's go home and see what's on the phone."

"You'll make a crime reporter yet." Cindy smiled. "And watch where you're going."

I turned my head and focused on the road. "What if the phone is locked?"

"Then we're shit out of luck."

"Shit out of lock."

She didn't laugh at my joke. "But I'm pretty good at guessing passwords. I had kids, too."

"I never read my kids' phones." I was a little shocked that she did this.

"I didn't say I read their phones, just that I could guess passwords."

"You're such a good liar, Cindy."

"I didn't lie." She beamed.

I left it alone. Besides, I was the one who had stolen the evidence. This, I knew, was a criminal act. God forbid that

I should accuse her of something as trivial as lying. "Maybe she didn't lock it."

Neither of us believed that. Everyone locked their phones.

"Maybe." She looked out the window as we made our way back to my cottage. We were okay.

As we drove down the long narrow lane to Pair o' Dice, I wracked my brain for passwords that Darlene might have used. I didn't know her at all, not even her birthdate or the name of her boyfriend. Well, maybe Sparling was an option. Or perhaps the name of her cottage. What was it again? Right. Moot Point. Cindy was working her phone. Maybe she was looking up the prison sentence for stealing evidence or obstructing justice.

When we arrived, I carried the phone into the cottage, holding it out in front of me as if it were the crown jewels and putting it down carefully on the dining-room table. Lucky jumped around and then followed me, tail wagging, up to my bedroom where I had left my phone charger. "What are you? My little shadow?" I crooned to him. He leapt onto the bed and tossed the pillows into the air with his nose. His idea of play. I took a second to pat him to calm myself down. What on earth was I doing? Me? Stealing evidence? In a potential *murder* investigation? I had never done anything like that before. Lucky looked at me with his big brown eyes. To him, I could do no wrong.

Downstairs, I could hear Cindy opening and shutting drawers. What on earth was she looking for?

I grabbed the charger and headed downstairs, Lucky following my footsteps. "What are you looking for? Redemption?"

"*Haha.* No, paper. I want to make a list of possible passwords. I think we're allowed three tries before the phone shuts down. Or maybe that's only for a bank password. Whatever. I want to make a list."

"There's paper in the sideboard. Open the centre door, you'll find it. Put 'Sparling' and 'Moot Point' on the list."

"Good ideas. You're not just a pretty face." She bent over

and opened the sideboard door and pulled out a huge roll of brown paper. "Geezus. I only needed a scrap. Like the back of an envelope or something. What the fuck do you use this for? Roofing the Taj Mahal?"

"Kids. They go through paper. It's been there for years."

Cindy thumped the roll on the dining-room table and tore off a teensy-weensy corner. She was making a point. Then she rolled it all back up and lugged it to the sideboard, grunting melodramatically, and hoisted it in with two hands.

"And you could try her parents' names. 'Sandraandharry.' All one word."

"Good thinking, Robin. Plug the damn thing in."

"There's an outlet behind the sideboard. I'll get an extension cord so we can look at the phone together at the table." I left Cindy writing busily at the dining-room table, her red hair framing her face as she bent over the miniscule scrap of paper, and went to the kitchen to look for the extension cord.

Suddenly, the screen door flung open and Ralph entered, brushing bits of wood bark off his chest. What the hell was he doing here? He was supposed to be in town, schmoozing with the local cops. We were caught, red-handed. I was rooting around in a kitchen drawer for a cord for stolen evidence. Shit. "What are you doing home? I thought you were going to the station?" I sounded shrill, even to my ears. I watched as his cop radar turned on.

"And what are you looking for? I thought you'd gone to Darlene's parents."

An impasse. As I coolly stood up from the open kitchen drawer, I tossed a hand in the air, hoping it looked casual as it floated by me, somewhat detached from my arm. My ears began to hiss. The snake was back. "Oh, we went all right, but they are very unusual. Creepy. I gave her a lasagna and we beat it of there. Hard to take, you know how it is." I could tell he knew something was up.

"I don't know how it is. Tell me." He leaned against the

fridge and looked straight into my eyes. I knew he was trying hard not to look amused.

Oh God, the phone was in the next room. I could see the cord in the drawer. Shit. Deflect. I decided on a frontal attack. "Why didn't you go to the station?"

Ralph picked some bark off his sweater and put it carefully in front of him on the counter. He then picked off two more pieces and started building a mound. "When I got to the station, I called Kowalchuk on his cell. He was out at a site, so we made a plan to get together for lunch. I came back to do some outside chores." He folded his hands in front of himself like a chairman of the board. Like a dog with a bone, he didn't give up. "What's going on? What are you trying to find? You seem jangled."

Could he hear that rattlesnake shaking its tail, too? "Oh, nothing. I'm a bit discombobulated because of that visit. They are one doozy of a couple."

"How do you mean?"

He was looking at me earnestly. I was fooling him. Maybe. I tried not to think of the phone on the dining-room table, one room away, or the cord in the drawer, in case he had ESP. I could do this. But I needed a plan. I needed him to think I was hiding something else from him, something I was working on for a story. That way I could veer him away from discovering the truth. When did I become so devious? I needed a foolproof theory. He was the fool and I was the proof. Wait. Did I get that right? Dyslexia strikes again. I was the fool and he was the proof? No, that wasn't right either. Whatever. Maybe I could act as though I was worried about him discovering that I was compiling evidence to support an alternative theory that a bear didn't kill Darlene, that her body was dumped and a bear ate her carcass. Dumped by her parents. Or someone else. Right. Perfect.

"Well, they didn't look at each other. They didn't talk to each other. They didn't touch each other. Plus, they had this thing going on where they would be full of grief one second and then be normal the next. I'm wondering about them as, well, sort of violent people."

"They were sort of normal?"

"Well, not normal normal, angry normal. Bitter or something."

Ralph cocked his head. He was the expert when it came to grieving parents. "Everyone grieves in their own way. People react differently to bad news." So, he wasn't buying my story. Not yet. But I had more ammunition.

"I know that, Ralph, believe me. Remember, my husband was killed by a drunk driver." I couldn't believe I was playing that card. It worked. He fiddled with a hangnail, thinking. I hoped my plan was working. This had to be his idea.

"They do sound pretty off. Do you really think that maybe they killed her?"

Now to solidify the idea. Reverse psychology. "No, not really. It was pretty obvious that a bear did. Isn't it?"

He continued to think. He was pretty cute with his furrowed brow. But I wasn't too happy. I didn't like that I could pull the wool over his eyes so easily. He said, "Well, I don't know about that. Maybe they killed her and put her in the woods, making it look like a bear killed her."

And just like that, he discovered what he thought I was trying to hide. But I wanted to cement the concept.

"Really? Would a bear eat a dead person?" I asked innocently.

Cindy walked into the kitchen, flourishing her tiny scrap of paper.

"Where's the cord? I have the pass..." She saw Ralph, "the pasta recipe." She tucked it into her back pocket. "Hi Ralph. You back already from the station?"

"Kowalchuk wasn't in. We're going out for lunch instead. I was doing some chores. Wood. Got it all over me." He indicated the small pile of woodchips built into a pyramid in front of him. "What did you need a cord for? Anything I can help with?"

Cindy smiled at him, sweetly, “Robin and I were going to look at some pictures on my phone, so I needed an extension cord. My battery is almost dead, and I wanted to download some images and videos.”

God, that girl could lie. I had to admire it.

“Oh, what of?”

Once a cop, always a cop. This was an interview.

She gazed at him, eyes wide. “My parents and I took a trip to Italy in March and Robin wanted to see the photos. Like I said, my phone’s almost dead, so rather than wait for it to charge, we were going to look at them together at the dining-room table while it was plugged in.”

“You were in Italy? Robin said you were working hard on a gang story.” He had such a suspicious mind.

Cindy was unfazed and said deliberately, “Italy. You know, Italy. Mob? Connection?”

She was good. A complete lie, from beginning to end. It wasn’t her phone we were going to look at. She had no parents. They were both dead. She hated travelling to foreign countries. And she told all these lies absolutely convincingly. He completely believed her.

Ralph tilted his lanky body off the fridge and scraped the pyramid of woodchips into the palm of his hand. “Okay, I’m off. I’m going to hang around with Kowalchuk this afternoon. He’s taking me to that Greek restaurant in town for lunch.”

Cindy said, “Fantastic. You’ll have a great time. Report back what you find out.”

He looked at her, his mouth a jagged line and an eyebrow raised.

“Off the record, of course.” Cindy gave him that sweet smile again.

Oh, how that girl lied.

“Sure, Cindy.”

“No, I mean it. We know she was killed by a bear. We need to know when she died and you know, the circumstances. Why she was in the woods, that sort of thing."

Ralph said, "I don't know she was killed by a bear. Maybe she was murdered and her body dumped in the forest for some animals to chew up the evidence."

I winced at the word "evidence."

"That's ridiculous. Who thought that one up?" I tried to give her a warning glance. "Who would want to kill her? I interviewed her for the Sparling case and she was such a sweet kid. I can't imagine someone killing her. It was an accident."

"Robin says her parents were weird. That they had unusual reactions to her death."

Cindy shook her curls. "Nope. Everyone reacts differently to hearing about the death of a loved one"

"That's what I said to Robin."

Cindy finally noticed that I was sending her the hairy eyeball. She figured out that I had been trying to distract Ralph from the phone on the dining-room table with a different theory. She changed her dance with lightning speed. "I mean, yes, they were edgy, and there was something odd going on, for sure. Who knows? Maybe she was killed and then dumped. But by them?" She pretended to think. "Well, maybe."

"I'll run the idea by Kowalchuk. Who knows what he'll make of the idea that Darlene was already dead and left in the forest for the animals to consume. We'll know more after the complete coroner's report. Pasta for dinner, did you say?"

I looked at him blankly. "Pasta?"

Cindy patted her back pocket. "Yup, I got the recipe. Off my phone."

Oh, right. The password pasta.

Ralph frowned. "I thought your phone was dead."

He really was being a pain in the ass. I said, "Dying. It was dying. Not enough power to download large files. I'm looking for a cord so she can download videos while we look at the photos. That takes a lot of power." Did it? I was guessing here. I knew nothing about phones. This lying business was tricky.

"Oh, I see. So, I won't order pasta at lunch. Maybe liver. Rare. I'll chew on it while asking Kowalchuk about my 'dumped in the forest eaten by bloodthirsty animals' theory."

I punched him in the arm. "You're a sicko."

"Everyone deals with death in their own way."

With that, he walked out of the kitchen, laughing. Cindy and I didn't say a word until we heard his car start. I slumped over the open kitchen drawer and pulled out the damn extension cord. "Phew. That was a close one."

"Pull yourself together. Let's plug that phone in and see what we got."

19.

EASIER SAID THAN DONE. Plugging this sucker in was going to be a trial. Pair o' Dice was a century-old cottage and the living room only had two sockets. One was behind the sideboard and another was behind the couch. The sideboard outlet would be somewhat easier to get to than the couch one. The wooden buffet was full of stuff and too heavy to move. I groaned while stretching over it and felt the air being pushed out of my lungs as my torso got squashed against the wood. I finally managed to reach halfway down the back of the piece of furniture to touch the electrical socket with my fingertips.

My stomach was cramping up. God. I tried not to moan. The plug wouldn't go into the socket. Why couldn't I lose fifty measly pounds? With my left hand, I grabbed one of the spare tires around my middle and shifted it out of the way of the lip of the sideboard. I hoped Cindy wasn't watching. I stretched my arm to its absolute limit, arched my wrist, and finally plugged the end of the fucking extension cord into the wall.

That done, I had to stand up. This was not going to be an easy endeavour. I could already tell that my arm was stuck. I twisted my body forward so I could get it out. And pulled. No luck. So, I jiggled it this way and that until it came free, badly scraped. Upon inspection, it looked like I had a foot-long hickey from my elbow to my armpit. Then, I heaved my body off the top of the sideboard and dropped the whole cord behind it. I collapsed on the floor like a deflated beach ball. I had a plan. I reached under the buffet, got the end of the cord, and wove it through the furniture legs until it was in the open. Finally, I stood up, waving the end of the plug like a white flag. Truce.

Cindy had been watching all this with undiguised amusement. "So. Congratulations. You win the grand prize. You made that look so easy." She shoved another cord at me. "Here's the charger. Plug the damn thing in."

I took the charger from her and tried to push the plug into the end of the extension cord, doing my best to ram it home with the palm of my hand. "This extension cord is old. It's hard to get this plugged in. It's so ancient, it only has holes for two prongs. Thank heavens the charger doesn't have a grounding prong. We'd never be able to do this." I grunted, still trying to get the charger plugged into the extension cord. "Man, this is stiff. These prongs won't go in."

"Hurry up, Robin, or I'll give you a stiff prong."

"*Hahaha.* Aren't you the funny one." I gave it a final slap. "There, good to go."

We were excited. What would the phone reveal? I inserted the charger into the phone's jack and sat down beside Cindy. I was trying not to puff. She took the device from me and held it out so we both could see the screen. We held our breath.

Nothing.

A second that seemed like an hour ticked by. Nothing. A completely black screen.

We looked at each other in dismay. The phone had crashed. It was useless. The black screen was the proof. Or maybe the extension cord was faulty. Maybe the plug didn't work. I'd be damned before I would find another and plug it in all over again.

But, suddenly, an apple missing a bite flashed onto the screen. I held my breath. Were we in luck? And then a charging icon appeared, a tiny battery with a small red stripe, indicating about a one-percent charge. Then the stripe widened. Two percent. We let our breath out in unison.

"It works," breathed Cindy. She pushed the home button to bring up the screen. Nothing. She pushed it again. And again.

I took the phone out of her hands. "You have to wait until it has a bit more charge," I said. "Be patient. It will only take a second or two. Don't push its buttons." I stroked the phone, trying to coax it along.

"How do you know this?" Cindy was worried and skeptical.

"I told you. I only charge my phone once a day. Sometimes it gets completely out of juice. When I plug it in to charge, I get exactly what's happening here. Wait a second or two." I stroked it again.

"Stop it."

"Stop what?"

"Stroking the phone."

"That's the difference between you and me, Cindy. I stroke. You push buttons."

"Stop telling me how to have a better sex life."

"I thought we were waiting for a phone."

We were crabby. This was stressful. She didn't wait very well. I was really good at it.

Cindy crossed and uncrossed her legs. Drummed her fingers on the table, itching to push the home button. Like a child, she needed a distraction. "What are your password ideas?"

She wasn't fooled; she knew what I was trying to do. She sighed. "Okay-y-y." She pulled out the shred of kraft paper from her back pocket and read, "'Sparling,' 'darlene,' 'mootpoint,' sandraandharry,' 'spooky,' 'philip,' 'bowser,' 'bernardo.'"

"The first five I know, but what about 'philip,' 'bowser,' and 'bernardo'?"

"Philip is her brother. I got that from her dad while you were upstairs. Bowser was her childhood dog. And Bernardo was a long-term boyfriend she had all the way through high school. I got that from her father as well."

"Let's hope one of them works. There's no way these Apple phones can be cracked."

Cindy said one word. "Alison."

Alison Trent was the researcher at the *Express*. She was a recent university post-graduate of about twenty-four who could find out anything, anywhere. Tiny Rasta braids covered her head, all finished off with coloured beads. Every time she turned her neck they swayed and clacked together. The last time I had used her services she had even found out the income of various suspects from tax returns. "Hack, hack," I said.

"Bad cough?" laughed Cindy.

Nonetheless, I doubted Alison the cracker hacker would be able to get into this phone. Not even the FBI could bust through the security on an Apple phone. I checked the charge icon. The red stripe had turned to green. "It's ready enough. Do you want to turn it on or shall I?"

"I'm better at turning things on than you are." She arched her back and threw out her chest.

Okay then. But probably true. Cindy took the phone back from me and ceremoniously pressed the home button with her pink nail. The phone sprang into life with all of Darlene's app icons scattered over the screen.

I was impressed. "Wow. Look at all the apps she had. Try the passwords."

Cindy looked at me, amused. She was grinning. "You really are a technotard."

"I don't think that's politically correct."

Her smile was patronizing. "Robin. Good news. She didn't put a password on her phone. See?" She held the phone up for me to see. "It opened up right way. Those are her apps. We can access all of her information. Photos. Facebook. Instagram. Twitter. And, best of all, her emails. See?" She tapped the blue envelope email icon and we were instantly connected to her inbox.

"Holy shit."

"Holy shit is right."

I shimmied next to her and scanned the emails. None of them had a blue dot, so all of them had been read. By her? I could only assume so. My eye snagged on one in the middle of the list that looked interesting Spar123. "Look, I bet that's Sparling. Open it."

Cindy tapped the email and began to read. "*Hi Babe.*" She gave me a look. "*I can't wait to see you again. Dinner and a little fun? Tomorrow night? At seven? Let's talk about your design job on my next production. Let's meet at our regular place.*"

"*Ugh. Babe*? Who says that these days? And it sounds a bit like emotional blackmail to me. It's almost as if he's saying, if you have sex with me, I'll make sure you get work on my next production."

"That's typical in the theatre industry. Rampant abuse of power." Then she made small circles with her thumb over the phone. She was scrolling. Suddenly she stopped. "Wait. There's something really strange about this. He said on the stand, under oath, that he barely knew her. That she was lying about them having a relationship. That he never used his position of power to influence her future employment. That they only saw each other professionally at the theatre."

"Really? Clearly that's not true. None of it. Why didn't her lawyer present these emails?" I grabbed the phone and scrolled down. "There are about thirty of them from him that show up right away. Probably more if we searched the history. This is way more than a professional relationship."

"Let's look at another." She tapped one from six months ago. "*Hey kitten, looking forward to spanking your mommy pussy tonight. Your reward will be???*"

"*Ew, ew, ew*. He's disgusting." Something inside me shrank.

"Oh, grow up, Robin. People talk dirty to each other all the time."

"Not like that. It's so um, so ... *ew*."

"Aren't we the expressive one this morning." Cindy thought for a moment and then ventured, "Maybe she was trying to protect him. Victims of a sexual assault from a person in power do that. And he certainly had power over her at the theatre. He was the lead actor and she was merely a lowly set designer. I wonder why she brought the case against him if she wasn't prepared to register all her evidence." She thought some more. "Maybe her parents pushed her to go to the police, but she didn't want to."

I sort of agreed with her. "That would make sense. Did I tell you that her parents moved her little girl bedroom from the family home into Moot Point? That's why Spooky was there. Maybe she didn't want her parents to know she was an adult, a sexual person. Maybe that's another reason why she didn't show these emails to her lawyer. She did what her parents wanted, up to a point, but held back so he would win and not be punished. She was probably still in love with him."

"But why not simply delete the emails? And why hide the phone at all? Maybe she was protecting the information so that it wouldn't disappear. Maybe her parents weren't involved at all. Maybe she thought she would win the case without the emails, but when she lost, she saved them for her lawsuit."

"When was that going to happen? The lawsuit? Didn't you say it was in June?"

"I'm not sure exactly. I'll have to look it up. Soon, though. June sounds about right."

Meanwhile, I was scrolling through her emails and noticed quite a few from MTPT@hotmail.com. I pointed them out to Cindy. "Who could that be? Sounds a bit like a bank or something. An investment firm."

Cindy was whispering to herself. Sounded like she was spitting. "If you say it fast it sounds like Moot Point. Open the last one sent. I bet it's from her mother."

I read it out loud. "*Hi, sweetie.*" I looked at Cindy. "You were right, *Just wondering how much longer it will take for you to finish up measuring the property beside Pair o' Dice. I can hold dinner for another hour, but after that it will be too dried out.* It seems this was probably the last email her mom sent her. That's so sad. Unless her mom was the one who killed her. And this is a decoy. Let's see. It was sent on the Saturday of Andrew's party."

"No one killed her, Robin. A bear mauled her to death."

"I don't think so. There's something off about everything. I mean, sure, if we were in British Columbia where there are grizzlies, then maybe a bear killed her. But here? In Ontario? Once in a blue moon, there's a rogue bear that will attack a human, but usually there's food involved. And there was no food involved here."

"She *was* the food, Robin. Don't waste your time on this theory."

A little flicker of annoyance flamed in my chest. Why was I always dismissed? Was it because I was fat? That my muffin top hung over my waistband? Or was it because my job was trite? That a person who knew what colours went together couldn't possibly figure out a mystery. I was certain something was mysterious here.

Cindy continued, "Besides, if that's your theory, how do you explain the bear going for Niemchuk? Two random attacks? I think there was simply a rogue bear out there."

"Maybe." I was sulking.

"Okay," Cindy said, relenting. "Maybe she was killed elsewhere and then brought into the woods as bear bait."

That was the theory I had implanted in Ralph, but I doubted it. It looked to me like the bear had targeted Darlene, exactly as it had targeted Niemchuk. But I wasn't going to split hairs. If she could accept that maybe Darlene was murdered, then at least she would be on the right track. "That's what Ralph is going to find out. The coroner will be able to tell."

"Lividity and blood splatter and pulsing veins and all that. *Yada, yada, yada.*"

Her attitude was pissing me off. "Arteries. Pulsing arteries, not veins. Veins don't pulse."

"Aren't you little Miss Perfect. But I still think we're both wasting our time. There was simply a rogue bear. Period. That's all." Cindy brushed some hair out of her eyes. "That has to be the explanation. Otherwise, why was Niemchuk attacked?"

This conversation was going in circles. Frankly, I didn't care what Cindy believed. The more I thought about it, the more I was convinced that Darlene had been murdered. How, I didn't know, but I would find out. Little Miss Muffin Top could be pretty smart. "Let's check out some more of her emails."

Cindy ran her finger down the list. Here's another from her mother. It's from over a year ago. She opened it with a tap of her finger and began reading. "*Darling, I know you don't feel up to talking to the police about Sparling, but really, sweetie, you should. The only people who are allowed to do that to you are your family. Sparling needs to be punished. I think you should move back home and let us take care of you. It's time to get back on the right path.* And so on."

Cindy and I looked at each other, dumbstruck. Neither of us spoke. *The family*? Had someone in the family abused Darlene? What exactly was going on here? That poor girl. She was being assaulted on not one but two fronts. And we had the proof in our hands. Cindy began to rapidly tap on the phone. What was she looking for now?

"Here, look Robin, in her sent messages, is the reply to that email from her mom. *Thanks Mom, for the invitation to move back home. I am quite convinced that the best place for me to be right now is in my own apartment with my own friends. I'm sorry I told you about Sparling. And no, I won't go to the police. I'd never win against him and he would go free.*"

"She got that right," I said.

"No kidding. She was torn into tatters by the judge."

"I wonder how she got from here," I tapped the email on the phone, "where she wouldn't move home, to her complete childhood bedroom being transported to Huntsville with her in it."

"Or from here, where she says she won't go to the police," Cindy tapped the phone, "to going to the police. Who knows? All I know is I feel sorry for that poor girl. First abused by someone in her family and then by Sparling."

"That's unlike you."

Cindy's eyes flashed. "I'm not a hard-hearted bitch, you know."

I kept the peace. "I know. I'm sorry." But not really. And she sure could be.

"Righto." She didn't believe me. But she let it go and turned her attention back to the screen. "Let's see what else we got here."

Cindy hogged the phone and tapped open Darlene's Facebook page. She scrolled through the postings with a practiced circular motion of her forefinger. Her hand stopped abruptly at an entry. I looked over her shoulder and saw that it was a picture of Darlene. "Look at this. Her last updated status. A photo of her in her new outdoor gear, announcing her new job. She's so cute, isn't she? She looks about twelve with that pixie haircut."

I took the phone from Cindy and saw that there were about fifty likes of her new status and one comment. I tapped on the comment to read it. My eyes widened when I saw what it said and handed the phone dumbly to Cindy. She read it and then whistled.

"Maybe you're right, Robin. Maybe she was murdered. This here's what you call a clue. It couldn't be clearer. *Your gonna die if you divided that land.* Spelling and grammar mistakes aside, I would say she had something to worry about here."

"Here, give it back. I want to see who wrote the comment."

But Cindy was already on it, peering at the small type. "Ursula Major. Not a photo, just a cartoon image of a bear wearing an army uniform. I'm going to search her profile. If it is a her." She tapped on the tiny cartoon to bring Major's page up. "Oh great. It's not a single person, it's a group of people." I watched as Cindy sped-read the postings. "Their mission statement says they are militant flora and fauna protectors. Animal rights people. I guess they took exception to the land being divided up into private plots."

"You think?"

She ignored me and read, "*We are dedicated to the preservation of land so that all species can live upon it in harmony without threat. We respect all life and expect it to be treated with dignity at all times. We will take extreme measures to ensure our beliefs are upheld.* Typical Facebook rant."

"Except she is dead."

"Mauled by a bear, Robin. By a bear."

I gave her a look.

She acquiesced. "Okay. Maybe dead before that. I'm sure we can figure out that rogue bear's part in this."

"And maybe she was murdered by one of the Ursula Major group. They sound very aggressive and militant."

"Lots of people might have motive to kill her, Robin, but it was a bear. Face it. I saw the claw marks."

I pursed my lips and held my hand out. I didn't think so. Cindy relinquished the phone. I scrolled through some of the photos that Ursula Major had posted. "No wonder they want to protect the land. There are some truly beautiful pictures here."

Ralph walked into the living room. "Hi girls."

Cindy bristled. He'd committed a sin.

"Are you looking at some photos of your trip?"

What trip? Oh right. Cindy's trip with her parents. "Oh, hi Ralph." I was trying to sound sincere. I'm sure my cheeks were burning, although not quite as hot as the hot phone I was holding. I stood up. "Yeah, have a look. Here are some pictures that Cindy's parents took. The Italian mountains." I was so calm. I was getting good at subterfuge. I wasn't sure if I was proud of it or not.

Ralph barely glanced at the pictures. I could smell beer on his breath.

"Good lunch?" I leaned into him, trying to distract him from the phone, my breasts brushing against his arm. I wasn't sure if he knew what Cindy's phone looked like.

"Kowalchuk didn't completely laugh me outta the ballpark when I brought up the idea that Darlene might have been murdered elsewhere. He's going to ask the coroner about it." He nodded toward Cindy.

"I'm sure you know how that will be assessed, being a crime reporter and all. Lividity. Blood pooling. Splatter."

Cindy rolled her eyes. "*Blah, blah, blah*. I can't *bear* it."

Ralph forced a chuckle. "Good one."

It took me a minute to get the joke. Maybe I was dim-witted. But maybe I was distracted by the *zing* between my nipple and my *zippity-do-da*.

Ralph gave me a wink.

Yeah, the sex was good.

20.

I COULD TELL RALPH was distracted by the *zing* between us and was amazed that he could keep his poker face firmly in place. Hmmm. Poker face. Now there's a concept. I wouldn't mind a little poke by the tongue in his face. While I was thinking lewd thoughts, he was chuckling at the dumb bear joke and looking straight at Cindy.

And I could also tell he didn't suspect a thing. Could he? Naw. Here I was, holding stolen evidence right in front of his nose and he was completely oblivious. Winking at me. Laughing. So unaware. What a cop he was. Or maybe I was way better at deception than I thought I was. When had I become so devious? And why did it give me such a thrill? I'm sure it was a bad thing to pull the wool over someone's eyes.

His breath wafted over me and I wondered how much beer he'd had at lunch. We made a fine pair, drinking away. I didn't know when I first met him that he drank as much as he did. He probably thought the same about me. This was not good. I would get help from my naturopath to halt my descent into becoming a homeless wino, but would he stop? And what if he didn't? Would our relationship last? On top of all that, I wasn't sure how I had become a person who could lie so easily to her boyfriend. This was all new to me and I wasn't sure I liked it.

Maybe he wasn't really my boyfriend. How often did I see him, after all? Three or four times a month? Sure, he'd saved my life, but he was a cop and that's what cops do. How had the last eight months actually been? Sure, the sex was great, well, better than great, but he didn't seem to be very, well, very what? What was the word I was looking for? Deep. He wasn't deep. Not that I needed depth, no, shallow could be fun, but our conversations weren't holding my interest. Is that why I could lie to him? Because we weren't really that close? Was he my soulmate? I was edging towards a 'no' on that one. Maybe I could lie to anyone now. Was my job more important than my ethics? Than my relationship?

Funny how fast thoughts can scattershot across a brain, in seconds, and yet everything keeps rolling on around you as if nothing had changed. Here we were, laughing at a dumb joke, standing so close our arms were touching, a little *zing* zapping between us, and I was thinking about ending the relationship. Was I? Is that what all this was about? I wish he hadn't said the L-word. I panicked when I remembered that and said the first thing that came to mind. Of course it was about food.

"What did you have for lunch?"

Ralph looked at me strangely. Could he guess what I was thinking? Or maybe he was surprised at my about-face in the conversation. What were we talking about, anyway? Oh right, the coroner. Blood splatter. Lividity. No wonder I forgot. No, face it Robin. The drinking is affecting your memory.

"The burger platter."

"I thought you were at the Greek restaurant."

"They do a great burger platter. Fries. Coleslaw. A nice fluffy roll. Gravy." Defensive.

"No spanakopita? A kebab?"

"I like the burger platter there. It's huge." Irritable.

"No stuffed grape leaves? Spicy lamb intestines?" I was teasing him.

"It was a great burger." He was getting downright prickly.

Were we fighting? I didn't want that. I tried to lighten him up. "So, the restaurant is Greekadian?"

He laughed, relieving the tension. "No, Caneek."

"What are you going to do now?" I asked while slipping the phone into my back pocket.

"I thought that was Cindy's phone."

Oops. Sometimes he didn't miss a trick. Caught by the cop. I laughed while digging it out. "God forbid that I should be a phone thief right in front of a police officer. What an arresting thought. Hahaha." I sauntered into the kitchen, my heart fizzing, where Cindy was banging around. "Here Cindy, here's your phone back."

Ralph followed me in. I could feel his body heat right through my clothing. And his beer breath on my neck.

She backed up, taking her head out of the freezer and nonchalantly received the phone from me and tucked it into her breast pocket. Now here was an expert in chicanery. "Thanks. Do you want mac and cheese for lunch or lasagna alfredo?" She held up two small boxes of frozen entrees, probably left behind by my brother who was many things, including a dipstick, but not a cook.

"I like both. Which one do you want?"

She put them in the microwave. "We can split them. And I'll throw together a salad."

"While you two girls are eating lunch, I'm going to check out where the body was found. See what I can see."

"Is the little boy going for a walk?" Cindy *hated* being called a girl.

Those two really got on each other's nerves. Maybe I should think about that, how my best friend had trouble with my boyfriend. Another black mark against him. I smoothed the tenseness in the air. "Are you sure you can find the location? Did you want me to come with you?"

He was dismissive. "It's along that same trail that you and I hike all the time, isn't it? The path clearly marked with those orange strips of tape?"

"Yes, but how will you know when you get there? The body's been removed." I was trying to be helpful.

"I imagine the crime scene tape is still up." He said it like he was saying, "*Duh.*"

Of course it would still be up. "Right. There's some bug spray on the windowsill." Still helpful, but my heart hurt a bit.

Ralph picked it up and read the label. "DEET. Should work." He sniffed the nozzle. "Disgusting." Was he blaming me?

"Yeah, put it on outside, will you?"

He turned and waved goodbye with the bottle as he moseyed out of the kitchen. "I'll put the bottle inside the door when I'm done."

The microwave *dinged* as the screen door slammed shut and Cindy put the two pasta dishes on the kitchen counter. A salad appeared out of nowhere and soon we were suctioning up our frozen noodle entrees.

"So, what do you think?" She asked me with her mouth full.

"Don't talk with your mouth full."

"Who are you? The Emily Post police?"

"I think I'm going to break up with him."

"No, you're not. You're doing the six-month assessment."

"Eight months. We've been going out since last September. So that's eight months."

"Whatever. He's a great guy. Despite the fact that I don't like him. Tall, dark, handsome, smart, big hockey stick. What do you think about what's on Darlene's phone?" She pulled it out of her breast pocket and put it on the table between us.

"I don't like that I can lie to him so easily."

"And so well!"

"Couples shouldn't lie to each other."

"Oh, Robin, couples lie all the time to each other."

I could see lettuce turning into pond scum in her mouth. My stomach lurched.

"It's not like you're lying about something deep. Everyone tells little white lies daily. They make a story better. They add colour. They can be funny. Relax. You're joining the human race."

"Really? But this is important. It's *evidence*. The police should have the phone."

"They will, but not quite yet."

I grabbed the phone off the table and pocketed it. "No, now. Right after lunch I'm driving into town and handing this over to Kowalchuk."

She lifted a shoulder and gave it a small shrug. "I have no problem with that, but hand it over to me first." She saw my look of rebellion. "I want to get a few copies of her emails."

"I don't have a printer here."

"Screenshots. Only a couple. Three from the mom and three from Sparling."

I reluctantly handed the phone back to Cindy and watched as she opened up Darlene's email and took screenshots of six emails. She then selected the photos from the photo roll and asked me for my email address.

"You already know it. And why?"

"I don't know it by heart, it's stored in *my* phone. This is not my phone." She waggled Darlene's phone as if to make a point. "I want them to go to you because this is your story."

That sounded more ethical than Cindy was. I wondered about her real reason as I gave her my address. If I got caught with this stuff, she wouldn't get in trouble? Was that it? My phone *pinged* with the incoming email from Darlene's phone.

"Now we have to cover our tracks. I want no email record of what we just did."

"What *you* just did."

She ignored me and tapped away. "Okay, I've deleted the photos from her camera roll and I've deleted the email to you from her sent box. Now I want you to open the email, save the photos to your camera roll and then delete the email that came to you from Darlene's phone."

I did as she asked and then joggled my phone at her. "But I have the photos of her emails. They're stored in my phone. So, there is a record. "

"But no *email* record on either of our phones. They can track emails through the server, but unless you give them your phone to search, they won't know you have the pictures."

I wondered if she was right. Alison could probably track right through this web of deceit. Take remote control of my phone or something. "Why do I need these pictures anyway?"

"I don't know yet."

Now there was an admission. "I should mark on my calendar the day you were flummoxed."

"I'm often flummoxed. I just don't advertise it. Something will come to mind."

Blackmail came to my mind. Imagine how much I could get from Sparling, the rich and famous actor, in exchange for these little bombshells. Or her mother. It seems my descent into the underbelly of the world was well on its way. Little goody two-shoes Robin MacFarland was long gone. But blackmail? No, this I'd never do. I wouldn't break the law I assured myself as I looked at the phone I had stolen in Cindy's hand. I felt quite light-headed.

Suddenly, Cindy stood up and zipped up her threadbare hoodie. "Let's get cracking. We can hand this phone over to Kowalchuk and then check out the Town Hall."

"I'd completely forgotten about the Town Hall. Shirley will have a fit that I'm not hot on the story of the murdered land surveyor." If Darlene was murdered.

The screen door whapped behind Cindy as she marched out the door. She called over her shoulder, "Mauled to death, not murdered. And that's not your story. You're hot on the story of bear safety in the woods."

She could believe what she wanted to. That was my cover story. I knew differently. I hurriedly gathered my jacket and raced out the door, following her.

Geezus. I almost crashed into her. Cindy was slowly backing up the porch steps into the cottage. At the bottom of the stairs was a smallish bear, a two-year-old cub it looked like, that was wrestling with the plastic garbage can, snarling and chewing at the lid. What the hell was going on? This would be the third time a bear had gone crazy.

Oh God. Where was Ralph? Had he run into this fellow? I speed-dialled his phone. Of course, there was no answer. Had he been killed? No, Robin, calm down, he had gone in the opposite direction, he was simply out of cellphone range.

The two of us crab-walked backwards up the stairs, careful not to stumble or make too much noise. The screen door squeaked on its hinges as I opened it slowly with one hand behind my back and the bear glanced up from the garbage pail for a second before renewing his attack. What on earth was he after? Once the main door was firmly shut, we stood by its window and watched the cub puncturing the plastic with its sharp teeth and scratching at it with his long claws. We gaped in amazement as he tossed the can over his head as if it were a marshmallow and heard a loud *thunk* as it landed on the metal-clad porch roof. Then there was a thunderous clatter overhead as it rolled down. And then, suddenly, it was deafeningly quiet.

The cub stood on its hind legs and sniffed the air. Again, I reminded myself that bears probably couldn't see worth a damn, but their sense of smell was legendary. His head swivelled this way and that until he beamed in on the garbage can stuck on the roof, lodged between the snow guards and the gutter. He grabbed a porch post with his paws and tried to shimmy up it, his paws slipping and sliding. Oh God, he wanted to climb onto the roof to get the garbage can. We had recently replaced the rotting wooden beams with metal posts, hard-baked with black enamel. I could see shiny white scars on the brand-new post from his hind feet. If Andrew were here, he'd have a fit, already planning the trip to the hardware store to get more Tremclad. But the bear couldn't get any purchase on the metal posts and threw back his head in frustration. He tried again and again, his nails etching the post, and I prayed that Ralph wasn't anywhere near the cottage. I kept speed dialing Ralph's phone repeatedly and finally got an answer.

Before he said anything, I shouted, "Stay where you are. Do not come home. There's a crazed bear on the porch."

"What? I'm barely out of the woods."

"Don't come home. I'll try to scare the bear away." I hung up before he could reply. My heart was banging in my chest. A crazed bear and my boyfriend were in the same yard, with only a cottage between them. Did he have his gun with him? I didn't think so. I tried to picture him before he left the cottage. Was there a bulge anywhere on him? My mind wandered to his most interesting bulge. Oh God, get a grip Robin. There's a bear out there. Why do I think about sex when there's a crisis?

My heart continued to jump around in my chest. I was going to have a heart attack one day. And where the hell had Cindy gone? What kind of friend deserts you when there's a catastrophe? I opened the main door and kicked at the screen door frame repeatedly so it would open and shut, open and shut, hoping the slams would cause the bear to run off. It merely looked at me, quizzically. I stopped and banged the main door shut. The bear kept trying to climb the post and then suddenly the garbage can clattered to the ground, its lid still stuck on. I was amazed. Rubbermaid sure knew how to build garbage cans. I should write an article on them. I couldn't believe I was thinking about the Home and Garden section while a bear was on the loose. Cindy reappeared behind me in the kitchen. Where had she gone?

"Did you see the look it gave you? He was not amused."

"It's not funny, Cindy. Ralph is out there with the bear. Where did you go? You can't disappear on me like that. I told you that already. This is serious. We have a big problem."

"Here, let's try this." She held a fire alarm in her left hand and handed me a rolled-up piece of paper towel. Light it."

I ran into the living room, grabbed the matches that we kept by the wood stove, lit the paper, and held the smoking paper towel under the fire alarm while Cindy opened the main door. A high screech slashed through the air, causing the bear to raise its head. On the second screech, it turned on its tail and ambled off into the woods. I dropped the smouldering paper towel into the sink, ran the water to put out the fire, and took a deep breath.

"Good idea, Cindy," I gasped. She must have gone to the base of the stairs in the living room to grab the fire alarm.

And then I speed-dialled Ralph. The coast was clear.

21.

RALPH EDGED TENTATIVELY around the corner of the cottage, looking this way and that, creases of worry bracketing his eyes. He lifted the garbage can that was lying at the base of the stairs and righted it neatly. Everything seemed so quiet, so still, after the chaos of the bear's frenzy. I opened the cottage door and watched him as he turned around several times to survey the grounds. With his hands on his hips, he scanned the forest surrounding the house. I followed his gaze and searched through the trees as well. Nothing.

Everything was so silent. Then, a squirrel chattered in a pine tree and a blue jay flew by with a long blade of dry grass dangling from its black beak. Blue jays were a sign of something, but I couldn't remember what. My brain was so fried. Change? Hope? No, wait, I remembered now. They symbolized clarity and determination. Communication. Assertiveness. Was that the message from nature that I was meant to receive right now? Perhaps in respect to my relationship with Ralph? Or even to my belief that Darlene had been murdered? And did I really believe in this symbolism stuff? I must, at some point, have had some faith in animal totems. I remember having looked up various birds in my past out of curiosity. I remembered that my naturopath had said I needed a new animal totem. I think I needed an eagle to swoop overhead about now, sending me vibrations of power.

I came out of my thought cocoon and glanced around. Everything had been restored to normal. My eyes rested on the garbage can. I couldn't believe what had happened to it. And yet there it was, at the bottom of the porch steps, as per usual, looking almost unscathed. What a feat of engineering it was. After being viciously attacked by a bear, it only bore a few puncture wounds and scratches. I really had to talk to Shirley about Rubbermaid products. I wondered if they were an advertiser. Oh my, how my mind wandered. Back to the present. Cindy was shifting from foot to foot beside me.

"That was a really good idea, Cindy, using the fire alarm."

She was jiggling her arms. Nervous. "I couldn't find the air horn."

"Sorry, we keep it over the sink so you can grab it on the way out." Most of the time. Now that I had stopped daydreaming, I felt like I was moving underwater.

"It wasn't there." She turned on her heal and went back inside.

I remembered I had left it on the sideboard. "Sorry," I called to her back, "I didn't put it back after our walk."

Perhaps that's why Ralph had gone into the woods without one. I was so stupid. That could have cost Ralph his life. My heart skipped a beat. But he was fine. There he was, standing in front of me, a lopsided grin on his face. I saw him through crinkly plastic wrap. What was going on with my eyes?

Ralph said, "If I hadn't seen the tooth marks in the garbage can, I would say it never happened."

I pulled myself together and laughed. "You think I'm a liar?"

"Oh, God no. You're as straight as a die."

If only he knew.

"Cindy and I are heading into town to check out the planning department and the ownership of the land next to ours. Large tracts of land being divided into small plots is a new trend. I want to make sure it isn't Crown land and to ascertain if Darlene was murdered because of her job." His head tilted. He didn't believe me. Thank heavens he let it pass. I had to admit it was pretty far-fetched. But not really. People became very passionate about protecting land. Ursula Major in particular. And even Dick Worthington. But I let it go. "What do you want for dinner? We can pick something up. We don't have to have Cindy's pasta recipe."

"Well, pasta is so heavy. And I think we should forget using the barbie outside. Too buggy. I don't want that bear to come back because of the enticing smells. Let's have something simple, like a roast-up. Chicken, zucchini, potatoes, and bang it in the oven. I can do it."

One thing about Ralph, he always pitched in. I put a mark on the plus side. "That's nice of you. It will give me time to work on the information I get in town today."

"Oh, and after you go by the police station to hand in that phone, would you mind picking me up some beer? I think we still have lots of wine."

I stared at him blankly. He knew?

"What? You think I didn't know? You told me you'd been to visit Darlene's parents and then the next thing I know you're futzing around with a phone, pretending it was Cindy's. It had interesting stuff on it, so I figured it had to do with Darlene. In fact, it's Darlene's phone. Isn't it?"

I whispered, "Yes." This was terrible. Straight as a die? I could have died on the spot.

"Don't worry, I'm not going to make a federal case out of you stealing evidence."

"You're not?" I couldn't make my voice any louder than a squeak. I had been caught lying.

"No. I figure you couldn't get it into Kowalchuk until later today in any event, what with everything happening around here. Bears. Garbage cans." He swept his arm around him to prove his point. "I would have to say that you were very diligent, getting it to him as fast as you could."

"Thank you." Oh my God, had I ever dodged a bullet. Sort of.

"On the other hand, I don't like being lied to. I'm a cop,

Robin. I can tell when someone is lying. Their face always gives it away. Don't do that again."

That was it? *Don't do that again*? "I'm so sorry, Ralph." I felt close to tears. "I don't know what's happening to me. I am always so honest."

"You still are. It eats you up to lie. I can smell the guilt. Sometimes, crime reporters have to be devious, and you certainly have been that, but in your personal life, no, you're honest. I'm just saying, be honest with me. This phone business? It's over. Let's move on."

"That's very generous of you."

"So, tell me. What's on the phone?"

I could have said "nothing," but he'd find out soon enough. Also, he'd know I was lying and I couldn't do that anymore. "There was a threatening comment on her Facebook page from an environmental animal rights group. Ursula something." I thought for a moment and tried to visualize her page. My mind was fried. More like pickled. "Ursula *Major.* Militant. You know, the type. Plus, Sparling had said on the stand that he hadn't had a relationship with Darlene outside of the theatre, but there are dozens of emails between the two of them, setting up places to meet and ah, you know, do the dirty. And her mother's emails to her made it clear that she had been abused in the family and perhaps bullied into starting a criminal action against Sparling."

"Really? All that paints quite a different picture about her death. So, as far as motive goes for someone to kill her, we now have three. There's a plot against plots, and two other possible plots. Ursula Major. Sparling. And a family member. I wonder why the police didn't figure this out." He paused and thought. "Maybe she didn't have a computer and did everything from her phone. Maybe it looked so obvious that she was randomly killed by a bear that they haven't bothered to pursue other possibilities."

"Here, let's go inside. I have to get my wallet." I said, as I opened the screen door. Cindy was in the kitchen, pretending to be tidying up. Eavesdropping. "There was no computer in her bedroom. And I know lots of people who do everything on their phone. Emails, banking, Facebook, searches. So that wouldn't be unusual," I said. "But, then there's Worthington," I added. "He pretty much said he'd kill anyone who meddled with his hunting ground.

Cindy piped up, "I don't have a home computer," picking up on the earlier part of our conversation. "I work on one at the office, but as for my personal life, everything is done on my phone."

"There, see?" I said. "But wait a minute. Cindy, you said 'personal' and that's reminded me that her mom said she had *two* phones. A personal one and a work one. Besides, the local police wouldn't think to check Sparling's sent emails on his computer because that sexual assault case was months ago and he was found innocent in Toronto, miles from Huntsville."

"Well, at least you'd think they'd check her Facebook page. If they'd done that, they'd have seen the threats from Ursula Major," said Ralph.

"Let me check something." Cindy took Darlene's phone out of her pocket and tapped on the Facebook icon. "They would never have found her page. It's not under her name. See?" She stuck the phone under Ralph's nose. "She's called *Darland*."

Ralph nodded. "Well, that explains that. But still, the local force should have searched her room more carefully. They should have found the phone. Where was it?"

To us it was such an obvious hidey-hole. Cindy snorted, "Up an ass."

Ralph took her tone as an *up yours* insult to him. "No, where was it?"

I intervened. "It was in a teddy bear that had a pouch in its bottom where you could hide things."

Ralph's face screwed up, trying to picture a stuffed bear with this anatomy. "I doubt I would have looked there either."

"It's was a thing from decades ago; there were a bunch of stuffed animals you could buy that had pouches built in for pyjamas and other things," I said.

"I guess that sort of excuses the locals. Not many people would have guessed to look *there*." He shook his head as if to clear his mind. "Well, girls, have a good time in town. Don't forget the beer." He walked back outside, letting the door slam behind him. Cindy and I both jumped. He turned and laughed. "I like the sound of a screen door slamming. It reminds me of my childhood."

Cindy and I walked towards my beat-up, rusted-out red Sentra. I called over my shoulder, "Take care of Lucky. Don't let her out."

Cindy shouted, "And I'm not a girl, *little laddie*, I'm a grown woman." Then she grunted at me. "I wish he'd stop calling grown women 'girls.'"

"He's doing it to bug you, Cindy. If you stop reacting, he'll stop doing it."

"Oh, and women get raped because of what they wear? He should stop doing it. I'm going to react every time. It isn't a game, you know. Men need to smarten up."

I put my hand on the chrome handle and paused. Should I say anything? Should I get into this? Or should I quietly get into the car? I got in.

Cindy reached for the door handle from her seat and tried to slam the door but it only creaked shut with a soft click. I did my best not to laugh and jab into her already edgy mood. The door had been askew on its hinges ever since Calvin, my oldest boy, had swung on it years ago. She crossed her arms with great deliberation instead. And stared at me.

Okay, I would get into it. "If you fight fire with fire, Cindy, you only get a great big fire. That isn't the way to create world peace."

"I'm not talking about world fucking peace. I'm talking

about men using diminutive names for women. Calling them 'girls.'" She snapped her head forward.

"If you ignore him, he will figure it out. If you keep fighting him, you put that negative energy into the universe and feed bad karma. Try it. Ignore him and see what happens."

"I'm not going to ignore it. I have a voice and I'm going to use it."

"Okay, do it your way. See if it changes him."

"You and your damn Buddhism."

I laughed. "Where do you want to go first, the police station or the Town Hall?"

"I think the Town Hall. It's getting late and they might close at four or four-thirty. The police station never closes."

"You still got the phone?" I'd lost track of it.

Cindy patted her breast pocket. "It's right here, close to my heart."

"I can't believe that Ralph knew about the phone all along."

Cindy said grudgingly, "He *is* a cop."

"Yeah, but still. I didn't think he was that smart."

"He's very smart, Robin. You're looking for reasons to ditch him. You're nervous of getting too committed. You can't accept that someone really likes you.""

As I drove along the dirt road, skirting muddy potholes and feeling the wheels slip here and there on sodden leaves, I thought about what she had said. Was I just merely nervous about taking the next step up in our relationship, or was the relationship in trouble?

"You might be right."

"I'm always right."

"Sure you are."

The car bumbled along the paved road into town while we sat in companionable silence. I yanked the wheel into a parking space behind Huntsville's Town Hall and we walked toward the very shiny and very tall glass doors. Cindy seemed so confident. Me? I felt like the unfortunate sidekick. But it was my story and I was going to chase down all the facts. I stood up to my full height, picked up my pace, and cruised through the doors ahead of her. My eyes quickly scanned down a list of the various offices, their names engraved on removeable black nameplates that were screwed onto an official-looking board. The Planning Department was on the third floor. I trudged up the stairwell, Cindy following me.

"They should have an elevator," she gasped. "It's a government building and they need to have complete access for everyone."

"They do have an elevator. But we're taking the stairs. It's way better for your health and therefore your outlook on life."

"Fucking Buddhism," she panted.

Finally, we stood in front of a fake wood counter. Behind a Plexiglas barrier sat a young woman of about twenty-five with blonde hair tightly pulled back into a ponytail. She was adding up a column of figures. Pinned to the lapel of her khaki blazer was a silver name tag with blue lettering. Elisa Lizette. I briefly wondered why Elisa was behind a Plexiglas wall. What was there to steal from a planning department? I imagined a robber sticking a gun through the little slot for paperwork at the bottom of the barrier, saying, "I have no future. Give me some plans or I'll shoot."

I spoke into the circle of little holes that had been drilled into the protective plastic glass. The holes hadn't been neatly done with a sharp drill and had small fibres around the edges.

"Hi, my name is Robin MacFarland. I would like to know who owns the land beside my family's property on Peninsula Lake."

Elisa stood up and straightened out her pencil skirt, smoothing the creases over her flat belly and trim thighs. I did my best not to hate her. She leaned over her desk to the furry holes and spoke loudly. Did I look old enough to have lost my hearing? "I'm going to go into the back room to look it up on the computer there. You wouldn't happen to know your lot number would you? Or your district?"

"No," I spoke just as loudly. I love sarcasm. "Sorry, I don't."

"No one does, don't worry. Your name's MacFarland?"

"Yes, Robin MacFarland."

"How do you spell that?"

I patiently spelled out my name and she leaned over her desk, exposing magnificent cleavage, while she wrote it carefully on a scrap of paper. I heard Cindy's sharp intake of breath behind me. Elisa scooped up the paper and waved it cheerily in the air. "It'll only take a sec. I'll go look it up."

As soon as she was out of earshot Cindy muttered, "I'd like to look her up."

"But what about Andrechuk?" I whispered out of the side of my mouth.

"I'm too old for Andrechuk."

"Sh-h-h. Here she comes."

"I'd like to see that."

God.

"So," Elisa chirped, "it was owned by a numbered company based in Toronto, and now it's owned by a new numbered company, based in Huntsville. Sorry, that's all the detail I can give you."

Fucking privacy laws. "It isn't Crown land, then."

"No, there isn't a lot of Crown land around here. You have to go further north for that. You are the third person to ask about this property in the past little while."

Interesting. "Can you tell me who else was asking?" I guessed one was Andrew.

"No. Confidentiality issues and all that." Elisa was trying to structure her face to look authoritative. She had almost pulled it off when it conked out from the effort. "But one guy? OMG, so handsome."

Who was it? Certainly not Andrew, who looked like a chipmunk. Then I remembered what Andrew had said that Sunday dinner at my house. If Sparling was Andrew's theatre friend, he was probably the one who had told Andrew the land had been sold to a developer. It was probably Sparling. "How long ago did he ask?"

"I guess I can tell you that. Let me check." She walked away into the back room.

"Nice little wiggle on her too."

"Give it a rest."

Elisa jiggled back. She was vying to be a future Shirley Payne. "After Easter weekend. Late April." She wasn't going to give an exact date. And then, as if to make up for her pigheadedness in following the rules, she offered, "He actually wanted to know about all properties near yours that were going to be divided up." Her mouth snapped shut. She'd said too much.

"A few weeks ago, then. About a month," I said. I did a calculation. This was right before Darlene went missing. What was he up to? He was rich. Maybe he wanted to invest in local property? What did all this mean?

Cindy modulated her voice. "And when was it sold?"

"I'll check." This time her flounce into the back room was a little less enthusiastic.

Cindy watched carefully. "Naw, she's not for me."

"She's way too young for you anyway, Cindy. She's half your age."

"Just having a little fun."

Elisa shimmied up to the desk. "It was actually sold almost a year ago. Before last summer."

Really? That was news to me.

Elisa sat down. She wasn't going to answer any more questions. She tapped her pencil on her column of figures. We'd worn out our welcome. But I had one more. "And the surveyor, Darlene Gibson? When did she start surveying the property?"

Elisa's eyes widened as she looked up, her pupils pulsating. "I'm not allowed to talk about her. Anyway, she wasn't a full-blown surveyor. She was an assistant. Measuring right of ways and stuff like that. She only measured stuff. She stopped showing up for work. Just like that! Her work phone and computer and bear spray? Gone." She snapped her fingers in the air.

The news hadn't got around.

I pretended astonishment and imitated her, adding a question mark. "Just like that?" I snapped my fingers.

"Yes, *poof*. She was here one Friday evening, handing in her clipboard and tape measure, and never showed up the following Monday. She'd been out checking that the new builds were fifteen metres from the water's edge. She was really good at measuring. People try to cheat, you know. This was like the beginning of May sometime. Maybe the end of April. So, we got a new assistant surveyor."

"The office didn't report her missing?"

"Why would we?" Elisa's eyes grew wide. "She went missing on the weekend. It had nothing to do with us. Unless it was overtime. Maybe she was working overtime. I doubt it though. Cut-backs. Anyway, I have to get back to work here." She squiggled on her chair.

Cindy and I said nothing as we clomped down the stairs in our hiking shoes and exited through the very tall and very heavy glass doors. Once we were in the car I said, "Well, that narrows it down. At least we have a bit of a time frame now. Late April, early May. Not that long ago. Right when the bears are good and hungry. On a weekend. But what was she doing with a clipboard?"

Cindy did up her seatbelt. "Measuring. Let's get that phone in."

The car coughed as I started it. "No. It doesn't make sense. She wasn't at work taking measurements, yet she had a clipboard. But Elisa said she'd handed hers in. What's going on here? Did she go back to get it?" I pulled out of the parking lot and headed over to Huntsville's cop shop.

Cindy said, "Probably she was working overtime. It's their busy time of year, before the summer building begins. She probably picked up her clipboard on Saturday. Whatever. The only thing I know for sure is that Darlene is dead. I guess she didn't measure up."

She was looking straight ahead. Every now and then, my politically correct friend was very politically incorrect.

22.

THE SUN WAS BEGINNING its slow descent by the time we reached the police station parking lot. We were just a month away from the longest day of the year, so it would be light for several hours yet. But I was hungry, of course. And now that we were in town, we had tons of fast-food outlets at our disposal. As soon as that bloody phone was handed in, maybe we could grab something to eat. My mouth watered as I daydreamed of crispy fries doused in salt and vinegar. Or a hot slice of pizza dripping in cheese. Of crunchy chicken smothered in gravy. Oh wait. Ralph. He was sitting at home waiting for me to arrive with food to cook for dinner. And beer. How easy it was for me to forget. Maybe he was the perfect guy, at least according to Cindy, but maybe I liked being on my own. I nosed into a parking spot between two black-and-white cruisers with O.P.P. stencilled on the side.

I turned to Cindy and held out my hand. "Here, give me the phone."

"Why?"

"So I can give it to Kowalchuk."

"But I'm coming in with you."

"I know that. But I found it and I'm handing it in." I couldn't believe we were having this conversation. "Hand it over." I jutted my hand at her.

Cindy slapped the phone onto my open palm. She didn't relinquish power with grace.

I stashed the phone in my purse and climbed out of the car, holding on to the door handle for support. I must have hurt my hip when I fainted in the forest yesterday. Cindy didn't get out. Geezus. Was she sulking? I limped around the front of the car and tapped on her window with my knuckle. "Let's go."

I saw her mouth move but couldn't hear what she was saying behind the dusty glass. She was frowning, her lips tight along her teeth. It sounded like she was talking underwater. I opened the door and the last of her sentence rolled across the parking lot in high volume: "...here."

"No, come with me. Don't be so stubborn."

She put her hands up while looking straight ahead. "That's okay, I'll wait."

Cindy hated not being in charge. She was so sensitive. For her, everything quickly turned into a rejection. No wonder, I guess, considering her husband's treatment of her. "No, no, I want you to come. I need the support." I didn't really, but it would help her feel wanted.

"Oh, all right." She snapped off her seatbelt and clambered out of the car. No flies on her.

"Thanks," I said. "I wonder if Kowalchuk will be there."

"He's probably sleeping off the huge lunch he had with Ralph."

Somehow, I doubted that. Although the man was enormous, he was charged with a nimble inner energy. There wasn't a lazy bone in his body. I replayed in my mind his shooting of the bear. It was so *accurate*. I wanted that guy on my side, but I'm not sure I liked him. As I stood in front of the doors to the station, I felt a bit light-headed. Perhaps my mind had escaped on the short journey across the parking lot, rendering me a true airhead. I felt giddy. This is how I was before encounters with the police. Guilty as not charged. I fingered the phone in my purse. It was still there. Amazing. At least I hadn't lost *that* between the car and the front door. Wonders will never cease. But Ralph was right, wasn't he? I only found the phone this morning. It wasn't as if I'd been secreting it away for days. I mentally rehearsed saying, "I came as fast as I could." Without laughing. This was a line I hoped I would only ever say to Ralph.

We opened the solid metal door into the station and banged smack into a counter that spanned the whole length of the small room. Running along the top of the counter was a yet another Plexiglas window with a cluster of speaker holes drilled into it. I looked at them more closely. They had the same fuzzy edges as the ones in the Town Hall. At least one guy in Huntsville had regular work, drilling holes into Plexiglas. Too bad he wasn't that good at his job. The only way into the room behind this wall of security was a door to the right that had a small window embedded with wire mesh about eye height. I guessed that the door was locked. The three brass keyholes were my clue. A five-year-old wearing a police uniform sat at the counter and behind him were a dozen or so playmates, all wearing the same costume.

"Can I help you?"

Oh, so the child had learned how to talk. "Sure, thanks. My name is Robin MacFarland and this is my friend, Cynthia Dale. I was wondering if I could see Detective Kowalchuk, or Officer Andrechuk." I didn't like the way this kid was looking at Cindy. Had Andrechuk blabbed about their date?

"And the nature of your visit?"

I was wrong. I thought he'd learned how to speak, but he was talking in that foreign tongue reserved for affected assholes, for children who wanted to sound as if they were really, really smart. *The nature of your visit,* my ass. "We have some evidence to hand in on the Darlene Gibson case."

The young boy looked up. "Darlene Gibson?" His freckled nose crinkled up as he made a show of thinking. He tilted his head, put a finger on his tongue, and then used it to flip through some pages on his desk until he found what he was looking for. "That case is closed."

"Um, no, I think there's more investigation going on."

His lips formed a compressed line as he read the sheet in front of him, "No, it says right here that the case is over. As of two o'clock today. *Kaput*. Anything else I can help you with?"

Really? They weren't going to pursue the case? I was so frustrated. Hadn't Ralph said Kowalchuk was going to look into the idea that Darlene had been murdered elsewhere and then dumped in the forest? Surely he couldn't have done that between lunch and two. "Why don't you ask Detective Kowalchuk to come out for a second?"

He raised his eyebrows apologetically. "I can't do that without a valid reason."

This guy had his head up his ass. "I understand totally. Rules and everything. The other reason why I'm ... I mean, why *we* are here is because we have something of his that I'm sure he would like to have." Cindy was poking me in the back with the hard corner of her purse. "A personal item."

This fell into the category of "lying on the job." I was okay with it. Ralph was right. I could lie on the job, but not in my personal life. But sometimes there was an obtuse grey area when the two overlapped, like in my relationship with him.

"Oh, why didn't you say so? I'll buzz him right away. Why don't you wait on the bench by the wall there?"

It wasn't a question, more like an order. "Thanks." What was with the police? Why were they so officious and controlling? Was Ralph like that? No, he seemed pretty laid-back. Then, why was I undecided about him? So many questions. Cindy and I arranged ourselves on the metal bench which felt cold through my pants. The quiet hum of a busy office settled over us. We couldn't see above the counter into the room behind it and I figured they had designed the counter height that way on purpose.

"He's coming." I whispered to Cindy, my head gesturing to the door.

"How can you tell?"

"The floor is vibrating. I can feel him walking. In there." I signalled with my head. "He's like a tank."

"I don't feel anything." She put her hand on the bench, trying to sense the vibration.

"Ever since I started chanting with my Buddhist group, I am really sensitive to vibrations."

Cindy snorted. "Or maybe the Robin-bird is listening for a worm."

"Not all cops are worms. I'm sensitive to vibrations. Really."

"You're sensitive to everything."

"So are you."

The door opened and the elephant rumbled into the room. "You have something personal of mine? Did I leave something on the table at lunch that Ralph picked up? I don't seem to be missing anything." He patted his pockets to reassure himself.

I stood up. Standing with him in the small foyer, there wasn't a lot of airspace left. "Actually, I thought you should have this," I said as I was digging in my purse. "It's Darlene's phone. I found it in her parent's house this morning." I had backed right into the counter, the edge digging into my hip.

His bushy eyebrows shot up to the top of his head. "We were looking for her computer and phone. Where did you find it? It was at her parents? But we searched that cottage from top to bottom. Are you sure it's hers? Besides, I've closed the case. Death by misadventure." A look of suspicion briefly flicked across his face. "How long have you had this phone? When did you find it?"

I put it into the palm of his outstretched hand. Even the thought of uttering my practiced line made me weak with silliness. I couldn't laugh. Not right now. "We are sure it's hers." I had to be careful here. No laughing. Plus, I had to include my protector, Cindy. She was already in a snit, I could feel her breathing down my neck. "We read some of her emails and looked up her Facebook, that sort of thing, to identify the owner. You know how it is."

His eyebrows lowered as he looked at the phone, tiny and black in his enormous paw.

"You might want to reopen the case. We came across some pretty compelling motives for someone to kill her." He towered above me. "We found it this morning and came as fast as we could." There. I said it. And I didn't laugh. I didn't have to tell him how I had entertained the idea of keeping it.

Cindy sidestepped from behind me and went around the man mountain to stand beside him. She was almost his height. Her eyes were wide and a very hot green in the flickering fluorescent lighting. She said, "I mean, we know a bear killed her. But perhaps someone manipulated the bear to attack."

In one concise sentence, Cindy had solidified the random thoughts that had been floating inside my head. Like little snowflakes they had drifted about on air. And now I had a snowball. Manipulation. Damn, I was such an airhead. Of course! Someone had manipulated the bear to attack. But how?

Kowalchuk laughed in her face. "I don't really think you can make a bear do anything. Bears are bears. They attack when they want to. And thank heavens it's not often."

"We've had three bear attacks in the last two months. Surely you must find that unusual."

"Three?" Kowalchuk gave his barrel head a shake as if to clear out cobwebs while at he same time mocking her.

"First Darlene, then Niemchuk, and then this morning, Robin's garbage pail."

He turned his watermelon-sized head to me. "Your garbage pail? Bears attack garbage cans all the time. Especially this time of year. They are very hungry and they want the garbage. What's so unusual about a bear attacking your garbage can?" He was dismissively shaking his head while sliding Darlene's phone into his shirt pocket.

"It was empty. It's been empty since last fall." I suppose it didn't matter that he hadn't put the phone in an evidence bag. Far too many people had touched it already, so there'd be a mess of fingerprints. But still, it was evidence. It should be in a bag.

"Garbage smell lingers." Kowalchuk wasn't being abrasive, just stating facts.

"Have you met my brother?" I, on the other hand, was being abrasive.

"What about him?"

"He's a cleaning fanatic. I bet that garbage pail was completely disinfected last Thanksgiving when we closed up the cottage."

"Even so."

I gestured to the phone, only a corner of it visible in Kowalchuk's pocket. "And there are four distinct murder suspects."

"Only four?"

Now Kowalchuk was laughing at me.

I decided to fight fire with fire. So much for world peace and Buddhist intention. Fuck that. This man was pissing me off. But I kept my voice flat and laid out the facts. "If you hunt, Detective," I kept the sarcasm out of my tone as I said his rank, although I secretly hoped some crept in, "through her phone, you'll discover threats from an animal rights group on her Facebook page. She was also involved in a sexual assault case against David Sparling who lied on the stand in court. The proof of his perjury is in his many emails to her. She was launching a lawsuit against him. Also, someone in her family could have killed her to silence her from exposing his or her sexual abuse. In addition to this, I personally heard Dick Worthington vow to kill someone who threatened his hunting grounds."

He listened to me with a sneer glued on his face. I had rapidly come to dislike this man, marksman skills aside. "Yeah, right." He slapped his palms clean, washing them of everything I had said. "Animal rights people don't kill, the Sparling case is done and dusted, her parents are odd but kind, and Worthington is a drunken blusterer. She was simply killed by a hungry bear." He chortled a bit and amended his sentence. "A very hungry bear."

Cindy face had turned slightly pink and a vein throbbed beside her right eye. She entered into the fray. She didn't like being dismissed. And she really didn't like the dead being treated with disrespect. It was okay for her to make jokes, but not someone else.

"Scoff all you like, but you'll be the one looking like a fool if you don't solve this case properly and leave it to journalists from *The Toronto Express* to investigate."

"What? You're dumb reporters for a useless Toronto rag. You think the *media* is better than the police?" He said "reporters" like he was saying "dog shit."

This was a side to Kowalchuk that I hadn't seen before. He was a bully. I turned my head to see the reaction of the young cop behind the glass partition. He was keeping his head down, although his ears were tipped red. Did he know this honcho was stepping over the line? Was that why he was hiding his eyes? He didn't want to witness this abuse of power? And how much of the conversation had he actually picked up? We weren't that far from the communication holes in the Plexiglas. Cindy and my voices had been quite quiet. Kowalchuk's, on the other hand, was rising with every minute. Why was he getting so riled up? Had he been burned by the media before? I'd google that as soon as I got out of here. After some pizza. Or fries. Fries would be faster. We could get some at the McDonald's drive-through.

Cindy didn't let it go. I knew she wouldn't. The words "letting go" weren't in her lexicon. "You may think we are run-of-the- mill reporters," she spat out the word, exactly as Kowalchuk had, "but we are investigative crime journalists. For the largest daily in Canada."

I had to stop myself from stepping back. Me? An investigative crime journalist? *Hahaha*. Nice of her to say so, really, but nowhere near the truth. I investigated fire retardants and lampshades. She, on the other hand, investigated gangs, drugs, robberies, fraud. She was brave. Tenacious.

I watched dumbstruck as Kowalchuk put his hand on his holster. I couldn't believe this was escalating the way it was.

He was going to threaten us with violence? "Don't lie to me. I know this gal." He removed his hand from his weapon and cocked a finger at me. Perhaps he had been merely resting his hand and not trying to intimidate us. Or perhaps he had been, but removed it because he sensed the young guy behind the Plexiglas had lifted his head and was watching the exchange. "Andrew's sister is no investigative crime journalist. Gardens are her forte. Flowers. This timid gal falls apart under pressure and we know how fond she is of the bottle."

Fuck him. Just fuck him. Fuck, fuck, fuck. So, he was going to play dirty. I was enraged. How *dare* he?

Now two veins were throbbing on Cindy's face, one beside her eye and the other right down the centre of her forehead. She would not tolerate this, that I knew. But I also knew he had a point. I *was* fond of the bottle.

Cindy hissed, "This timid *gal,*" she jerked her thumb at me, imitating his rudeness, "solved those two Everwave murders in Toronto last year, virtually on her own. She was the one who figured out the murder weapon. She was the one who figured out who had used it. She was the one who figured out the motive. So, watch your step, *fatso.*"

With that, she turned on her heel and marched out. I resorted to my default setting of shrinking violet and followed her for a few steps. But then I held my head up high, despite the snickers and sneers that I could hear from the rookie cops behind the Plexiglas. As if that would protect them from Cindy's wrath. Or mine. Little did they know. I was a force to be reckoned with. Right, Robin, righto. Whatever you say. But still, I held my head up.

Cindy was right. I did figure out that case last year on my own. Mostly. Her words echoed in my ears as I approached the exit. And then an arrow shot through my heart, deflating the balloon of pride. How did Kowalchuk know I was fond of the bottle? Someone must have told him. Ralph? It must have been Ralph. Would he do that to me? No, Kowalchuk had been at Andrew's party. Could it have been Andrew? No, I couldn't imagine Andrew dirtying his own nest. He wouldn't say that about me. More than all Kowalchuk's bullying about the case, the fact that he knew I drank too much ate away at my gut like battery acid. No way would I turn around to say goodbye to him. I was so embarrassed I thought my face was going to pop off from the sudden rush of blood to my cheeks.

My mother wouldn't approve of my bad manners, so in deference to her, I tossed an arm in the air and waved. It took some effort to not give him the finger. I followed Cindy in her wake out into the parking lot and then hurried to keep up with her long stride. Some people could walk so fast. "Hey," I puffed, "hey, thanks for the support in there. You told him."

"Pompous, narcissistic, bully, asshole, fuckhead."

"Oh, tell me how you really feel." I made light of it, but I felt exactly the same way. What a colossal jerk.

"I wish we hadn't given him the phone. Did you see him put it in his *pocket*? No bag? He's so convinced he's right he won't do anything with it. Some people are like that, Robin. They have to be right. But I think he's wrong. I think you're on to something, Robin. I really do. That garbage can thing really made me think there is something weird going on. What bear attacks an empty garbage can? There's a reason why all this has happened. That was a stupid argument about lingering smells. I highly doubt it."

"I'll ask Ralph to get Kowalchuk to investigate what we discovered on the phone."

Cindy waggled her head back and forth and imitated me in a singsong voice, "I'll ask Ralph to get Kowalchuk *blah blah blah*."

"Okay, okay, you're right. The boys have lost their chance. We will take this on. First thing I'm going to do when we get back to the cottage is smell that garbage can. I bet it's clean as a whistle. But someone is doing something to the bears to make them crazy. And I'm going to find out what it is."

"Beep the doors," Cindy said as she approached the car.

"They don't beep. That feature died."

"What, you can't lock your car? You've left it here in the lot unlocked, all this time?"

"It's a *police station.*"

"Criminals hang around police stations, Robin. Duh."

"I can lock it manually, but not with the key fob. The power locks are no longer."

"You should get that fixed. It's a safety feature."

Cindy folded her long legs into the car and hitched the seat back as far as it would go. She needed to stretch out. I heard the mechanism scraping as it slid back, metal against metal, when I opened my door to get in.

We drove along in silence to the first set of lights through the town and then I said, "You hungry?"

Cindy said, "Ralph. Beer. Dinner."

"An appetizer? Like some fries from the drive-through?"

"Oh, all right. After we pick up what we need for the evening."

"No, before."

Cindy and I squabbled a lot.

23.

THE SETTING SUN CAST long shadows that criss-crossed the driveway as we crunched up the gravel toward Pair o' Dice. We were surly and fighting after our horrendous meeting with Kowalchuk. Cindy and I had had a spat about what to get for dinner that would make fighting cats proud. In the end, we decided that instead of buying food to cook we would pick up some curry takeout from the local Thai restaurant, The Purple Elephant. The smell of coriander and lime floated over the smell of wet dog in the car. It made me feel a little sick. I wasn't a fan of Thai food, but I didn't want to admit it because that would make me look uncool. Cool people liked Thai food. And sushi. I hated sushi. And dumplings. Slimy, boiled snot. I was so uncool I should just wear a fur coat and let someone put me out of my uncool misery.

Ralph must have been watching for us because as soon as we parked, he appeared at the screen door. Lucky was yipping at the handle, as if his bark was a remote control, and Ralph opened the screen to let him out to greet us. Sharp needles of annoyance prickled the underside of my skin as he bounded to the car. Didn't I tell him not to let the dog out? There was a fucking bear roaming around. The last thing I needed was Lucky heading into the woods, chasing a bear. I hurriedly got out of the car and grabbed his collar as he leapt at me, tongue hanging out, leaving Cindy to carry in the beer and brown bag of takeout.

Hunched over, with my hand grasping his collar, I walked to the house. Lucky was dancing on all fours and straining my arm. I yelled, "There's a demented bear out here. Why did you let him out?"

He stared at me with steely blue eyes while he held the door open for me. "Someone's in a good mood."

Fuck that tone.

"Did you remember the beer?"

"Can't go a night without your beer, can you."

"Look who's talking."

"Did you tell Kowalchuk that I was fond of the bottle?"

"We were discussing life."

"Keep my life out of your conversations."

Pain flittered in his eyes. He looked away. "Hey Cindy, can I help you?" He reached his hand out to take the case of beer from her as she passed him into the cottage.

"I'm okay, thanks." Cindy stalked past him and plunked the beer on the kitchen counter.

Ralph let go of the screen door and spread his hands. "Okay-y-y. How did the town trip go? I'm thinking not that well."

I was throwing dishes onto the table, marching back and forth between the kitchen and the table. "We can talk over dinner." I held up the bag. "Thai."

"You don't like Thai."

"It's dinner."

Lucky was on his bed in the corner of the living room, wisely staying out of my way. But when he heard the word "dinner" he jumped up and ran to me. I absent-mindedly patted him. "Don't worry, I'll give you your food. Poor doggy. You can't run outside." I patted his silky ears. "We don't want that big bad bear to get you." I looked pointedly at Ralph while I said all this. Nothing like a little passive aggression. He ignored me. But then, I suddenly remembered the garbage can. I wanted to smell it and see what was so interesting to the bear.

I slipped around Cindy who was dishing the curry into bowls

in the kitchen. "I'm going to check out the garbage can. See why the bear was trying to kill it."

I could barely see in the fading light, but to the right of the steps below the porch was the can, right where Ralph had placed it after the bear's calisthenics. I undid the handles that snapped over the lid to hold it in place and carefully lifted it off, my eyes peering into the forest, my ears on high alert, pinned back against my head. Emanating from the can was a slight odour, one that I vaguely recognized from my recent memory, but I couldn't recall what it was. As my eyes adjusted to the gloom, I saw at the bottom of the can, the empty bottle of insect repellent that Niemchuk had tossed there. Oh, that was the smell. Other than that, the container was empty. As I had said to Kowalchuk at the station, the container was pristine. There wasn't a crumb of food. You could eat off of it. And the bear was trying to.

Cindy's tall, lithe figure was silhouetted in the screen door's square of light. "Clean?" she called out.

"Nothing. Not a morsel of food. Only that finished bottle of insect repellent that Niemchuk used. You know, the one we found in the woods." I lifted up the whole garbage can and gave it a shake so she could hear the bottle rattling around in the bottom.

"Kowalchuk is an asshole."

She was right. That he was. Over dinner, I stuffed the Thai food in my mouth like a robot. The rice was dry and the always surprising bits of chili in the inadequate supply of curried chicken would haunt me all night long. I wished we'd ordered pizza or even fried chicken. But no, Cindy wanted to be urban. Huntsville didn't do urban off-season. Maybe in a month when the population exploded with summer residents there would be fresher food. The three of us sat at one end of the large harvest table and ate in silence, looking down at our plates. At least no one had brought out their phone. I'd had enough of phones for one day. The quiet was punctuated by the sound of silverware clinking against dishes and the rattling of Lucky's kibble as he nosed around the flotsam for the tastier bits. The tension in the air was so thick you'd need a nuclear missile to blast through it. I was so pissed off at Ralph badmouthing me in public I couldn't even look at him. I wish he'd leave. Finally, he threw down his napkin.

"Look. I know you're angry. Obviously what I told Kowalchuk at lunch was used against you. I shouldn't have said anything about your personal life to him. Yes, I told him you liked your wine. But there are two sides to every story. I thought he was a compassionate and trustworthy guy. I didn't know he'd turn the information into a weapon. I misjudged him. We were talking about issues we were dealing with. His, obviously, is weight. Mine, just as obviously, is alcohol. Your wine drinking came up, but only because I said I didn't know if you thought my drinking was a problem because you enjoyed drinking as well. I wasn't gossiping. I was trying to figure out the problem." He let out a long sigh and spread his arms wide. His chest deflated.

Cindy said, "Pass the hot sauce."

I was flabbergasted. Ralph knew he had a drinking problem? Plus, he hadn't told Kowalchuk about my drinking to bad mouth me at all. He was exposing himself. But now that I'd had that encounter with Kowalchuk and seen his nasty side, I wasn't sure it was such a good idea for Ralph to tell him such an intimate detail about himself. Even though they were in completely separate jurisdictions, word got around. The police force in general was a small community full of blabbermouths. I didn't want Ralph to get a bad reputation as an unreliable cop because he might be tipsy. And that Kowalchuk, man oh man, he would do anything to win.

"Okay," I said.

"Okay? So, I'm forgiven?"

"I didn't say that. I said 'okay.'"

Cindy piped up, "And I said, 'Pass the hot sauce.'"

I handed it to her. "You didn't say, 'please.'"

"Pulleezzzee." She rolled her eyes.

"What do I have to do to be forgiven?" He looked so remorseful. I thought I even detected a tear. What? The big bad cop was crying over spilt milk? Probably not.

I winked at him. Cindy kicked me under the table. Ralph's face uncrumpled. It was time to move on.

Cindy said, "The handing in of the phone wasn't a raging success."

I butted in. "Darlene's case has been closed. I doubt Kowalchuk even looked into the idea that she was murdered elsewhere and her body dumped in the forest with the hope that an animal might eat up the evidence."

"Really? He said he would." Ralph had parked his dry curry inside his cheek. But I could see it. I'd talk to him about that later. Maybe when his tongue was in cheek. My cheek.

"Well, I don't think he did. The case was closed at two o'clock this afternoon."

"Two o'clock? I left him at one forty-five. He said he'd investigate it. Who told you two o'clock?"

And now Cindy was talking with her mouth full. I was going to gag. Next thing you know they'd be licking their knives. "The youngster behind the Plexiglas. There's a real attitude in that cop shop. Anti-gay. Misogynistic. Territorial. Close-minded. A bunch of fucking assholes."

Ralph looked at me for confirmation.

"Yeah," I said. "They snickered when we left."

"Oh. I'm sorry." He looked like he was apologizing for all cops everywhere. "What exactly did Kowalchuk say?"

"Basically, he said that the investigation was closed. That there weren't any suspects. That a really hungry bear, quote unquote, attacked Darlene. That he wasn't going to do anything more about it."

"Did you let him know you were journalists?"

"He wasn't impressed. Especially since he knows I work for the Home and Garden section."

Ralph tilted his head on a slant. "But not all the time."

"He wasn't interested. Cindy told him all about Everwave, but then the snickering started. She called him *fatso*."

He laughed. "Well, that probably upset him more than anything else she could've said, unless of course he was lying to me about worrying about his weight. Maybe he was trying to find out dirt about me, so he could use it somehow."

"I think that's more likely, Ralph." Cindy was squirting hot sauce over her whole plate. "Plus, it's obvious that he has a short penis."

Ralph choked on his food, but then recovered, saying blandly, "Oh? Short penis?"

"Yes, I have a short penis theory. He's one of those cops with a short penis. He needs to act big and to break the rules to get where he wants to get."

"I've never heard the short penis theory before." Ralph was all ears.

"Really?" She raised an eyebrow. "I think when guys have short penises they have to puff out their chests and abuse their power. Like this Kowalchuk asshole? While Robin was talking to him, he put his hand on his gun to intimidate her. Any guy with a decent-sized penis wouldn't do that. They wouldn't feel the need to act like a bully because they wouldn't feel the need to overpower. They would want the truth and they would want to get to it without threatening someone. Like you, Ralph. You don't have a short penis."

Oh my God. Did she really say that? I mean, I knew it was true, was it ever, but still, commenting on my boyfriend's penis? How embarrassing. I stuffed a forkful of rice in my mouth as if nothing had been said. Not many people would talk about the length of a person's penis. Yet here she was, eating her food like it was nothing. It was more than a little disconcerting and yet her short penis theory was interesting. I was surprised that my best friend had kept her short penis theory from me. Maybe that's why she didn't feel threatened by Kowalchuk when he put his hand on his gun. She had distance. She had knowledge. She had power. She knew what was in his pants. A short penis!

"Ah-h-h," Ralph spluttered. "Thank you. I guess."

Cindy looked up from her plate. "Anytime, big guy."

Geezus. I pushed myself away from the table. "Dessert anyone? We have ice cream. Maple walnut."

"Sure," said Ralph, "that should cool things down a bit." He looked deliberately at Cindy. A secret smile played around the left corner of her mouth. "And then maybe after dinner we can talk about what was on Darlene's phone. I'm sure you had a good look."

"We even took some pictures," I said. "Screenshots of some emails and a comment on her Facebook page. They'll prove a lot." I counted on my fingers as I stood at the head of the table. "One, Sparling knew her in the biblical sense, despite saying under oath that he only had a professional relationship with her. Two, I think members of her family had reason to want her dead. And three," I bent back the third finger, "there is a militant animal rights group that wanted her dead. So, three potential suspects from her media alone. Maybe someone else did it. Like Worthington. He threatened to kill whoever took away his hunting ground. I mentioned him before, Ralph. That makes four suspects. We have to figure out which one did it."

Ralph handed me his empty plate and said, "Well, actually, we have to figure out *how* they did it. I'm sure the autopsy won't reveal anything from her remains. They've been too chewed up. Any knife nicks or even bullet grazes will be masked by the bite marks."

As I swooped Cindy's plate from under her, she scraped off a last forkful of curry and smacked her lips around it before tossing the utensil on the plate in my hand. "You're still working on the idea she was murdered elsewhere and then left in the woods? Sorry to disappoint you, Biggy, but the bear did it."

Biggy?

"You can't make a bear do anything."

"That's what Kowalchuk said. Robin and I know differently. That bear was manipulated to kill Darlene."

"How?"

"That's the question."

After eating ice cream, we all huddled around my phone on the couch, looking at the screenshots Cindy had taken of Darlene's emails and Facebook page. Lucky growled periodically from the chair he had taken over and I hoped it wasn't at a wild bear. Were they nocturnal? No. It was probably just the wind. Ralph went over and scratched behind his ears to calm him down. He was so good with Lucky. Anyone who loved animals was okay by me. And that apology of his today was so heartfelt. He really was remorseful. How did I really feel about him? Was he the one with intimacy barriers, or was it me? Was I still recovering from Trevor? Or maybe it was from stuff in my childhood. So much baggage. I couldn't even handle an "I love you." I kept lifting the glass of wine to my lips and taking big gulps. Why was I even drinking? What was I hiding from? Ralph? Me? My past? My future?

Ralph rubbed his hand over his forehead, sweeping his hair out of his eyes. He was tired. "I can see why you think there are four suspects. Sparling. The animal rights group. Someone in her family. Worthington. I still think she was murdered elsewhere and then dumped. If she was murdered, that is. I looked at the place where she was found and there isn't any blood around. You'd think there'd be lots of it."

Cindy acted impressed. "You're right, Ralph. Why didn't I think of that? Maybe it wasn't from the bear attack that there was that large bloodstain on the back of her jacket."

He snapped back. "We don't know that it was blood in the jacket. The results haven't come back from the lab yet. And I was talking about blood on the ground. There wasn't *any*."

I said, "Rain." I thumbed through google and found the chart I was looking for. "Look." I held my phone up for everyone to see. "There was a record amount of rain in the last two weeks of April, the first week of May. Two huge storms with over a total of two hundred centimetres."

"How did you think of that?"

"The driveway had washed out and we had to repair it before Andrew's party. He called me for a contribution to the repair."

Ralph said, "And now that the case is closed, Kowalchuk won't bring in forensics for trace." He yawned. "I have to go to bed." He looked at me, and said, "Coming?"

Cindy laughed. "Not yet."

Such a dirty mind.

"Oh, yeah," I said. "I'm done. Let's tackle this in the morning."

Ralph and I snuggled a bit until his deep breaths floated in and out of his chest. He was dead to the world. There was no way I could fall asleep. I tossed this way and that, trying not to bounce on the mattress with my enormous weight. I dozed off, thinking of how I believed I wasn't worthy and comparing myself to Cindy and her short penis theory. She had power. She had it figured out. She was worthy. My mind drifted. Kowalchuk's gun. Hunting. The bear charging. I was garbage. The word "unworthy" travelled across my mind, over and over. *Unworthy. Unworthy.* Worthington. The neighbour. The guy who hunted and had bought new gear for next fall. The guy who had bought bear bait and a great big knife. What a creep.

My mind wandered on the edge of sleep. Garbage. Garbage can. No food. I pictured myself shaking it for Cindy. Just an empty bottle of insect repellent rattling around. With the word DOG on it. Insect repellent for a dog. Someone loved their dog. What was that joke about God spelled backwards? Dog, God. Next time I was at my desk, I would look it up. Words. But was it a word? Maybe it was initials. Desk. Suddenly, the white desk in the Gibson's cottage with a name carved in the upper right-hand corner drifted across the film screen of my eyelids. Darlene Olive Gibson. *Oh-h-h.* D.O.G. That bottle of insect repellent wasn't for a dog, it was for Darlene. She was worthy of insect repellent. And then Worthington again. Knife.

Bear bait. Wait. What was the smell in the garbage can? Was it only insect repellent? Maybe it was bear pheromones. What did that smell like? And how would bear pheromones get in the garbage can? I would have to ask Worthington. Maybe it was his garbage can? No, it was ours. Don't be stupid, Robin. Of course, it was ours.

Suddenly my eyes flew open. Holy fuck. *Bingo*. I'd figured it out. All at once, I knew what had made the bear attack. I knew how the bear had been manipulated to kill. Someone had put bear pheromones in Darlene's bottle of insect repellent. Which had then been used by Niemchuk. So both had been attacked. Well, fuck me sideways. That was so clever. What a perfect way to murder a person. But who had access to her insect repellent? And who would do this? Worthington?

Worthington had bear bait. Did he kill Darlene? Was he the one? Not Sparling or her parents or an animal rights group? Creepy Dick with his rural application of justice? But maybe not. Was he smart enough to plan something like that? Maybe. Maybe not.

This was so exciting. I had figured it out. Should I wake up Cindy and Ralph and tell them how a bear had been manipulated to murder? Naw. It could wait. Everyone was tired. I'd tell them in the morning. God knew I was exhausted. But who had filled the bottle with bait? With question marks floating in my head, I finally fell dead asleep.

24.

THE SMELL OF COFFEE floated up the stairs as I staggered down on my sore hip to the living room. Getting old was such a bitch. I rubbed my hands together in front of the roaring fire in the woodstove. I wasn't cold. It was simply a nice habit, something I've always done in front of cheery flames. I looked around. Ralph had been busy this morning. He'd even refilled the wood box after building the fire. Expecting to see him in the yard, I looked out the window over the couch but only saw a bright and sunny day. No Ralph. There was a slight breeze on the lake and the buds on the trees were almost completely open. How fast the spring was turning into summer. It seemed as if it was winter just yesterday and now I was itching to swim in the inviting lake. I was also itching to tell Cindy and Ralph what I had figured out last night. About how the bear had been manipulated to kill.

But where was everyone? Not even Lucky was home. His bed had been abandoned in the corner by the sideboard. I lumbered over and touched its red plaid flannel cover. Still slightly warm. Not long gone then. Next, I hobbled to the harvest table. Ah, a note. Damn, I'd left my glasses upstairs. I squinted my eyes and peered at it. It said, I thought, that Ralph was in town, picking up the phone. Really? Is that what it said? I picked up the piece of paper and held it at arm's-length so I could read it. There was nothing wrong with my eyes. My arms weren't long enough. But yes, that's what it said. Interesting. I wondered if Kowalchuk would let him have it. I guessed that because the case had been closed before the phone had been handed in, the phone wasn't evidence. I knew nothing about police procedure, but this made sense. Besides, Ralph wouldn't be bothered to go get it if he thought it was a lost cause.

But where was Cindy? My slippers scuffed the pine boards as I shuffled through the kitchen and over to the back door. Maybe she was out back, playing with the dog. But the hook beside the door where Lucky's leash usually hung was empty. So, she must be out walking with him. That was nice of her, if not a bit stupid. Her acknowledgement of danger was a tad in the sparse department. But then, she didn't know about the bear bait. Not yet, anyway. And the offending bottle was right by the house in a garbage can, not up the road where she'd be.

I couldn't wait to tell everyone about my startling epiphany last night. That the bear had been manipulated to kill Darlene because someone had filled her insect repellent bottle with bear pheromones. At least I thought so. The residue in the bottle would need to be analyzed. But it made so much sense.

The question was who? Who would be devious enough to think of such a thing? What kind of person would subject someone to the terrifying torture of being mauled to death by a bear? This person would have had to execute the plan well ahead of time. My mind considered the alternatives. Who had access to her stuff? Her family, for sure. Sparling? Maybe not. And the Ursula Major crowd? Who knew? I didn't even know where they were located, although from the comment on Darlene's Facebook page, they looked local. Worthington? Well, maybe. He was in the neighbourhood. Maybe he'd run into her. I would never forget the look in his eyes, the rage, at the thought of losing the land where he hunted. This was a premeditated murder for sure. Not an accident. There was no way her death was an accident. Bottom line, the bottle would have to be tested for pheromones. Maybe Ralph could help with that.

I had to get the bottle, so that I could give it to him. I saw through the window in the kitchen door that the garbage can was still sitting at the bottom of the steps where Ralph had righted it. Did I dare take off the lid and remove the bottle of insect repellent? I'd taken off the lid last night and nothing happened. But now there was no one was around to help me if anything happened, except Mr. Worthington next door. And he might have put his bait in the insect repellent. Some help he'd be. What if the bear was lurking in the woods, its tiny eyes zeroed in on the can? Did I defy the bear and go out and grab the bottle?

I stood by the door and thought about all the risks. Then I slapped my forehead. Oh God, I was so stupid. I didn't have to take to take the lid off *outside*. I could bring the whole can inside and remove the bottle in the safety of the cottage. I was so smart. No, I wasn't. The bear had attacked the can with the lid on. Oh, what to do?

If I brought it inside, would the bear attack the cottage? I thought about this for a minute as I stood by the kitchen door. Would it or wouldn't it? Probably not. The insect repellent had been on the kitchen windowsill before the Niemchuk incident and the bear hadn't attacked then. The best plan, the safest plan, probably, was to get the can and bring it inside. *Probably* was good enough for me. Kind of.

As I opened the kitchen door, I was terrified that I would be attacked and my mind went into safety mode. This was the place where my brain retreated when it was frightened, into a la-la land of inconsequence, where it tried to find a place to relax. This place in my brain was close to the place where the snake lived, hissing away at me, if I let it. The snake was pretty much under control, but I felt its rattle right at that moemnt.

Not to put too fine a point on it, I was frightened out of my skin.

The first thing that crossed my mind as I opened the screen door was the riveting question. Why do we say *the* bear? Why not *a* bear? It was always *the* bear. Like there was only one. For years I had been saying to my kids, "Watch out for the bear." But it wasn't only me. If anyone saw a bear around, they would say, "I saw the bear," and look terrified. And when I had purchased an air horn at Canadian Tire last fall, I'd said to the salesperson that I needed it to scare away *the* bear. As if there were only one bear in the woods. But now I knew better. Now I had proof there was more than one bear. Oh, yes, I did. That event with Niemchuk was a clincher. With this not-so-relaxing thought in my mind, I clutched the banister and shambled down the porch stairs as quickly as I could, my feet swimming in my fake leather slippers. I tripped on the last uneven board, felt my arms windmill as I tried to regain my balance, and fell on my hands and knees in the yard. Fucking slippers. Fucking hip. Fucking getting old. I picked myself off the ground, checked out my palms for bits of gravel embedded in the torn skin, grabbed the garbage can, and hurriedly limped back up the stairs, the garbage can in front of me like a huge pregnant belly.

"Yoo-hoo."

Cindy. Shit. Did she see me fall? How embarrassing. I nonchalantly turned my head and said, "Oh, hi. Thanks for taking Lucky out for a walk. Weren't you worried about the bear?" My left hand was bleeding and my hip hurt like hell.

"Naw. I'm more worried about the person who made the bear kill Darlene." Sounded like Cindy was now firmly onside with the bear manipulation theory. "And I doubt that person is anywhere around here." She clambered up the steps with Lucky and held the door open for me. Her eyes travelled up and down my dishevelled body. "Interesting look."

I was a sight. Naugahyde slippers streaked with a smear of dirt. Stiff hair standing straight up. Worn cottage pyjamas with a faded SpongeBob motif. Ratty old maroon terrycloth housecoat complete with pulled threads. A bleeding hand. And, as a finishing touch, the garbage can. Dressed for success. "I figured out the murder weapon."

Her eyes widened. "Really?" She followed me into the living room and turned her head suddenly to the window. "Oh, there's Ralph."

She was right. He was walking in front of the cottage. I hadn't heard his tires on the gravel. Great. Bad eyesight and dim hearing. Ralph flung open the kitchen door and barged in, holding Darlene's phone in the air. "Got it!"

"Great," said Cindy, meaning not great. "What do you need it for?"

Ralph did an exaggerated Road Runner screeching stop in front of me. "Hi sweetie. Just getting up?"

"I know I look fetching, but I figured out the murder weapon." I gave them a hint by thumping the garbage can on the floor so the rattle of the empty bottle was clearly heard.

Ralph looked at me quizzically. "No offence, and I don't mean to cast aspersions on your puzzle-solving abilities, but we all know she was killed by a bear." He was patting my hair, trying unsuccessfully to tame it.

"True enough. But the bear was made to kill her." I snapped off the black handles holding down the garbage can lid, reached my arm in as far as it would go, and pulled out the empty bottle of insect repellent. I gingerly held it out in front of me as if it were a bomb on a short fuse. In a way, it was. "With this."

Ralph scratched his chin with the edge of Darlene's phone, a smile playing on his lips. "Hmmm. Insect repellent keeps away bugs. It doesn't attract bears."

"Let her explain," said Cindy, my protector.

I padded into the kitchen and got the other bottle of bug spray off the kitchen window ledge. It was comparison time. "We'll do a little test." I took the lid off the empty bottle and held it first under his nose and then under hers. Then I took the lid off the newer bottle of repellent and held it under their noses. "What do you think?"

"All I see is that the old bottle stinks worse, probably because it's old." Ralph had never been hunting in his life, being a city boy. Well, except for criminals, of course. But they weren't attracted to pheromones.

Cindy took a second whiff of the empty bottle and wrinkled her nose. "Wait a second. That empty bottle smells as bad, but it's different. It's sort of musky."

"*Bingo,*" I shouted. "This bottle," I held it up as if I were holding up the hand of a boxing champion, "the one that has the word DOG on it, probably contains bear pheromones. I'll bet any money that if the residue were tested, that's exactly what would show up."

Ralph had not quite bought in to the idea. "So-o-o-o, how did the bear know to attack Darlene and not someone else?"

"D-O-G," I said, spelling it out for him slowly.

He cocked his head, trying to make sense of it. "Did she have a dog? The bear was going for her dog and she tried to save it, getting killed for her trouble?"

"Her initials were 'D-O-G.' *Darlene Olive Gibson.* She'd written 'DOG' on her bottle of insect repellent so no one at work would take it. But someone did. And they filled it with bear bait. She didn't have a chance. Just like Niemchuk didn't. She must have sprayed herself with it before going into the woods, and that's why she was attacked. I am sure. If you google 'bear pheromones' it says to not get it on your clothes or skin for that very reason. Bears go wild over that stuff and will move mountains to get to it."

"But how do you know the bottle was used by her? And why is it in your cottage?"

Sometimes I got so frustrated by Ralph. Why couldn't he believe me? He wanted fucking details. I hoped I was smiling patiently but my voice sounded a little clipped, even to my ears. To be fair, he didn't know the bottle's history.

"Cindy and I found it in the woods when we were out exploring the next-door property. The same day we found her body. Who else would it belong to? Not many people go into those woods except us. Not many people have the initials D.O.G. I guess we could have it checked for fingerprints, and if hers are on it we would know for sure. I mean, go ahead and send it to the lab." He nodded, so I was halfway there to getting it analyzed. "So, we brought it home, rather than have it littering up the environment. Also, I doubt many people would write the word 'DOG' on their insect repellent. I mean, who puts insect repellent on their dog?" I thought about this for a second. "I guess lots of people do, but not this kind. They use citronella and geranium oil and various natural alternatives. But not this commercial brand. It's way too poisonous for dogs."

Cindy huffed. She was always hammering away at me about how I fed my dog organic food, but thought nothing of eating a full bag of neon-coloured cheese puffs myself.

"Anyway, that's why I think it was her bottle. I found it in the woods and brought it back here. Niemchuk saw it on the windowsill and used it up, throwing the empty bottle into the garbage can. That's how it ended up in our cottage. That's why he was attacked as well."

"Let me get this straight. You think someone took her bottle, probably from her work or home, filled it with bear bait, and then put it back so she would use it in the woods and get killed by a bear? Is that what you're thinking?" Ralph was shaking his head, digesting the information.

"Exactly! But why are you looking like that?"

"I believe that it's certainly a possibility," he was being polite, "but who would ever think of such a thing? I've seen a lot of despicable actions, but this is disgusting. It's a sociopath's idea of a practical joke."

"But you think it's possible? I do." This from Cindy, the world's best skeptic. She had seen things that other people could do to each other and was no longer surprised by truly cruel acts.

Ralph hated to give her an inch, but he said, "It makes more sense than any other idea we've had." He reached into his pocket. "Here, Robin. I have an evidence bag. Give the bottle to me and I'll take it to the lab. I'll get it worked up. Contents, fingerprints, the whole enchilada. I'm heading back to Toronto later today for an early shift tomorrow."

He's leaving? News to me. But did I hear him say "the other ideas we've had?" There was no "we" about this. *I* thought of it. I stood up for myself. "*I've had.* Any other idea than *I've had.*"

He looked sheepish. "You're right. Your idea."

I accepted this apology and let it go. Thank heavens for my Buddhist practice. Then I said, "Kowalchuk gave you the phone." It wasn't a question.

"He said the case was closed. The phone was redundant."

"I don't know why he's so shut down over this. I find it bizarre. You'd think he'd want to solve her death. What's wrong with you cops, anyway?" Cindy had a hand on her hip, challenging Ralph.

Ralph met her head-on. "He believes what he believes. That it was an accident. Pure and simple. Me? I'm open to other ideas. That's why I wanted to examine her phone myself. I doubt he even looked at it." He sat down at the table and tapped the phone open. "I'm going to look at all her digital stuff, going back about six months. This is going to take a little time." He sighed and took off his jacket.

I looked at Cindy. "While he's doing that, did you have breakfast? I'm starving."

"I had a piece of toast, but I could eat some fruit or something."

I beelined into the kitchen, my hip feeling more mobile now that I'd been moving around a bit. "How about bacon and eggs, pancakes and maple syrup?"

"You won't want to eat any lunch if you eat all that, Robin. Have a small bowl of cereal or a piece of toast."

"What? Are you my mother?"

Cindy sighed. Loudly.

But she was right. I definitely had to get my weight under control. But I loved maple syrup. Maybe I could put some on my cereal. Or my toast. I know: I'd fry the toast in some egg and put maple syrup on that. French toast. "How about some French toast?"

"Robin."

"Oh, okay, you're right. Lunch is in a couple of hours. I'll have cereal." With some maple syrup on it, I added mentally.

Cindy and I placed our bowls of cereal at the pine table while Ralph sat at the far end thumbing through the contents of Darlene's phone and writing notes. He had great hands. His sinewy fingers dwarfed a small pen as he wrote a word or two. From the frequency of the taps he made on the phone, I could tell he was searching through her Facebook, going through all the comments to her posts. Lucky was lying on his bed in the corner, his soft snores picking up pace when he dreamed, his paws twitching while he chased imaginary rabbits. Every now and then, Ralph looked up and smiled at me, causing my heart to beat a little stronger deep in my chest. It was a peaceful scene and I could feel myself settling down after my adventure of getting the garbage can. Even my scabbed-up hands felt better. There was no hissing snake, or stupid thoughts, merely the comforting sounds of spoons tinkling against the sides of bowls, a dog's snuffles, and the scratching of pen on paper. Even Ralph's tapping on the phone had slowed down. He was probably going through her emails now. Life was good. I was sitting at a beautiful wooden table with two of my best friends.

Wait? Did I say "two?" Was Ralph now a friend as well as a lover? I'd have to think about that. And Cindy? She drove me fucking nuts. Taking risks and telling me what to do. But she was such a support and I loved her. I gave her a smile and she smiled back. Hard to imagine that a day ago, we had witnessed a truly violent act of a bear attacking a person. Cindy had been so kind to me, with the blanket and the tea. And poor Darlene. Poor, poor Darlene. Her final moments must have been horrible.

"Holy shit."

I jerked my head toward Ralph. He never swore. Never. He said cops can't swear on the job and he had gotten out of the habit. Me? Journalists swore all the fucking time. Whatever he read must be big. "What have you found?"

"I guess the two of you didn't look at Darlene's most recent emails. You did a random sampling?"

"That's right." Cindy was on the edge of her chair, leaning forward. She didn't like not being perfect. Me? I didn't give a rat's ass. I was never perfect. Unless I was drunk, and then I was perfect all the time.

"Why Ralph, what did you find?" I was so curious.

He leaned back in his chair. "Her very last email to Dave Sparling. Let me read the whole thread to you, starting from the beginning." He leaned forward, tapped the tiny screen to open the email, and then scrolled through to the bottom. "This is from her to him. *Hi, Tiger*." Ralph looked up at us. "*Hi, Tiger*, he read again, *sorry about that court business, my family made me. But I didn't let on that we were an item. No one saw your emails. So, don't worry about evidence for the civil suit either. I've missed you so badly. I had to move to Huntsville,, but I was wondering if you could come up and we could meet, you know, in secret, like we used to. Love, your pussycat*. That sure sounds to me like she loved him. Looks like he's off the hook as far as a suspect goes."

Cindy fiery temper was unleashed. "Are you crazy? Even if she did love him that doesn't mean he loved her. He was probably using her. Famous stage star? Lowly set designer? A classic abuse of power. Plus, you don't know if she loved him. Maybe she *thought* she was in love with him. Maybe she was actually terrified of him because of things he'd done to her. Fear and love are easy to confuse. They're both strong emotions. We know nothing. Or maybe she was luring him here, so she could confront him. Who knows. We can't ask her. She's dead."

That was quite the speech from my politically active friend. But maybe I disagreed with both of them. Maybe she was luring him to Huntsville to get more evidence, not relying just on the emails in her personal phone for her civil suit. It was interesting that she said there was no evidence against him. That was a flat-out lie. "Read his reply, Ralph," I said.

He pushed his glasses up the bridge of his nose with his forefinger and looked at Cindy before he started to read again. "*My dear little kitten, I'd love to see you. I understand from friends that you're working for the town, measuring plots in the wilderness. Maybe we could walk in the woods. I'll bring a blanket for us to lie on. I have to be in Huntsville on Saturday to go to a party on Peninsula Lake. Love, Tiger Boy.* Any comments?"

Fear was prickling my skin. The only party I knew about on Peninsula Lake was my brother's annual bash, the first Saturday in May. "My brother has an annual party on the first weekend of May every year. Sparling was invited this year." I saw Ralph's puzzled glance. "He manages Sparling's money," I said by way of an explanation. "So, he was here, and I guess he met her then."

Cindy was clicking her long nails on the table. She was thinking. "This doesn't mean he killed her. There are other suspects. Someone in her family. Ursula Major."

I piped up. "And don't forget creepy Dick Worthington. He insinuated he would kill anyone who came between him and his hunting ground. He lived in her neighbourhood. He had motive. He had opportunity."

Ralph looked at me, taking it all in. "Let me read you her reply to him." He sat forward and found his place on the phone. "Okay, here it is. *I can't wait to see you! You're talking about*

Andrew MacFarland's party, right? I'll be working right next door that Saturday, overtime, measuring plots. Why don't we meet in town at the Swiss Chalet at 12:30 and then head out there for a walk in the woods? I can show you how I do my new job!"

I was holding my breath. Had my brother somehow been involved in this murder? "What did he say?"

"*Hi Puss in Boots, won't people recognize me there? Do you know a more out-of-the-way place?*" Ralph looked up at us, then continued. "And she replied, *This is Huntsville before tourist season. No one would recognize you. I'll wear my boots. Puss.*"

Ralph knew I was having difficulty and gave me the sweetest smile. It didn't calm me down. This was terrible. He said, "Just because they met didn't mean he killed her, Robin. There are three other suspects."

Cindy nodded in agreement.

I whispered, "What did he say, Ralph?"

He grimaced and then read, "He wrote, *Meow. Swiss Chalet it is. Bring your computer so you can show me all the places you work while we eat. And then a lovely walk. Don't forget your phone so we can text each other if we get separated in the woods. We can lie down on my blanket under the trees. It'll be buggy but I would love to lie down in the woods with you and have some fun. Bring your insect repellent! I can't wait to eat you all up. The tiger is as hungry as a bear.*"

"The guy's a sicko," I said. I felt like throwing up.

25.

"WELL, THAT KINDA sews it up," I said.

"Not really," said Ralph. "I say 'hungry as a bear' sometimes too. It's a common idiom."

"And no," agreed Cindy. "No, it doesn't sew it up." Cindy spoke as if she was correcting a toddler. Sometimes, she really did drive me fucking nuts. I felt like they were ganging up on me.

"Not really," she said, probably because she had caught my look. "Simply because he had motive and opportunity doesn't mean he did it. I mean, you have to admit, it is pretty incriminating. But I think we should research Ursula Major, find out where they're located, see if they had any opportunity. Plus, there's Worthington to consider. And of course, we need to talk to Sandra and Harry."

Ralph asked, "Who are Sandra and Harry?"

"Her weird parents," she replied.

"Okay, well why don't you two research the Ursula crowd, talk to the parents and Worthington, and get back to me."

"Actually, why don't you get the contents of that bottle analyzed and get back to us?"

There was always a power struggle between those two.

Ralph shook his head, put the phone on the table, and said as he was walking to the stairs, "I have to get packed. I need to be in the city by four o'clock to get this to the lab and to see my kids for dinner. I made a Thursday night plan with them weeks ago."

I didn't blame him for wanting to get back to Toronto. He and Cindy just didn't see eye to eye. "I'm going to be heading home in a few days, so I'll see you soon," I called up the stairs after him. No answer. Maybe he didn't hear me.

Cindy said, "Once we talk to the parents and Worthington, there really isn't much more to do around here. That Kowalchuk is a piece of work and Andrechuk and I would never be an item. She's way not my type. But maybe you and I will have fun. With the blackflies."

Cindy looked a little wistful as she said this. I tried to console her. "I'm sorry it's been so hard for you to find a partner, Cindy. But don't worry, someone will come along who you'll find completely charming."

"Right," she said briskly. "Do you want to go to the Gibson's now, before lunch?"

She was asking me, not telling? Well, wasn't that different. "Sure, I'll get myself together." I headed to the stairs as Ralph was coming down, his overnight bag clutched in his hand. "See you soon, sweetheart," I said. I knew that a "sweetheart" didn't quite match the L- word. But it was the best I could do.

He stopped at the bottom of the stairs in front of me. "This hasn't been the greatest visit, has it?" He took my face in his hand and tilted it so that he could kiss me. He whispered in my ear, "I do love you, you know. We will work out this drinking problem together."

Every time he said the L-word my innards cringed. How did I feel about him? I really didn't know. I stuttered, "Sure we will. We can talk about it later," and then I croaked, "honey."

One evening, after I'd had a few drinks.

He kissed me again at the bottom of the stairs and I could feel his body pressing against mine. Naturally, I pressed back. And there it was, that *zing* again. "See you later, alligator."

I stroked his bum and said, "Safe trip" over my shoulder as I climbed the stairs.

When I came down all spruced up, I could see Cindy playing

with Lucky off-leash in the yard. She was tossing him a ball. I paused for a minute as I watched them through the window over the couch. She was laughing at him gamboling around and he had his tongue hanging out with a big smile on his face. They were so cute together. But why did I get angry at Ralph for letting the dog off his leash and not Cindy? The universe was a mysterious place. I threw on my jacket and met them on the sodden grass. "Hiya. I'll take Lucky inside and meet you in the car."

"Car? You're calling that jalopy a car? Isn't that a bit of a reach?"

"Layoff my wheels. I love that car," I shouted as I dragged Lucky inside. After settling Lucky on his bed, I picked up the garbage can that was still in the living room and placed it at the bottom of the porch steps where it belonged. Cindy was leaning over the gear shift and putting some lipstick on in the rear-view mirror.

"Your visor doesn't have a mirror on the flip side."

"Duh. Have you finally stopped looking for one?"

I clanked the car into gear and headed out to the Gibson's for the second time in two days. This time, I didn't call ahead. I wasn't in the mood for talking about precious Andrew and more importantly, I wanted to catch them off-guard. I wanted to know exactly what it was that the Gibson family had done to Darlene that Sparling shouldn't have done. If they were unsettled by a sudden visit, they might blurt something out. While I drove, Cindy focused on her phone, her long nails hitting the screen with sharp little clicks.

"What are you looking at?"

"I'm googling *Ursula Major*, and I found them. They're a very small group of left-wing activists in Maine, USA. They were founded about twenty years ago to stop logging and logging roads through the Allagash Wilderness Waterway."

"Never heard of it. But more importantly, how did they hear about Darlene?"

"We can ask Alison. She'd know how they were made aware of her, but I'm guessing that they have alerts on their computers for certain words like 'wilderness' and other things that would threaten habitats."

"That makes sense. But wouldn't there be thousands of hits? Thousands of alerts?"

"They probably used two or three additional words to narrow it down like 'lake,' or 'river.' And maybe they divided North America into zones, with each member taking a zone to monitor." She focused on her tiny screen. "Doesn't look like they had anything to do with Darlene's death. They're miles away." I could see out of the corner of my eye that she was looked at the scenery around her. "Sure is pretty around here. I love the rocky outcrops."

"Yeah, me too. But I think we need to ask her parents if she had come in any contact with them."

"Hey, isn't that Worthington up there walking ahead of us down the road? Sure looks like that ratty bush jacket he was wearing the other day."

I peered through the windshield at the figure sauntering along the side of the road. "Yup, that's him. Should we talk to him now or get him at home?"

"Now. He seems to be on the road a lot. This way, we can catch him. Besides, it'll throw him off-balance."

I slowed the car down and crunched to a stop on the gravel beside him. Cindy rolled down her window, so he could hear us. "Hi, Mr. Worthington," I shouted over her.

"What do you want now?"

Friendly sort. "Only wondering how you felt about that land being sold beside us." Why bother beating around the bush?

He leaned into Cindy's window. "I don't give a shit."

Really? I was speechless. This from the guy who had threatened death if someone destroyed where he hunted? I was completely taken aback. Cindy rescued me.

"But what about your hunting grounds?" She was pressing

against me, trying to get away from Worthington who was bent over with his arms on the ledge of the car window, breathing his disgusting fumes into the car.

"They can have the fucking land. What do I care? Not much deer or bear around here now anyways. Heard the cops shot one over there. Assholes. I saved up some money. I'm going to buy me a camp up near Novar. A buddy of mine wants to sell up. The cancer got him."

"Sorry to hear about your friend. So, you're buying another hunt camp? You don't care about the land beside us?" I was incredulous.

"That's what I said, missy. You deaf?" Some spittle flew out of his mouth onto Cindy's arm. She didn't flinch.

"Well, glad you're okay with it. See you around." My car stunk. I couldn't wait to get away.

He extricated himself from Cindy's window as I pulled off the shoulder. It wasn't until we were out of his sight that she pulled a tissue out of her purse and wiped the spit off her arm. "*Ugh*. That poor man. He really has gone way down."

Every now and then, Cindy surprised me. "Yes, he has. But it looks like he didn't have anything to do with Darlene's death either. No motive. So that's two suspects down. Ursula Major and Worthington."

"No, he's simply a sad old man."

The minutes ticked by and we drove in silence until we were at Moot Point. "Here's the Gibson's driveway."

As I drove the car through the brush-lined lane, once again Cindy's head snapped back every time a branch flicked at the car. "Slow the fuck down," she barked.

"I can't go any slower. This is it. Otherwise, the car will get stuck in the ruts."

"You're already stuck in a rut."

We were nervous about trapping the Gibsons in their web of lies. Had they murdered their own daughter? That would be an efficient way to hide family secrets. Their cottage loomed up ahead. My hands were sweating on the steering wheel. "What's our approach?"

"South by southwest."

"Cindy. Stop kidding around. We're almost there. We need a plan."

"Honesty is never the best policy."

"C'mon Cindy. We need a plan."

"Let's see how it unfolds. We know what we want." She talked in a falsetto. "Put it out there into the universe. The answer will come back. The wisdom will float to the surface. The courage will appear to act on the intention. Chanting will reveal all."

"Don't make fun of me."

She laughed. "Okay, Miss Sensitivity. But really, let's see how it unfolds. We want a motive and a confession."

"Good luck with that. And I mean it. Don't make fun of my Buddhist practice."

"*O-o-m-m-m-m.*" She hummed. "That's a dyslexic cow. Get it? *M-o-o-o-o-o?* Backwards? *O-o-m-m-m-m.*"

Geezus. I tried to ignore her. "There's Harry, still scraping away at that old boat. And yikes, here comes the giant spider."

"She better not try to hug me."

Sandra teetered on her heels, waving her arms and signalling for me to stop. "Hello, don't come any further, it gets muddy here. You'll get stuck."

I obliged and parked the car between two trees. "Hi, Mrs. Gibson."

"Sandra."

She stepped forward, arms out for an embrace. I stepped backwards.

"Thought we'd come back and clear a few things up."

"What, as journalists? About Darlene's death?" Red-hot emotion flared across her face.

Harry had put down his scraper and was walking over to the car. "Hey, honey," he said, putting his arm through his wife's. "What's going on here?" He'd sensed the pulsating reverberations in the air.

Cindy stepped forward, overshadowing the couple. With her imposing height and sinewy muscles, she probably looked quite threatening. Well, good. If these two were murderers, I wanted Cindy around. "Just a few questions."

"We've been hounded by the press enough. We don't have to answer your questions. I don't want any more written about poor Darlene. Imagine a bear killing her. That was a horrible death." Sandra's face crumpled and she clutched at her chest. She looked like she was preventing her heart from shattering. Harry rubbed her back in an ineffective gesture to soothe her, his own face contorted in grief.

While watching Darlene's parents grapple with their overwhelming grief, my suspicions about them as murderers drifted out the window. They weren't acting. They might be unusual in their behaviour, but that didn't make them killers. I didn't think they had done it. That was my instinct. But then again, there was that email. I lightly tugged Cindy's arm to let her know I wanted her to step back and give the Gibson's some breathing space. She stood firm.

"How did you learn she was killed by a bear?"

Sandra looked surprised by the question and glanced at her husband. He shook his head. "That huge police officer told us. What was his name, honey?"

Sandra answered, "Kowalchuk. I didn't like him much. Officious."

Sandra went up in my estimation.

Harry continued, "Yes, Kowalchuk. When he came to tell us about Darlene's remains. I don't know why she was attacked. She always carried bear spray. She knew what to do if a bear charged her. It's too much for me to fathom." Harry's eyes widened in an effort to keep the tears that were swimming around his rims from escaping down his cheeks.

Sandra wept openly, her sobs punctuating her words. "She

was in the woods working. She worked all the time. Overtime. She was such a good person. Even on weekends, she would go out and do her measuring. There was so much to do, you know. She really wanted to do a good job. Such a good girl."

There was no way these two had killed their daughter. One by one, my questions were being answered. Darlene was no neophyte in the woods. But where was her bear spray? I didn't see it near her body. And what about that email from her parents? The one that said only they were allowed to do what Sparling was doing to Darlene? What did they mean by that? Why had Mrs. Gibson, Sandra, written that?

Like a radar-directed missile, Cindy whizzed out the next question. "What was Sparling doing to Darlene that only her family should be allowed to do?"

The blood drained from Sandra's face and her husband clutched her arm tightly. Was Sandra going to faint? "How do you know about that?"

"Emails." Cindy was triumphant.

"But we couldn't find her computer or her phones. She had two, you know. Work and personal. Both are missing. How do you know about her emails?"

I stepped between Cindy and the parents. "I found her personal phone, Mrs. Gibson. Yesterday, when you were showing me her room, I found it inside Spooky's hidden pouch. I'm sorry." I felt as if I had violated her daughter. I felt terrible.

"No, don't apologize, dear. At least it was finally found. But how did you read her emails? Wasn't her phone password protected?"

Cindy answered, "No. But what was Sparling doing?"

"That was just like her, our Darlene, just like her. Trusting the world. I told her to put a password on it. She only laughed at me."

So far, they hadn't answered Cindy's question. I softened my voice. "You can tell me, Sandra. What was Sparling doing that only her family should do?"

"He was paying her rent." She spat out the words like a ball of slimy phlegm.

I was floored. Really? They were hiding this measly fact? *This* made them encourage her to charge him with sexual assault? "But why would you encourage her to have him charged for sexual assault? Surely, this was a nice gesture on his part?"

"I disagree. If he's paying her rent, what does she owe him? What was he making her do? And we couldn't come out and say we believed he was abusing her because maybe he wasn't. She wouldn't talk about their relationship. We really didn't know what the story was. So, we had to couch it in normal terms."

"Normal terms?" It was hardly "normal" to me. I had interpreted that email to mean that only they were allowed to abuse her. All my ideas supporting their guilt in killing their child were shot down. And if Darlene was working overtime on Saturdays, that would put Sparling in the frame. He was in Huntsville on a Saturday to go to Andrew's party. I wondered if Cindy had caught the reference to overtime.

Throughout the conversation Harry had regained his composure. "That's why we wanted her to come home. If she couldn't afford Toronto rent, then she should be with us and make her way in a town where she could build a life and become financially independent."

Sandra shook off her husband's arm. "I don't understand why she hid the phone. I don't understand why she didn't give the police all the evidence she had. Was there incriminating evidence in her emails that Sparling was taking advantage of her?"

Cindy finally stepped back. I felt she was coming to the same conclusion I had. These people were innocent. Odd, but innocent. She spoke softly in a soothing voice. "Sometimes, not all the time, but sometimes, when there is an abuse of power, the abuser seems to have an almost magical power over his victim. Sort of like the Stockholm Syndrome. You've heard of that?"

They both nodded. Sandra said, "Patty Hearst, right? She fell in love with her kidnappers."

"Sort of like that. Her kidnappers gave her food and water and she depended upon them for her survival. She was terrified of them because of their power to cause her death, but she interpreted her powerful feelings for her captors as feelings of love in order to survive. If she had acknowledged the powerful emotion she was feeling for what it truly was, fear, she would have to acknowledge her situation, which would have been too terrifying. It would have driven her crazy. It was like that for Darlene. Sparling had power over her. He controlled her job and her housing, and she was dependent upon him. She was deeply frightened of him because of what he could do to her. He could destroy where she lived. He could destroy her job. But like Patty Hearst, she interpreted her fear as love in order to stay sane. He took full advantage of that. I'm sorry to say that he did in fact, use, and abuse, her."

Harry Gibson's eyes looked upwards as he was working it all out. "She hid her phone and the evidence because she was protecting him. She thought she loved him and he loved her."

"Exactly," said Cindy.

"All this is fine and dandy, but our daughter is still dead." Harry's eyes bugged out as anger overcame him. "So, I want to know why you came by here asking all these questions. She was mauled to death by a bear, and yet you're acting as if there was foul play." He put his hand on his chest. "Surely you didn't suspect me. Us."

Sandra was strutting around in circles, flapping her arms. She squawked, "Fowl play, fowl play, fowl play." The woman had lost it. Harry was looking at her in alarm.

I nudged Cindy. "I think it's time to go."

"Wait," she whispered, "I want to ask them about Ursula Major."

"No, Cindy. It's time to go. Give these poor people their privacy."

"You're a scaredy-cat. She can deal with a few more questions," she bickered.

My snake was hissing in my head. Sandra was winging her arms wildly. Harry was staring at us accusingly. I walked slowly backwards to the car while Sandra flapped and walked in circles. Cindy shook her head once and then gave up, following me reluctantly.

Behind us, I could hear Sandra laughing her head off. "Oh Harry, don't you see how funny it is? Fowl play."

Cindy snapped her seatbelt on, looked at me, and said, "Chickenshit." Then she hooted at her joke.

I was surrounded by hilarity.

Harry's reply to his wife seeped through Cindy's mirth. "It's okay, sweetheart. It's okay."

As I reversed the car out from between the two trees, I watched him leading her to the house, patting her shoulder. My heart went out to them. There was probably no greater shock than losing your child the way they had. They were odd, but they did love her.

Sometimes, Cindy was really harsh.

26.

CINDY SETTLED BACK into her seat, a smug smile on her face. She thought she was so amusing. I didn't like it.

"Listen Cindy, what happened back there wasn't funny. Sandra's heart has been broken and she's coping the best she can. The last thing I wanted to do was escalate the idea that Darlene had been murdered. That I was casting around for suspects. That she was one of them. That would have been too much for her to bear."

Cindy mimicked me, "To bear," and laughed again. "Get it?"

It was like being with a six-year-old.

"Okay, now that we all know what a great sense of humour you have, let's move forward. I liked your summary of why Darlene hid her personal phone, but still, I'm wondering if she hid it because she was planning to use those emails in her civil suit. She wanted to keep her phone safe."

"I doubt it," said Cindy. "I got to know her a bit during my interview and she was really just an innocent young woman. I don't think she was conniving like that."

"Whatever. We may never know. Anyway, it doesn't look like Ursula Major had anything to do with Darlene's death, and I really don't think her parents did either. Dick Worthington might have anger management issues, but he doesn't have the smarts to plan such an attack. Plus, he bought a new place to hunt. So, there's no motive. What do you think?"

Cindy was rubbing her arms as if she were cold. Maybe

joking around was her way of coping with horror. She had been like that in the forest, a professional clown, after discovering the torso. "I agree with you, Robin. I don't think her parents could have done it. They somehow don't seem capable of planning something this intricate, although they would have complete access to her bottle of insect repellent. But no motive. That idea has flown the coop." She chuckled at herself. I pursed my lips.

"And the Allagash people? They are simply too far removed. They might have the motive, for sure: They don't want wilderness divvied into plots of land for sale. But there are a lot of people who believe that as well. And besides, the Ursula Major group are too far away. Wrong country, for a start. Maybe there are some people here in Huntsville who hold a strong belief about preserving wilderness, like you and me, but basically the people around here, I'm guessing the cottagers anyway, are more sophisticated than murdering to achieve an end. They'd rather litigate people to death while drinking glasses of white wine. And Worthington is a misguided redneck. So, I agree with you. The parents didn't do it The environmental group didn't do it. And Worthington didn't do it. So, maybe we were wrong. Maybe her death was simple. Maybe the bottle smelled awful because it was simply old. No pheromones. Death by misadventure looks pretty good."

"Not really." I knew the bear had been manipulated. "That leaves Sparling," I said decisively.

"Sparling? No way. How do you figure that? He was found innocent. He had no motive. He can't be retried for the same crime."

"I know-w-w." Did she think I was stupid? "He was supposedly innocent of criminal sexual assault. But, now, we're looking at a murder. He can be tried for something different. Besides, Darlene could have launched a dynamite lawsuit. Think about it. There was an email trail of their relationship a mile long. I think she had two email accounts, one on her computer, which is missing, and a personal one that was only on her phone. People do that. So that might be why his emails to her never surfaced at his trial. He had to get rid of her before that evidence came to light before the lawsuit. Maybe he caught wind of what she was planning."

Cindy looked thoughtful as she checked her makeup in the rear-view mirror. "True. Yeah, you're right. That would make him nervous. He could lose everything, including his reputation. Assholes with no respect for women and no boundaries don't stop at just one. If he's done it once, he's likely guilty of doing it more often. Other victims of his might be motivated to come forward and press sexual assault charges if he lost a lawsuit. And that would certainly open up a whole new can of worms. He could end up in jail after all. But good luck proving he murdered her."

"There could be more evidence to be found. Somewhere." I knew I was reaching. "Maybe his fingerprints will be on the bottle of insect repellent. Maybe there will be some security film coverage of them in the Swiss Chalet. Maybe it will show him doctoring up the bottle. Maybe there will be some trace evidence of him being in the woods with her. Maybe tire tracks or something by the entrance to the property. Maybe they could match the soil type with what's on his hiking boots to place him at the scene. Maybe her computer is in his house. Maybe her work phone is there. And maybe that's where her bear spray is."

"Soil trace? That's pretty clever. How did you think of that?'

"I saw it on *Law and Order*. Surely there'll be some evidence. And there's always the emails. He was in the neighbourhood, so he had opportunity, right about the time it's figured she died. He met with her for lunch. They had a plan to walk in the woods. Right where she died."

"Kowalchuk closed the case. Remember?"

"It can be reopened. It's not like he was tried for murder and found innocent. He was tried for sexual assault. A completely different kettle of fish. Ralph is taking the bug spray bottle to forensics. Who knows what they will find."

Cindy's phone belted out "Jingle Bells." Really? "Jingle Bells?" It was almost summer. I gave her a look.

As she was thumbing in her password she said to me, "What? I haven't had time to change it." She lifted the phone to her ear. "Hello?... Okay... Right... I think so... Three hours... Thanks for the tip, Doug." She disconnected and looked at me, "I guess you figured out that I have to go back to Toronto today. That was Doug. There's been a gang-style execution. Restaurant owner on College Street. I have to cover it."

I hated it when her phone rang. Every story she wrote put her close to danger. I hated it almost as much as I hated Ralph's phone ringing. Ralph. He'd only been gone an hour and I missed him already. But, I didn't want to leave quite yet. I had a full week booked off with pay. And a gas card. But then there was Ralph. He was probably passing Barrie on the highway right about now. I guess I could cut my week short. Three more days of being in the cottage alone didn't sound like fun. But I'd have to do laundry and tidy up the place. That would take at least a day. Right, I'd stay one more day. "I'm going to stay another night. But I'll drive you to the bus." Cindy hated the bus.

"What time will you leave tomorrow?"

So, she was going to negotiate. Well, I wanted her to stay tonight, at least. As lovely as Pair o' Dice was, I had been thoroughly unsettled by the events of the past few days. A night alone wasn't that attractive. There wasn't anything more I could do on the Darlene story here. The bug spray bottle was in the lab in Toronto. Everything was going to be revealed in the city. Besides, I could see Ralph. "I could go in the morning if we rush around cleaning tonight."

"Thanks, that might work." She did a quick google search of the gang hit and then pressed redial. "Hi Doug, I spoke too soon. Robin and I have been working on a story here in Huntsville and I need the rest of today to wrap it up.... Yes. I know it's good to be on it, but the gang story's already broken at the other three papers and I'm better at the analysis anyway. It's not like we're going to be scooped.... Good idea, no worries, she's doing a good job. See you tomorrow.... Thanks."

"Well, that sounds like you can stay another night. I'm glad. I didn't really want to stay by myself. Lucky's great, but he isn't a scintillating conversationalist."

"I was planning on reading."

"Bitch."

She laughed. "What do you feel like for lunch?"

"Oh, nothing difficult. I have no idea what's in the fridge. Maybe a salad?"

"Great idea. Grilled cheese it is."

"Right," I said, smiling. As I pulled up to the cottage, Lucky came bouncing off the porch to greet us. Lucky was outside? How could that be? I watched him bound over to the car, worry coursing through my veins. "Cindy? Why is Lucky outside? I put him in, didn't I? Before we left? I'm pretty sure I did. You were playing with him in the yard and I dragged him in. I shut the door behind me firmly. I haven't lost my mind completely, have I?"

Cindy was opening her car door. "No. I saw you put him in the cottage. This is giving me the willies. But there's no car here. Maybe he escaped."

I grabbed Lucky's collar and pulled him back up the porch steps while Cindy followed behind. I immediately saw the back door gaping wide. I knew I had shut it. As I opened the screen door, my heart was rattling around in my chest. Worry about a heart attack zipped across my mind. Then I detected a man's figure silhouetted in the living-room doorway. My heart thudded even harder in my chest and I signalled for Cindy to stay behind me with my hand. As if I, at five-foot-two, could protect her, at six feet. Lucky was straining to get into the cottage. I called out, "Hi Ralph, we're back." I hoped my voice sounded confident. Whoever was in the living room would be tricked into thinking there was a guy around. I hoped.

The figure loomed closer. I still couldn't make out his features. My eyes were having trouble adjusting to the comparative gloom from the brightness outside and the man was backlit by the living-room window. I stood as tall as I could while holding on to the dog's collar.

"Hi ,Robin. Cindy. Where have you been?"

I knew that voice. It was Andrew. That dickhead, frightening me like that. "You nearly scared the shit out of me, Andrew. Why didn't you call? You knew I would be here."

"You've made such a mess." He flung his hand wide. "There's dirt on the kitchen floor and devices scattered everywhere."

Pompous asshole. Be kind, Robin. He's OCD. "The police brought in that dirt. But how did you get here? I didn't see your car in the driveway."

"I came with a client. He's in town getting some sushi and wine."

"Oh, a rich kind of client. *La-di-dah.*" I was making fun of him. He ignored me.

"That's why I left the place pristine. Our retreat was planned weeks ago at my party."

"We were talking on the phone a few days ago. You didn't mention you were coming up. Not that I don't appreciate all the cleaning you did."

"It must have slipped my mind. And I cleaned after the party because theatre people are very sensitive to their surroundings."

Theatre people? As far as I knew the only theatre person at his party was Sparling. I was getting a very bad feeling about this. "Oh," I asked nonchalantly, "who's with you?"

"You wouldn't know him. The last time you saw a show was in the fifth century.

He was right. But still. "Whatever. What famous actor drove you up?"

"Dave Sparling. He was the star of *Cruise Away*. Remember? Ran for months. He's got millions."

Oh great. Cindy and I were going to be in the same cottage as a guy we thought was a murderer. A smart one. "Well, isn't that niiiiccce." "You staying the night? We're not leaving until the morning."

"Why? What have you got against him? He's a great guy."

"I don't know about that. But I thought you didn't like him because of the way he behaved at your party. Oh right. He has moooolahhhh." I drew out that word too, to make my point. "And he was in that court case. Charged with sexual assault."

"*Pfft*. That was dismissed. No evidence. He'd never do that. Just a bunch of women jumping on the entertainment industry sexual assault bandwagon. It's all the rage."

Cindy stiffened. "Yes, Andrew, 'all the rage' is right."

He raised his hand with disdain and banished her comment with a deft flick of his fingers. "I've tidied up and let's hope the place stays that way."

"Cindy and I are going to make lunch. Maybe your rich and famous actor will be back in time so we can all eat together." Joy of joys.

"Look, you know I don't really like him either, but he is a client, and that means money for me. It was my money that put on the new metal roof."

I loved emotional blackmail and gave him the finger. Andrew huffed out of the room. Cindy was digging in the fridge and slapped the cheese on the counter. "God, what a misogynist."

"Oh, yeah." I whispered so he wouldn't hear. He was my brother and I had to get along with him, at least a little. "And look, here comes another one."

A shiny BMW was pulling up beside my car in the driveway and stopped at the very edge of the grass. The long, lanky figure of Dave Sparling emerged carrying a black cloth shopping bag. He took his own bags to the store? A murderer with a conscience? I looked him up and down. He was wearing cowboy boots, a checkered red shirt, faded jeans, and there was some grey stubble on his square chin. About six-foot-two and a hundred and eighty pounds, he was the epitome of The Marlborough Man. His tight little ass strutted across the gravel driveway onto the sodden grass. I was pleased to see mud oozing over the edges of his tooled leather boots.

Andrew called jovially from the living room, "Speak of the devil!"

Yeah, right, speak of the devil. This should be a barrel of laughs. Sparling flung open the kitchen door and then stood stock-still, arms slightly raised. He was making an entrance. Geezus.

His voice boomed, "You must be Robin, Andrew's sister, and you," he turned to Cindy, "are Cynthia Dale. The notorious crime reporter for *The Toronto Express*. I recognize you from your online profile. Looks like the picture was taken some time ago." Cindy bristled. He stretched out his arms and clasped Cindy's hand in his left and mine in his right. I felt like puking. "How nice to finally meet you, Robin. You're with the Home and Garden section? Am I right?"

I withdrew my hand and molded my face into what I hoped was a smile. Fucking jerk. "That's me." I was playing the innocent. "Flower shows and home decoration."

Cindy had turned her back on him and was slicing thin slivers of cheese off the block. Every time her knife *thunked* against the bread board my heart jumped.

"Oh, lovely." He swept a speck of dust off his plaid shirt. "*Moi?* Although I'm an actor, I'm not into that sort of thing." He made a limp wrist and laughed.

Cindy's head jerked up. "Not all actors are gay. Not all people into home décor are gay. Plus, you never know who might be gay. Watch it buddy." She chopped the hunk of cheese with vigour.

He laughed, so amused. "Oh, aren't you the feisty one. Me, I prefer male activities. Hunting, fishing, dirt biking."

My ears perked up. "Hunting? You like to hunt?"

"Oh, sure," he said, snatching a piece of cheese off the cutting board. If he tried that again, I was sure Cindy would hack off his finger. "Every fall, me and some buddies head into the bush. In fact, I picked up some hunting stuff in town. It was on sale." He held up his black fabric shopping bag. "So much easier to find here than in Toronto."

Andrew had finished plumping the pillows and was now in the kitchen as well. The place was getting crowded. "Hey Dave, glad your trip was successful. The girls are about finished making lunch. Hand me the sushi and I'll put it on the table."

"Sure." He took the plastic containers out of the black bag and reached behind Cindy to give them to my brother. Andrew was doing his best to not look at the mud Dave had dragged in. "I'll put the rest of this stuff in my car. I'll get some wood for tonight while I'm out, if someone would show me the woodpile."

Andrew said, "Robin, you go. You still have your outdoor shoes on."

Outdoor shoes? What was this? Kindergarten? The last thing I wanted to do was go outside with Sparling. "Sure Andrew, no problem." I either had to go or make a scene.

As we walked across the muddy lawn, I casually asked, "So David, how long have you been a hunter? And what do you hunt?" Other than women.

He puffed out his chest. "I'm not into deer, moose, or wild turkey. I prefer wildcats, bears. You know, big animals that are in the real wilderness."

"You hunt bears?" I was feigning indifference. "It's now illegal to hunt grizzlies in British Columbia." Just a fact. "Did you know that? And a woman was killed by a bear next door." Another fact. Making idle conversation. "Aren't you scared of them? Or do you have bear spray with you all the time?" I scanned his face for any reaction to my reference to bear spray.

Did he have Darlene's? But he was a very good actor. His face was completely neutral.

"I always carry bear spray. Bears need to be treated with respect, for sure. Andrew told me about that woman. Poor thing. Bears don't usually attack."

"Not unless they have a reason." Was I pushing it? Probably. "Did you know the woman? Darlene Gibson?" Definitely pushing it.

"What a small world. Andrew mentioned her name. It rang a bell. She was an employee of the theatre I was working in at the time."

Did he really think I didn't know about his sexual assault case? Maybe he thought the Home and Garden section of the paper was only for lining birdcages. "Oh, come on. She pressed sexual assault charges against you. Of course you knew her!" I was pushing it.

He merely shrugged his shoulder and brushed it off. "People like me have to deal with all sorts of accusations. Jealousy is rampant. The case came to nothing."

So that was how he was going to play it? Like it didn't exist. I was getting pissed off. I decided to change tack and get back to the bear topic. "I'm sure it's bothersome. How on earth do you get near enough to a bear to shoot it? They are so skittish." Dangerous ground?

But he was eager to show off his expertise to the little lady. "Bear pheromones." He held up his bag. "I got some in town. You put it on a tree and the bear comes out of the bush."

"Bear pheromones. They must have a strong scent to lure a bear out of the bush."

"Oh yeah, it really stinks. I'll show you." He reached into his bag, pulled out a bottle, and took off the lid. "It really reeks."

I pretended to take a whiff. I don't know what possessed me, but I said, "What a stench. It's so strong. You sure wouldn't want to get that on you. That would be pretty dangerous. It could make a bear maul you to death."

We were standing beside Sparling's car on the gravel. Perhaps I was being naïve, but I honestly didn't feel I was in any danger. There were witnesses for heaven's sake. I could see Andrew's blue oxford cloth shirt through the living-room window; he was fussing around the table. And although Cindy had her back turned, I could see through the kitchen window that the door was open and I knew that her hearing was acute. But Sparling had frozen still. His piercing blue eyes had turned laser-cold and his breath was coming in jagged bursts as he controlled his anger. Without warning, he pitched the contents of the bottle at me, splashing my sweatshirt and jeans with the noxious liquid. I slowly backed away from him, acutely aware of the danger he had placed me in. That young bear was no doubt close by.

"Fuck, Sparling. Are you crazy? A bear could come out of the bush and kill me at any moment."

Sparling laughed. "How terrible that you tripped on the wet grass beside my car while smelling the bottle of pheromones and grabbed my hand, causing it to spill all over you. What an awful, awful accident."

I heard crashing in the bush behind me and watched as Sparling slid easily into the passenger side of his car. I heard the automatic locks go down; he was locking me out. An arctic grin froze on his face as he looked at me through the windshield. My car was parked on the far side of the BMW. I took flight. I needed to get inside my car. Thank God, I never locked it. My feet slid on the muddy grass as I desperately raced around the nose of his car to the passenger door of my car. My sore hip was burning with pain and my ankle twisted in the muck. A spasm of agony sparked up my leg. Behind me, I could hear the bear snorting as it pounded the earth toward me. It seemed to take me a million years to reach the pitted chrome handle of my car and tug it open, all the while praying this was not one of the times it had decided to seize up. Mercifully, it squawked open and I dove inside, pulling the door shut behind me.

When I turned around and looked through the window, I saw the bear's jaws snapping at me, revealing its huge canines embedded in red gums, surrounded by wet black flesh. Its beady eyes bore into mine as it clawed at the passenger door. I leaned over the centre console and pressed hard on the horn. It emitted a pathetic whimper, but still loud enough to be heard in the house. Out of the corner of my eye, I saw Cindy seemingly drift down the porch steps and then abruptly turn around and run back up. I didn't blame her.

The noise inside the car was incredible. Every time the bear swiped a paw against the door, there was a loud screech of nails as they scratched against the paint. With every strike, the Sentra rocked on its wheels. Would the car roll over? I kept pressing the horn, hoping the pitiful bleats would scare the bear away. Finally, above the mewing of the horn, I heard the howl of sirens approaching. Cindy must have called the police. I glanced in Sparling's direction. Behind the reflection of the crazed bear on his window, I could see him smoothing down his hair.

27.

TWO O.P.P. CARS CAREENED down the driveway, sirens whooping and lights blazing. The first one skidded on the gravel as it flung sharply around the front of the BMW. Then it fishtailed wildly on the slippery grass until its brakes screeched, stopping halfway in front of my Sentra. The second car spit out small stones as it shrieked to a halt behind me, effectively cornering the bear between the two cars. A third car pulled up beside my driver's side door. Ralph's Jeep? What was he doing here? I thought he'd gone to Toronto? Relief flooded through me. Ralph was here. He wouldn't let me die. He'd told me he loved me.

Rearing up on hind legs and roaring over the scream of the sirens, the bear shook its whole body. Six feet of fur brushed against my window, leaving smudged lines of oil. Oddly, I felt like I was inside a fishbowl at a car wash, the brushes beating at the sides. My old friend, the hissing snake, circled my brain. Oh, God. I couldn't faint. Not now. I took a deep breath. I was safe inside the car. The bear couldn't get me. Ralph was here.

The car began rocking violently, and I watched with amazement as the bear climbed onto the hood, its seven hundred pounds denting the metal. For a brief second, I admired the animal's problem-solving skills. Blocked between Sparling's car and mine on both ends by the cop cars, the bear's pea-brain had figured a way out. Part of me cheered it on, hoping it would get away. It was such a magnificent, glorious beast. The beautiful creature wasn't crazy—it was only doing what it was supposed to, be attracted to bear pheromones. I muttered under my breath, "Go, go, go." Ralph started honking his horn and the bear, surprised at this new noise, went stock-still on all fours for a second and then slid down the hood of my car. I breathed a sigh of relief as it took off toward the path into the woods.

Through the windows of the cop car in front of me, I could see Kowalchuk getting out of the passenger side. His huge head appeared over the top of the car while Andrechuk's hands gripped the wheel, her knuckles white. Niemchuk must be in the car behind me. And then I saw the barrel of Kowalchuk's gun resting on his hand that he placed on top of the car.

"No," I screamed. "Let the bear go. It's not crazy. It was baited."

Kowalchuk, of course, couldn't hear me inside the car. I wound down my window a crack and shouted through it, "No. Don't shoot the bear." My pleading was impotent. I pounded on the windshield.

A shot boomed through the air.

I watched the bear disappearing into the bush, his hind legs pushing hard into the mud. I couldn't believe Kowalchuk had missed. But then I saw why. Ralph had jumped out of his car and was waving his arms. He was hopping up and down right in Kowalchuk's line of fire.

Ralph was shouting, "Don't shoot. It's not a rogue bear. Don't shoot."

Puzzlement distorted Kowalchuk's beefy features. But he put down his pistol and yelled, "Get out of my way. It'll attack again. Stay in your car. Get out of my way."

Ralph brushed the air in front of him with both hands, as if to iron out the tension and fear. He made a turning motion with his fist at Andrechuk, telling her to turn off the siren. He then made the same motion to Niemchuk behind me.

All of a sudden, the air was deathly quiet. "No," I could hear Ralph say, reason personified. "The bear won't attack again. It went after Robin because she is probably covered in bear pheromones."

Ralph had believed me about the contents of the insect repellent bottle! He'd assessed the situation and knew what had happened. He didn't know why or how, but he knew I was a walking target, a bull's eye for the bear.

"Bear pheromones?" Kowalchuk was disbelieving.

"Kowalchuk, let the bear go. I'll explain inside."

"This better be good," Kowalchuk muttered. He thumped over to Sparling's BMW and tapped on the window with his knuckle. "Sir, the coast is clear, for now. You can come inside with us. You'll be safe."

Sparling's doors unlocked with a *clunk* and he got out of his car, shoulders hunched. He was pretending to be frightened, but he knew that as long as I was inside my car there was no danger to anyone. He looked over his shoulder at me, trying to hide his smirk as he walked away, the three police protectively huddled around him.

I watched from inside my car as the four of them headed into the cottage. Ralph tapped on my window and shouted through the glass, "You're covered in bear pheromones, right?"

"Yes," I mouthed. No sound came out.

"You can't be in the open or the bear will come back. I'm going to open my passenger door. You scoot over your centre console and quickly get into my car. And I mean *scoot.* I'll drive you to the porch steps. Then you run inside, okay? You got it? Run. Put your clothes in a plastic bag and have a shower with that great shampoo of yours."

Shower and shampoo talk at a time like this? I looked up at him and nodded mutely. "Got it," I finally managed to mumble a few seconds later.

Ralph's Jeep was parked beside mine, his passenger door level with my driver's side. I was sitting in the passenger seat of my

Sentra, and he wanted me to climb into my driver's seat and then quickly get into his car on his passenger side. I completely understood what he wanted me to do.

But I wasn't so sure about the *scoot* part. I eyed the gearshift with trepidation. Then an interesting thought swept through my mind that had something to do with Ralph's gearshift being in the shower with me. No, no, no, Robin, don't think like that. You are in danger. Focus. But I knew the danger was over. The bear was gone. Sparling was with the police and I was with Ralph. My big, strong man. What had come over me? I tamped down the hysterical giggles that were blooming in my chest. This would not do at all right now. I had a job to do. I had to *scoot* over the gear shift. Easy-peasy. No problemo. *Scoot* here I come.

I put my hands on the driver's seat and hoofed my rear end up, hoping it would follow the momentum of the top half of my body. My knees creaked and my shoulders almost collapsed. I was on all fours, the gearshift poking into my hanging belly. I knew in my heart of hearts that this was not an attractive sight. There was no way I was going to be able to somehow move my legs over the gearshift and onto the driver's side of the car. I felt giddy. Weakness was flooding my body as helpless giggles threatened to explode from my throat. What a way to cement a relationship. God, I was so stuck.

Ralph flung open my car door. "Oh Robin," was all he said as he put his hands under my armpits. He pulled with all his might. Was I sweating? I hoped not, but somehow that seemed to be the least of my problems. I slithered out of my car like a newborn baby whale entering the world. Ralph moved to my side, grabbed my belt, and tossed me headfirst into his car like a football. God, he was strong. My sore hip banged on the handle of my car door. Surely, it would have a bruise later. As he stood behind me I was glad I wasn't wearing a skirt he could see up, but I was also painfully aware that my jeans were threatening to split. I bet my bum crack was showing. I heard a small squeak. Ralph was trying not to laugh. He whipped the car door shut behind me.

"Oh, for heaven's sake," he cackled as he got in the car, panting and screwing up his face. "You stink."

Oh really? This was news? I knew I stank to high heaven. I had landed on his car seat in a heap and was valiantly trying to adjust my body parts. "Thank you," I said.

He guffawed, covered his nose with a tissue—not that that would work—and drove me to the porch steps. "Tell me how you got covered in that shit." Over the tissue, I could see that his blue eyes were laughing.

"Sparling. He threw a bottle of pheromones at me."

Ralph went perfectly still. "Oh. I see. That's not funny. That's attempted murder."

"He's going to say that he was showing the pheromones to me and I slipped on the wet grass, grabbed his hand, and made the bottle dump all over me. He told me that's what he was going to say. And he's famous. I'm a Home and Garden reporter." I burst into tears. It was all too much. "It'll be his word against mine."

Ralph patted my hand awkwardly. He didn't want to touch me and I didn't blame him. "You're safe now. It's okay." *Pat, pat.* He got a whiff of his hand and stopped patting. "But I can disprove that."

He could? "How?" I stopped crying. "Why are you even here? You're meant to be in Toronto." Where my kids were, worrying about the land beside their cottage. I could only do so much. Hopefully, nothing would happen to it.

"When I left here, I was bothered by that bottle. I decided to take it to the police station in Huntsville. They ran the prints on it right away through their computer system. Sparling's showed up. Once Kowalchuk saw Sparling's fingerprints were on the spray bottle, he was convinced to take a serious look at Darlene's phone and saw the emails. He offered his lab as well. It doesn't have a backlog like ours. We'll know the contents of the bottle in a day, max. Anyway, while I was there, your call came in."

"I didn't call."

He brushed that aside. "Whatever, it was this address. Anyway, I'm going to get out of the car now. I will watch you as you run up the steps. And, I mean, *run*."

"I can't run. I hurt my ankle."

"Go as fast as you can. Go straight upstairs and take a quick shower. Put your clothes into a plastic bag. When you're done, bring me the bag. They're evidence. Don't take too long. Speed is important. I don't want Sparling to have time to convince the others of his innocence."

After my shower I limped downstairs on my sore ankle. My living room was packed full of people, all, it seemed, expectantly waiting for me. Perhaps Ralph had told them not to talk until I was present. I had hurried, as Ralph had asked, but there were consequences of this. My wet hair was plastered against my skull. One sock was inside out. My buttons didn't line up. What a way to make an impression. Sparling did an eye-roll and sat back, allowing a tickled expression to settle on his pretty lips. Kowalchuk raised his unibrow, sighed, and got out a pen and paper. I found an empty cushion on the couch beside Cindy and settled onto it. She moved an inch or so away. I guess I still stunk. Lucky, my faithful pet, came up to me, sneezed, and went back to his bed, head hanging low. Would they believe me? Not a chance in hell.

Ralph had come back in and he was now standing behind his chair at the dining-room table and began what was going to be a very interesting meeting. I was guessing Kowalchuk let him take charge because Ralph had proved him wrong. "Robin here," he gestured at me, "was outside when she was covered with bear pheromones a little while ago. I am trying to figure out how it all happened."

Andrew butt in. Naturally. "My good friend," he looked at me pointedly so I would know whose side he was on, "Dave

Sparling, the lead in many stage shows, kindly offered to bring in some wood after he deposited his shopping from this morning in his car, a new BMW."

Andrew was impressed by cars. I wasn't. Obviously. Sparling drove a sleek BMW i8 and me? I drove an clunky old Sentra.

"He didn't know where the woodpile was, so I asked my sister, Robin, a Home and Garden reporter for *The Toronto Express*, to show him where it was. That's why she was outside."

At least he left out the bit that I had my outdoor shoes on. But he was setting up the Who's Who parameters.

Then Cindy came to life. "Robin is an investigative crime journalist for a major Toronto daily, the largest in Canada. She single-handedly solved two mysteries last year due to her investigative abilities. She is now in the process of solving the murder of Darlene Gibson."

Kowalchuk harrumphed, "Attacked. She was attacked by a bear." Until the lab results on the contents of the bottle came in, he was sticking to his story.

"Murdered," insisted Cindy.

"Mauled to death. Misadventure." It was a sparring match.

Sparling interrupted, waving away the topic of Darlene's death as if it were irrelevant. "While I was taking my shopping to my BMW," here he paused, making a point about how rich and famous he was, "Robin asked me about hunting and my hunting purchases from town. She was very curious about bear hunting in particular and wondered how I got bears to come out of the bush. I told her about bear bait and she wanted to smell it. Before I put the shopping bag in the car, I opened the bottle and the smell must have been so overwhelming that she slipped on the wet grass, grabbed my arm as she went down, and tipped the contents all over herself. That's how the bear pheromones got on Robin." He sniffed and looked at his manicured nails.

I hated him.

Ralph was standing by his chair, his head tilted, as if trying to visualize the scene. He turned toward Sparling and said, "You opened the bottle beside your car, put it under her nose, she slipped on the wet grass, grabbed your arm, and it dumped on her. Is that the general gist of it?"

"Yes, you heard me accurately." Sparling seemed fascinated by his nails.

Ralph proceeded to nail him. "To be clear, you were standing right beside your car, your BMW, when this happened. And she slipped on the grass?"

"Yes," he lifted his head. "I was right beside the car door when she slipped on the grass and fell, grabbing my arm. I was worried she had sprained her ankle."

"And she got covered with pheromones."

Sparling was getting irritated. He snapped, "Yes."

"You were worried that she had twisted her ankle."

Sparling now looked a little wary. I could see he was trying to figure out where Ralph was going with this. "Yes," he nodded. "She's the younger sister of a very good friend of mine." He nodded at a preening Andrew. "I didn't want her to be hurt. But she was hurt, you saw her limping down the stairs, poor thing." He was Mr. Compassionate. "It all happened so quickly, but I could see from the tracks in the muddy grass beside the car that her foot had slid quite badly from under her."

Ralph nodded his agreement. "Good observation." He turned to me. "Robin did you hurt your foot?"

I had, but later, when I was running in front of the car. Suddenly, I got it. There was no wet grass *beside* Sparling's car. It's gravel. "Yes, I slipped on the grass." I smiled sweetly, giving Sparling a sense of security. He was safe. I was collaborating his story. His fucking pack of lies.

Kowalchuk stopped writing in his notebook and looked up at Sparling. "We will get your statement later, Mr. Sparling."

"Of course," he blustered.

Cindy had sensed the change in me and gave me a little smile.

She knew Ralph was onto something, but still didn't know what. She hadn't been there.

"So, Dave, I can call you Dave, can't I, being a family friend and all," he drawled, looking at my brother's arrogant face. "You were very worried about Robin. She had a twisted ankle and you were especially concerned because she was covered in a substance that potentially could cause her immediate death."

"Oh, I know," said Mr. Know-It-All. "They are very strong, those pheromones."

"I see." Ralph stared hard at him. "I'm curious. Why didn't you let her, with her twisted ankle, get into your car, which was closer?"

Mr. Smarty-Pants looked away. A small gotcha.

Ralph continued, looking at me. "Where did you slip on the grass, Robin?"

Here we go. "In front of Mr. Sparling's BMW."

"Not *beside* his car?"

"Why would I slip there? It's gravel. The parking area is gravel, not grass. No, I definitely slipped in *front* of his car."

Kowalchuk looked up at this, the truth of what happened today beginning to dawn on him. It was sliding through small cracks in Sparling's story. I watched his mind process the details. First of all, why hadn't he let me into his car, the closer one, if he were concerned about my injury? Secondly, there was no way I could have slipped on grass where he said I had, beside his car. There was no grass there. It was in front of his car. I would have been nowhere near him, so how did I grab his arm and cause the bear pheromones to spill on me? Sparling stopped looking at his nails and was eyeing me with a tiny flicker of fear on his face. Or so I hoped. Cindy elbowed me in the ribs.

"But Robin, why," Ralph was doing his best to look flummoxed, "were you running in front of his car? Why not get into the closer car, Mr. Sparling's, Dave's? Was his car locked?"

"It was." I was just answering his questions, offering nothing more. I was enjoying watching the two fat cats in the room squirm. My brother was finally figuring out that all was not as it seemed. He was picking specks of dust off his jeans, a clue to his level of distress. Sparling's fixed smile was faltering. And Kowalchuk was sitting forward, listening hard.

"Where was Mr. Sparling?"

"Inside his car, on the passenger side. He'd locked the doors. I couldn't get into the back seat. The doors were locked."

"He'd locked the doors leaving you outside his car, far from yours, covered in an agent that would attract bears." A large gotcha.

"Yes."

"And that's why you had run to your car."

"Yes." I smiled. We'd got him.

Kowalchuk had made a decision. It was his territory and his collar to make. He heaved his colossal body out of my father's reading chair and stood in front of Sparling. "You're under arrest for the attempted murder of Robin MacFarland."

Sparling's eyes bugged out. "What? She tripped and grabbed my arm. It was an accident. I wasn't trying to kill her."

Kowalchuk snorted. "Tripped? On what? The gravel beside your car? I doubt it. I'm betting you tossed the contents of the bottle at her. In any event, you deliberately put her in mortal danger when you locked your car doors. You might think it's your word against hers and that you will win because of your fame. But *I* saw where you were. Inside your car. *I* saw the locked doors. *I* saw where she was. Inside her car. Many steps away. It's your word against mine. The police. You put her in mortal danger. Get a good lawyer. And fast, because I'm shortly going to be charging you for that Darlene Gibson business as well."

"Who?" Sparling looked wildly around, the whites of his eyes flashing. "That kid who charged me? That was already thrown out of court."

Andrew, the legal authority in the crowd crowed, "He can't be charged again for that."

"Oh, I know. But, this time, it's a murder charge. When Detective Creston here gave me Darlene's bottle of insect repellent to check for prints we found Sparling's. They were on file from the sexual assault charge. And once the lab gets back to us, I'm sure we will find it contained bear pheromones. You've used the same murder weapon twice. Bear bait. Darlene sprayed herself with it before your little promenade with her in the woods."

"What walk in the woods?"

"Don't act the innocent with me. You're a good actor, but the evidence won't lie. We have her phone, which tracks all her emails to you. They give us motive and they prove you were planning to see her. This was premeditated. I'll bet if we ask around town we'll discover that you've been here before. Planning it all out. There's closed-circuit surveillance footage in the Swiss Chalet where you met her for lunch. I have no doubt it will show you rummaging in her knapsack *and* doctoring her insect repellent while she's in the can. Just because this is a small town, don't mistake us for yokels."

I wanted to roll my eyes, but Ralph had made a small gesture with his hand. Let it go.

As soon as Kowalchuk said "planning," I remembered that Elisa had told us he'd been at the Town Hall, asking about the properties near ours.

"He *had* been planning this."

Kowalchuk looked at me as if I were an irritating gnat.

"Talk to Elisa at the Town Hall. She can confirm this." He could eat shit. "And," I added, "I bet Darlene's computer, work phone, and bear spray are in his house somewhere."

Cindy was taking notes on her phone and then pretended to read them while holding her phone up in front of her face, tilting it this way and that. She was secretly taking photographs for the story. The story that I was already composing in my head. Shirley and Doug would love it. Sexual assault. Violence. Murder. Wealth. Wilderness. Wild animals. Famous actor. It was front page all the way.

Kowalchuk handcuffed Sparling and led him out the kitchen door and down the porch steps. Andrew trotted behind him, promising to help find him the best criminal defense lawyer in Toronto. He was probably worrying about the loss of his income. Niemchuk and Andrechuk followed mutely. Niemchuk's silence I could understand. He'd been severely traumatized because he'd used Darlene's insect repellent and nearly died. Andrechuk was quiet, probably because of the tension between her and Cindy. She'd get over it. As they headed to the police cars, I could hear Sparling complaining about the bugs swirling around his head. Andrechuk smacked his ears with a little more vim than she had to.

"Well, I'd better get going," Ralph said easily, as if it was all in a day's work for him, which of course, it was. "Dinner with my kids, you know."

Cindy hopped off the couch and plunked herself down on a chair at the dining-room table. "I'm going to make a timeline for the story. It'll help."

"I guess I'll let you," I said to her. I put my hand in Ralph's. "I'll walk you to your car."

"No, rest your foot." His finger brushed my lower lip.

"It's fine. Much better." I loved looking in his eyes. We were standing so close together that the energy between us was palpable.

"Get a room, you two," Cindy chortled.

Ralph grinned. "Okay, we'll stop. I really have to be off."

"You are off." Cindy held her nose. Hard to tell if she meant it. "Robin is the one who's off."

"Come on you two. Stop it. Let's go, Ralph." I pulled on his arm.

He stopped at the kitchen door. "You can't go out Robin, not until that smell wears off."

"You really do care about me, don't you?"

His brows knit. "Of course I do. We'll work out our issues, Robin. I'm up for that." He bent over and kissed me firmly on the lips and I felt my skin melting into his. Yes, he certainly was up for it. What did they say about the foundation of a good relationship? Sex and money? We'd got the sex part down pat. We'd be fine. He put his lips right by my ear. "I love you, Robin."

My stomach clenched. Why did he have to ruin everything? Fuck. I kissed him.

Andrew was walking toward the porch after seeing Sparling to the police car. Always the perfect host. "Germs," was all he said as he scurried around us, head down.

I watched Ralph through the kitchen window as he headed to his Jeep. He must have felt my eyes on his back because he turned and gave me a small nod as he opened the car door. Then he repeatedly opened and shut the door while waving his hand under his nose. I guess I'd left a lingering odour in his car. I stood still, waiting until his car disappeared down the driveway, my thoughts swirling. When I went into the living room, Cindy was still sitting at the table, tapping on her iPad.

"Where's Andrew?" I said.

"Upstairs packing."

"Oh good." I watched her writing the timeline, my stomach still clenching.

"What?" she said. She always knew when I was upset.

"Ralph used the L-word."

"Don't you hate that shmaltzy shit?" She brushed an auburn tendril from her green eyes. She tapped away and looked up again. "Are you going to help me with this timeline or what?"

I laughed. "Okay, bossy."

"I love you, too."

"Fuck off."

But I did love her. And I loved Ralph, too. Maybe.

Acknowledgements

I would like to thank the people at Inanna Publications for all their editorial and promotional support for this book, with a special thanks going to Editor-in-Chief Luciana Ricciutelli and Publicist/Marketing Manager Renée Knapp.

I am deeply grateful to my Buddhist friends for their constant encouragement, positive outlook, education, and inspiration. I would like to give a special acknowledgement to Silvia Granata who introduced me to the Nichiren Buddhist practice.

Thanks also to my friends and family who love me with very warm hearts.

Photo: Phil Brennen

Sky Curtis divides her time between Northern Ontario, Nova Scotia, and Toronto. She has worked as an editor, author, software designer, magazine writer, scriptwriter, poet, teacher, and children's writer. Sky has published over a dozen books and is passionate about social justice issues and the environment. Her poetry has appeared in several literary journals, including *The Antigonish Review, Canadian Forum*, and *This Magazine*. Her debut novel, and the first in the Robin MacFarland Series, *Flush: A Robin MacFarland Mystery,* was published in 2017 (Inanna Publications) and was short-listed for the 2018 Arthur Ellis Award for Debut Crime Fiction.